Caution

Caution

by
Franco Ford

iUniverse, Inc.
New York   Bloomington

Caution

Copyright © 2009 by Franco Ford

iUniverse books may be ordered through booksellers or by contacting:
iUniverse
1663 Liberty Drive
Bloomington, IN 47403
www.iuniverse.com
1-800-Authors (1-800-288-4677)

Because of the dynamic nature of the Internet, any Web addresses or links contained in this book may have changed since publication and may no longer be valid. This is a work of fiction. All of the characters, names, incidents, organizations, and dialogue in this novel are either the products of the author's imagination or are used fictitiously.

ISBN: 978-1-4401-6810-9 (pbk)
ISBN: 978-1-4401-6811-6 (ebk)

Printed in the United States of America
iUniverse rev. date: 8/27/2009

1

The digital clock on the dashboard displayed 10:08 p.m. My shift was nearing an end. It was the time of the night when things were likely to become real busy, real soon. It seemed everything jumped off at shift change. The only question was, where would the traffic hit?

I was one of few Border Patrol agents who preferred to back up my service-issued Jeep Wrangler to the fifteen-foot galvanized fence in the area we referred to as "Dog Gate," which was my assignment for the evening. Different areas along the border often got quirky names that agents could easily relate to. When the secondary fence first went up, it became a gathering place for stray dogs along the border that no longer had the pleasure of international travel.

The top five feet of fencing was slanted at a forty-five degree angle to deter illegals from climbing, but they still found creative ways around or over it. The metal fence was also fitted with dimple-like holes just large enough to make out someone on the other side, but small enough to prevent anyone from scaling it. It was one of several lines of defense.

From my Jeep, I could look east for a quarter of a mile down the fence line before the terrain took a dip. Directly to the west, I could look down into the San Ysidro Port of Entry, just a few miles south of San Diego, California. Someone without the proper documents, but with enough desperation, might choose to bypass inspection by customs officers and drop into the courtyard just outside the port, hence my positioning. The feat is often accomplished by first simply jumping the initial fence that is only about ten feet in height with rigid indentations that unintentionally aid in climbing. From there, a makeshift ladder made of rebar bent at the end to form hooks, brought over by groups of illegal immigrants attempting to cross, helps with advancing past the newer, taller second fence.

I put down my latest Dean Koontz novel in anticipation of the movement soon to come. Radio traffic had been very minimal throughout the night, so I grabbed the Jeep's service radio and called 8-2-7, dispatch's radio call number. "8-2-7, can I have a radio check?"

After a brief moment, a husky male voice replied, "10-2, on channel one," letting me know that I was receiving radio transmissions and I was also on the proper channel.

From my elevation I could look down at the lines of cars waiting to enter the United States. Though the port remained open through the night, it was only late at night when the lines ever disappeared or the foot traffic going into the port ceased.

Several roadside video screens on the Mexico side of the border advertised commercials for plastic surgeons, gentlemen's clubs, and beachfront resorts in the local Tijuana area. The largest screen was above a mercado and was currently displaying full-figured Latinas in tiny bikinis. Vendors walked the lanes selling piñatas, chicle, sombreros, and cobijas, while immigration officers used drug sniffing-dogs to select cars for secondary inspection. It was an area that reminded me of purgatory—not exactly Mexico, not quite the United States. It was complete with tourists and commuters left to suffer the wait in their cars for what seemed an eternity. With the border fencing as a backdrop it was like a Third World Las Vegas strip minus the casinos.

I got out of the Jeep to stretch my legs. It was a necessity after hours of sitting at a time. I turned on my handheld service radio on my gun belt so that I remained in radio contact. No one nearby, I relieved myself behind the Jeep's back tire. Dog Gate was only slightly visible from the lanes of traffic below, but far enough that the naked eye couldn't make out a Border Patrol Agent urinating behind his vehicle. A port-a-potty was considered a luxury in our line of work.

"Agents in the field, be aware that RVS is down," came over the radio's speaker. RVS, or Remote Video Surveillance, was the system of cameras manned mostly by National Guard personnel until they were pulled from supporting Border Patrol operations which we would then take over RVS operations. I was working in one of the few areas that had RVS support. As long as those on the south side of the fence didn't suspect anything was wrong, it was business as usual. The RVS was a fairly new tool for us, so we weren't dependent upon it, especially since it went down frequently.

The outermost edge of the San Ysidro Port of Entry courtyard is lined with bars much like those of a jail cell but much thicker and square in shape. Where the bars met the secondary fence is where I stood at a hinged opening, which gave me access to the courtyard. It was there, overlooking the port of entry, just a few feet from my Jeep that my cell phone began to ring. I retrieved it from my uniform's cargo pocket; the caller ID lit up with the name Michael.

Michael was a colleague as well as a friend. We had met at a club almost two years ago. Although we worked at different stations and never worked together directly, I had recognized Michael from our post-academy training days before actually meeting him. Post-academy training was held weekly at our sector headquarters for trainees within their first probationary year. At post-academy we had continued our study of the Spanish language and immigration law, but we were long past those days.

A couple years ago, I began seeing Michael at different clubs, so eventually I gathered the nerve to introduce myself. He was a little apprehensive since I claimed to have known him from work and he had no idea who I was. We exchanged numbers, and after much persistence on my part, we soon started hanging out. From there, Michael introduced me to Rafael, another Border Patrol Agent. Not one of us was "out" at work. We knew there were others, but not any that managed to infiltrate our group. Michael insisted that one day the three of us would take a picture with our handguns. He didn't have to say it, but I knew secretly he wanted to recreate some type of homoerotic Charlie's Angels poses, and I wasn't having it.

I answered the cell phone, "Wassup?"

"Hey, Puta, whatcha doing?" Puta was Michael's term

of endearment for me. It was basically Spanish for slut. He rarely called by my name—Devon—it was always Puta or Bitch.

"Solving world hunger as we speak," I said. "What do you think I'm doing? I'm at work, bored as hell."

"You haven't caught any Mexicans today?" he asked.

"No, I'm hoping maybe I can pick one up at *Numbers* tonight." *Numbers* was one of the gay dance clubs we often frequented.

"What time should I expect you?"

"I hope to be there no later than 1:00 a.m.," I said. "Is Rafael going?"

"Yeah, she's going." Michael was the classic example of a modern day queen, so *her* and *she* escaped his mouth quite often no matter whom he was referring to—male or female. I often wondered about his ability to conceal his sexuality at work.

"Well, I'll see you guys there."

"Ciao," he said.

"Later."

Back in my Jeep, I scanned the FM radio dial for a station capable of playing a hip-hop song that I hadn't heard eight times throughout my shift already.

My search for a radio station was interrupted when I heard, "Dog Gate, we have traffic between us. Looks like two bodies." The transmission was from Rodriguez who was sitting at "The Tank," another position. He sat about a quarter of a mile down the road from me in-between the fences. I didn't have visual of the two individuals he referenced since I was north of both fences. More than likely, they were merely the decoys.

"10-4, let me know if you spot a ladder," I said. "I'll keep an eye on the courtyard." Decoys are often deployed to distract us from the groups they are really pushing through. If they didn't have a ladder, most likely the two spotted wouldn't advance past the second fence.

I was still looking into the courtyard, but now from inside my Jeep. It wasn't long before I spotted two men in baggy jeans and sweatshirts running. They were probably not our two original decoys.

As always, I immediately felt the adrenaline rush as the chase began—I grew flushed and my heart raced. I quickly put the Jeep in drive and headed north (a strategic advantage of backing in). I grabbed the service radio to alert Rodriguez of my intentions. "Cover me at Dog Gate. I have two bodies heading for the boulevard, one wearing gray over black and the other white over black."

I maneuvered down a dirt road that led to a cul-de-sac with two outlets. The first outlet, which was an alley between local shops, would be where I would attempt to cut them off before they mixed in with the street traffic on San Ysidro Boulevard. Upon reaching the end of the alley, I turned the corner and drove up the drive way that led to the employee parking lot at the port of entry. A mechanical arm, similar to those at railroad crossings, and a code prevented me from driving in. I saw the two men dropping over a brick wall into the parking lot; they were headed in my direction until they spotted me. The man in white was up and back over the wall like a trained soldier on an obstacle course he had conquered many times over. The other was heavier and struggling to get back up the wall. His buddy tried pulling him up, but was unsuccessful. I easily ran up and grabbed him by his belt pulling him back down. The white sweatshirt disappeared behind the wall, but not before calling me a *pinche negro*—another term of endearment I was becoming quite accustomed to hearing from the south side of the fence. He would most likely be what we called TBS, or turned back south to Mexico, left to try again later if not picked up by Rodriguez before he made it back over the fences.

Gray sweatshirt was heaving and breathing frantically from his trek from Mexico just yards away. I ordered him in Spanish to place his hands on his head as I grabbed his sweatshirt and belt from the back and backed away using his body as a shield, a precaution just in case his friend returned to the top of the wall with rocks in hand.

Back at my Jeep, he was sweating profusely. Like many,

he clearly wasn't physically prepared for the running and climbing involved. I frisked and cuffed him then called out my apprehension on the radio and reported the one running back south. Rodriguez confirmed that the second individual returned to Mexico along with the two decoys.

"Como se llama?" I asked the man still panting.

"Ignacio," he answered as I helped him climb into the small caged area in the back of the Jeep. "Tiene agua?"

In Spanish, I informed him he would get water at the station during processing.

At Dog Gate, I asked Ignacio for his biographical information in order to fill out paperwork; it would also be used for his processing. Within minutes, he was picked up by our transportation unit along with my zone activity reports. I hoped Ignacio was telling me the truth when he said he had never been arrested by immigration or the police. There was a saying on our shift, "The longer the record, the longer the night." Individuals with extensive criminal or immigration history usually required pages of paperwork to set them up for deportation or criminal prosecution.

My relief drove up at 11:40 p.m. Shortly afterwards, I pulled into the station driveway and punched in the code to open the security gate. I drove a few yards by the main building where a supervisor was waiting outside on a bench to account for all the agents on our shift as we drove in. I gave him a wave and he scratched my name off his roster. I continued up the road, passed the processing building, and stopped at the personnel lot where I placed my backpack and lunch cooler in my pickup. In my backpack, I kept a back-up flashlight, flexi-cuffs, binoculars, books for entertainment, and anything else I may need in the field. To Border Patrol Agents, this was referred to as a "tricky bag."

The next parking lot was the service vehicle lot. I parked my Jeep in the designated area and walked back down to the main building to turn in my keys. Along the way, I saw Ruiz leaving the processing building. Ruiz came to the unit shortly after me, so he too was fairly new as far as agents went. It was a fact that our jobs weren't the least bit secure until we made it through our probationary year. We were no longer on probation, but we weren't exactly untouchable either. We were the ones expected to help in the processing area after shift. I guess we all had to pay our dues.

"Hey, Ruiz. Any casework?" I asked.

"No, it's clean over here."

"Good."

We were headed towards the main building when Ruiz asked, "Any plans tonight?"

I gave my usual response, "No, I'm kinda of tired.

I think I'm going to call it a night." If I lied half as well as I thought I did, I was a saint in the eyes of my co-workers.

"Lopez and I will probably head to T.J.," he said.

I wasn't thrilled about partying in Tijuana considering our line of work, my poor Spanish, and the recent rise in crime. The majority of the clubs along the border in Tijuana catered to the U.S. clientele, but I seldom went. The club I did go to on two occasions, *Club Ecstasy*, a gay club, wasn't exactly popular with the other agents. That wasn't entirely true since it was Michael and Rafael who took me to *Club Ecstasy.* I always stuck to the story that I had never been to Tijuana when asked by my co-workers, which seemed shocking to many because most agents had at least been to a strip club south of the border. As far as I was concerned, a gay bar or strip club didn't constitute a visit to a foreign country.

"Stay out of trouble, man," I said.

Ruiz grinned. "We got to find a little. That's why we're going."

Maybe that meant they were going to *Zona Norte*, a part of T.J. where you can get a girl to do whatever you want for the right price.

We both entered the building and headed to the issue room to turn in our keys to another supervisor, who in turn scratched us off another roster. This roster was more of a vehicle inventory than an agent inventory. We waited in the computer room with some of the other agents from our shift waiting to be released. A few discussed their plans for the night, while others busied themselves on computers. I was just about to log onto a computer and surf the internet when word came down. Someone from the hallway yelled, "We're cut."

The words "We're cut" could start a stampede on a Saturday night. I briskly walked to the backdoor that led to the personnel lot. I purposely mixed in amongst the cluster of green uniforms heading out the door. There were a couple of agents, academy classmates, I tried to avoid because I knew they would try to get me to have that beer after work. I wasn't opposed to that—I did it on occasion—but I wasn't going to surrender to them tonight. I needed a Saturday night out in an environment where I could be myself.

2

Because I worked second shift—and so late when most people had normal day jobs—little time was left for a social life. I was determined to go out, even if it was for less than an hour. Most of the bars in San Diego closed by 2:00 a.m., so I had to get moving. I got into my pickup and started the engine. It was already 12:03 a.m. I could be home by 12:20 and if I took a boot camp shower, meaning quick fast and in a hurry, I could be dressed and ready to go at 12:30. That would get me to *Numbers* by 12:45 and I could have a drink in my hand at 12:50. I really had to adhere to a strict schedule to have any kind of social life.

Showered and moisturized, I threw on a pair of Diesel jeans and a plain black tank top, which clung to my torso.

In the mirror, I noticed the signs of what I coined a "BP tan." Border Patrol agents are often prone to it. My left forearm, which was normally a medium shade of brown like the rest of me, was now Hershey-kissed by the sun. This happened from hours of sitting in my Jeep during daylight hours at the beginning of my shift; hours of such exposure baked my left arm as I occasionally let it hang out the window. I just hoped no one else noticed. I slipped into a pair of black Steve Madden sneakers and hurried out the door.

After arriving at Numbers, I waited in line several minutes, paid the eight-dollar cover charge, and entered the nightclub. Fat Joe's *Get it Poppin'* was blaring from the speakers while the video was being shown on several of the overhead flat screen televisions throughout the club. *Numbers* had two dance floors. On Saturday night, hip-hop pulsed on the smaller dance floor, and dance music blared on the larger floor. I was fond of the mix of music as well as the mix of people the club provided. Much like the surrounding population, the crowd at *Numbers* was diverse.

I made my way through the crowd—mostly men. Because it was a warm July night, many were in tank tops and tight tees if they had tops on at all. The air in the club was humid and carried a blend of the latest fragrances and scents that intertwined like potent pheromones.

Maybe it was more hormones than pheromones, but the club oozed of it.

I knew Michael would probably be on the patio smoking, so that's where I headed. Patios and smoking areas provided better lighting for sizing up prospects than the dimly-lit bar area. The only drawback was that your potential suitor was probably a smoker. I grew to love the fact that you couldn't smoke in the clubs or restaurants in California—you didn't *have* to go home smelling like smoke. Not a smoker, I nonetheless made frequent trips to the patios and outdoor smoking areas with Michael … and still came home smelling like an ashtray. If I was drunk enough, I suddenly wanted to be the Marlboro man, and I'd bum a cigarette from the cutest guy I could find, as if Michael's cigarettes weren't good enough for polluting my lungs.

I opened the door to the patio and stood in the doorway briefly scanning the patio for Michael and Rafael. The heavyset bouncer standing just inside grunted something about keeping it moving and not blocking the doorway. I spotted Michael and Rafael toward the back of the patio. Michael was holding his cigarette like a 1950's movie starlet. To say Michael was flamboyant was an understatement, though I suppose he could turn it off and on like a light switch. Being in law enforcement, I guess he knew how to play the game—he knew how to pose, act cool, and command attention. His looks topped off the act. No matter what time of day, he always seemed to have a five o` clock shadow. His thick stubble grew relentlessly, and his dark, thick, curly, hair gave him an exotic appeal. Though Michael wasn't Latin (I think he would give his right arm to be), he was fluent in Spanish. Michael was a country-fed white boy who grew up in South Texas, so most of his friends were Hispanic. Early on, he made it a point to fit in, and learning Spanish was part of fitting in.

Rafael was fair-skinned and the baby of our group. He was in his early twenties while Michael and I were both on the threshold of thirty. Rafael was Puerto Rican, slender, and spoke with a slight accent. He looked quite reserved with his tight military fade haircut, but he was probably the most outgoing among the three of us.

Rafael spotted me as I approached. He smiled and kissed me on the cheek. "Hey Papi," he said.

Michael took a long drag from his cigarette and exhaled before saying, "Hey, Bitch." Michael's personality could sometimes be described as abrasive; he could sometimes push my buttons. Deep down, though, I knew he would do anything for me or Rafael.

"What's going on?"

"Nada," Rafael said, still smiling.

"Mr. Man is here," Michael informed me, with a

slight grin.

"And who is Mr. Man?" I asked, although I knew exactly who he was referring to.

Michael exhaled another puff of smoke. "Don't go getting all hot and bothered, but Tony is here."

I tried not to look excited. "You serious?"

"As a heart attack," Michael said.

"Which you will be having soon if you don't quit smoking," I scolded. "I'm tired of coming to crack corner so you can get a hit."

"Secondhand smoke is more deadly than smoking," Rafael added.

"You two sound like a public service announcement," Michael said. "Anyway, are you going to speak to him?"

"Of course, I'll speak," I said.

"What's the big deal?" Rafael asked.

"It's his ex. A girl needs to be prepared for all chance encounters with an ex," Michael explained, putting out his cigarette in a nearby ashtray. "You don't want to run into an ex with no makeup on and rollers in ya hair."

With a look of confusion, Rafael simply responded, "Oh." Sometimes I wasn't sure if Rafael understood Michael's campy sense of humor.

I hadn't seen Tony in two months, since we last had lunch together. Tony and I had met online in one of those notorious hook-up sites over a year ago. After meeting in person we were inseparable. Tony was thirty-eight and stood at 6 foot 2 over my 5 foot 9 frame. He had a broad chest and shoulders, and skin the color of hot chocolate. I used to love running my hand over his shaved head, as if I didn't have one of my own. I would lose myself in his deep brown eyes. He was my Adonis, my black knight.

Tony and I had slipped into the relationship role quickly. It was something magnetic between us; I'm not just talking sexually either. We spent all of our free time together. Tony was active in the gay community by helping to raise money for various charities, which was a great way for him to reach potential clients for his particular profession. He worked for himself as an event planner. He took me to different parties and fundraisers; some he planned, others we merely attended. This was a side of the gay community I didn't have much knowledge of. One event in particular that he took me to—the Humane Dignity Society's annual fundraiser at the Art Museum—was like a gay prom. The Humane Dignity Society fundraiser was a black-tie affair with dinner and dancing. I met couples who had been together for several years, and to be honest, I had never been exposed to that side of the gay community.

After several months of dating, I had thought maybe I could spend the rest of my life with this man. In an instant, that all changed. After visiting my family in

Chicago, I had returned a day early in order to surprise Tony. I was the one surprised when I walked into his bedroom, a bedroom that was practically mine too since I spent all of my time at Tony's. I walked in to see Tony being ridden like a rodeo animal—unprotected no less. My boyfriend was having unprotected sex with someone that wasn't me. I didn't even have unprotected sex with Tony. I nearly went into convulsions and wanted to vomit like I was in some Lifetime movie. It was a hurt like I had never experienced. I felt disposable, like the condom he should have been using.

Silly me forgave but didn't forget. I had rationalized it by saying, "Gay men will be gay men." It's in our nature to spread our seed. Right? But wait … I wasn't doing it. I fought off temptation on many occasions, so why couldn't he? The next couple of months were like a tennis match in my head. Monogamous me versus my inner ho.

Stay or go?

I found my answer when I found Tony with rodeo rider number two. I gathered my belongings, my pride, and left.

Months later, when I had finally gotten over my feelings of wanting to see him suffer, we eventually did lunch as friends, per his request. That was a long road. It was good to see him, and not once did I get the urge to stab him with my fork. I knew one thing from that lunch and that was that I still had feelings for him. I was way too stubborn to tell him that and too smart to act on it.

The old saying goes, "What doesn't kill you, makes you stronger." Well, by now, I certainly was stronger—no longer having a man to entertain, I was spending a lot more time in the gym. It was a much healthier response to a breakup than a stabbing or shooting. I started to be more aware about the foods I ate, something I picked up from Tony. Between the diet and exercise, I was developing rather nicely—a broader chest and shoulders, and a sculpted the ass that could only have come from my mother's side of the family. It had gone from Jell-O to J-Lo acclaim. I was in better shape than when I left the Border Patrol Academy; there I gorged myself on anything I pleased. Now, I lost eight pounds and could see definition in my abs again. My physique was more toned and taut, and I was going to make sure Tony noticed.

"Let's go get a drink," I suggested, breaking out of my trance.

Michael perked up. "Do you have a sinister plan of revenge?"

"A plan? What are you guys talking about?" Rafael asked, looking more confused than ever.

"No, no revenge. I just want him to see what he's missing."

Michael brought his hand to his mouth and faked a yawn. "Sounds boring."

"First, I need a drink. Second, we are going to hit the dance floor—"

"Let me guess ... then your shirt comes off. That's not a plan, you do that every week," Michael interrupted. "Gay men think pecs and a six pack will bring them the world."

"Fuck you! I told you I didn't have a plan. Besides, do you have anything better?"

"Just go slash the muthafucka's tires," Michael suggested.

Rafael interjected, "No. Talk to him, tell him how you feel."

Michael and I stared at Rafael with blank faces as if what he was proposing was against the law. "I don't feel anything for him," I said, all the while wondering if I sounded convincing.

"Then why are we talking about it?" Rafael asked.

"You know, I heard about enough from 'Dr. Phil,'" I said. "I need a drink."

We left the patio and went to the main bar for drinks. The music was thumping rather loudly as we arrived at the bar and stood in line. I inconspicuously scanned the room looking for Tony ... with no luck. Soon we reached the front of the line.

I turned to Michael and asked, "Tonic, cranberry, or Red Bull?"

"Surprise me."

I turned to Rafael, "What do you want?"

"Give me a Long Island."

For the second time tonight, Michael and I stood there bewildered. "I guess she's stepping out tonight," Michael said.

Michael and I always drank vodka, the official drink of the gays; it was just a matter of deciding what mixer we were in the mood for. Rafael, on the other hand, rarely drank. Since Rafael wasn't much of a drinker, we often made him the designated driver, while Michael and I were usually the designated drunks.

I ordered and paid the bartender for two vodka cranberries and a Long Island Iced Tea. We grabbed our drinks and I left two dollars on the bar. The shirtless, muscular, bartender, winked and scooped up the two dollars placing it in his tip jar. Rafael moaned lustfully, watching his every move. I knew tactics like winking were purely for the sake of boosting his tips. I guess Rafael didn't care.

We ventured to the second dance floor on the other side of the club. To get there, we had to walk through a dimly-lit corridor, where I heard some mix version of Madonna's latest single being played. I wondered why dance songs had to be re-mixed into "dance songs."

We settled in a spot near the dance floor. Michael and Rafael moved to the music, while I continued my search. I had nearly given up … when I spotted him. "There he is," I shouted over the music.

Shaking his head in disbelief, Michael said, "Let the games begin." Rafael just laughed.

I watched him for a few moments trying to determine if he was there with anyone. I did notice Keith and Byron. Keith and Byron were both friends of Tony. They were a couple whom he'd known for years. They seemed to be the perfect couple, and they were too nice for me to hate them for it. Both in their late thirties, they owned a furniture store together, worked out together, and partied together. It was *way* too much togetherness. The icing on the cake, of course, was they were both gorgeous. They were always friendly to me, even after Tony and I had parted ways. There was none of that, "I don't know you anymore now that you're not dating my friend."

I looked down at my glass. It was what I liked to call half full instead of half empty. I downed the rest of my drink. "I'm going in," I said.

"You're asking for trouble," Michael admonished, with his arms crossed, looking like someone's mother. "Revenge is so much easier. This game of seduction is going to get messy."

"Don't listen to him. Go talk to Tony," Rafael encouraged.

Like Moses, I tried my best to part the crowded dance floor … but with no success. I suspected the club had to be breaking some serious fire regulations as I squirmed my way through the crowd. As I made my way over, I pulled my tank top off and stuffed the end of it in my back pocket so that it was hanging. Now I looked like every other twentysomething on the dance floor.

I hadn't eaten in a few hours, so on my empty stomach I was already starting to feel the effects of the vodka cranberry. I approached Tony, Keith, and Byron as if it was my first sighting of them.

"Hey, wassup?" I greeted, pretending to be surprised to see them.

"Hey, baby," Byron said. I exchanged hugs and kisses with both Byron and Keith.

"How's it going?" asked Keith.

"I'm good," I said. Then I turned to face Tony.

I tried to plan it so I would move directly into the pulsing light from the overhead strobes. Call me pathetic, but I was hoping the lighting would accent the toning I had worked so hard on. Tony began grinning ear to ear as he looked me up and down. I would say he noticed.

"You're looking good. What have you been doing, purging?" he asked.

"Funny! Strictly hard work, but thanks. You're not looking bad yourself."

I leaned in for a hug just before a set of massive arms from out of nowhere embraced Tony from behind. Those arms were attached to a guy that began kissing Tony on the back of the neck. Whoever he was, he was unaware of my presence. Tony turned around, and their lips met. Tony whispered something in his ear, and they both turned back towards me.

"Devon, this is Pablo; Pablo this is Devon," Tony introduced us.

Pablo was a mound of muscle, a Latin hottie. Pablo extended his rather large hand, and I lost my hand in his.

"Nice to meet you," he said, with an enticing accent.

I knew at that point that I was jealous, but at the moment, I couldn't figure out if I was jealous because Tony had Pablo or because I didn't have Pablo. Pablo was taller than Tony, and his rather large physique was now blocking my stage lighting. It was like an eclipse. I looked up at him silhouetted in the light; he appeared to be angelic.

"Good to meet you also," I said.

Looking at Tony, Pablo asked, "Is this *the* Devon?" Tony grinned and nodded.I needed to leave while I still had some dignity. "Well, I just wanted to say 'Hi.'" Rafael and Michael are around here somewhere. I better find them. Again … good to meet you Pablo."

"Come on. Dance with us," Pablo invited, grabbing my arm and pulling me closer to the two of them like a rag doll. I was a sucker for his accent.

Before I knew what was happening, I was in the middle of a Tony-and-Pablo sandwich—not that I was complaining. I couldn't have been happier at that moment if I were in a professional basketball team's locker room after a winning game—hell, after any game. I let the bass of the music course through my body as I savored the moment. I didn't know what I expected to happen: we would go home together, have a threesome, and live happily ever after … or Tony would be so moved by my dancing and toned body that he would leave with me. Not that I would have gone home with him. What *did* happen was … they soon forgot that I was there. They began making out like two bitches in heat. I slowly moved toward Keith and Byron, and I danced near them for a short while. Finally, I excused myself saying that I needed to use the restroom. I reached for my tank top which was now dangling like a tail between my legs as I scurried off.

I reached the edge of the dance floor and Michael was exactly where I left him still sipping his drink. Rafael was nowhere in sight.

I quickly put my tank top back on. "I could have used backup," I said, taking his drink and helping myself to a gulp.

"Didn't look like you needed any help from here."

"Anyway ... where's Rafael?" I asked, handing Michael his glass back.

"I don't know he disappeared...." Michael swallowed another sip then asked, "So?"

"So ... what?"

"Who was all that hunk of a man?"

"Oh, the Jolly Green Giant. I don't know. I guess it's Tony's new trick," I said.

"Looked like you were feelin' the Jolly Green Giant a minute ago. You were all ready to eat his vegetable."

"Shut up!"

Michael grinned. "So, if that's his new trick, does that make you the old one?"

I gave Michael my best "don't fuck wit' me" look. "You're in rare comic form tonight."

"Well, you're *easy*," he said, and chuckled. "There I go again."

"Let's dance," I suggested, trying to free myself from his annoying banter.

"I need a smoke."

"We were just out there. Can't you wait until we leave, Nicotine Nancy?" I sighed.

"No."

"Well, you go smoke, and I'm going to go walk around."

"Ok, but its almost closing time. Let's rendezvous at the sidewalk sale," Michael suggested.

"Should we synchronize watches?" I said with a hint of sarcasm.

"See you at 1:50; don't be late."

"Later."

Typically, after everyone was kicked out of the club, a large majority of the patrons would loiter out front. It was the bouncers' job to keep everyone moving to their vehicles and clear the sidewalks since *Numbers* is surrounded by residential residences. Of course, everyone would resist because it's the last chance to hook up, if that's what you were looking for. The game was referred to as "the sidewalk sale." This also gave you a better look at the merchandise before making any major purchases.

I moved to the front bar so I wouldn't run into Tony and Pablo again—not that they would have noticed me anyway. They would have been too busy giving each other throat cultures with their tongues.

I walked around alone, pathetically, until last call and then followed the herd out to the next holding area as bouncers yelled, "Let's go … you don't have to go home, but you can't stay here."

I saw Michael and Rafael as I exited the club. Michael was puffing away on yet another cigarette. Rafael stood next to him with his hands in his pockets.

"See anyone interesting?" I asked as I approached.

Michael exhaled. "We're still looking."

"Let's go to *Bacchus' House*," Rafael suggested. *Bacchus' House* was another dance club, but it remained open until five o'clock in the morning.

"I don't want to go to *Bacchus'*. Why do they charge eight dollars to get in and they can't serve alcohol anymore?" Michael complained.

"That's precisely why they charge eight dollars. They have to make a buck somehow if they stay open later.... I'm not really for it. I think I'm going to call it a night," I yawned.

"Well, let's go eat," Rafael suggested, making every attempt to keep the night from ending.

"No, I'm going home."

After a night of partying, it wasn't uncommon for the three of us to grab some Mexican food at, *La Fuente* on University Avenue. I guess if closing time at *Numbers* was the sidewalk sale, then eating at *La Fuente* was the going out of business sale since several club patrons ended their night there. I was pretty good with my diet, but there had been countless nights when I just gave into the urge and had a carne asada burrito since, obviously, I had no luck finding a different type of burrito.

"You see what's happening," Michael explained to Rafael, "He let Tony get to him again."

"Look, I'm fine. I'm just tired. I'm going home." I wasn't sure who I was trying to convince, me or them. Michael was right; I did let Tony upset me—again. It was my own fault, trying to show him what he was missing. It backfired. Big time!

We said our goodbyes, and I walked the few blocks to my truck. I drove back past *Numbers* to head home. Contrary to the prodding of the bouncers, the crowd showed no sign of thinning.

3

My run-in with Tony left me feeling a little nostalgic. I reached for a CD from the organizer attached to my sun visor and placed it in the CD player. It was a compilation I had made with some of my favorite soul-stirring love songs. I figured if I was going to wallow in self-pity, I should have a soundtrack. I enlisted the talents of a few Divas for my party—Track one: Mariah Carey, *Shake It Off*; Track two: Toni Braxton, *Un-Break My Heart*; Track three: Brandy, *Broken Hearted*; Track four: Macy Gray, *Why Didn't You Call Me*; Track five: Lauryn Hill, *When It Hurts So Bad*; Track six: another dose of Lauryn Hill, *I Used To Love Him*; Track seven: India.Arie, *Brown Skin*; Track eight: Destiny's Child, *Through With Love*; Track nine: Mary J. Blige, *I'm Going Down*; Track ten: Alicia

Keys, *If I Ain't Got You*; Track eleven: Aretha Franklin, *I Never Loved a Man*. Track twelve: Tina Turner, *Let's Stay Together*. Many nights, those ladies sung a brokenhearted, going down, let's stay together, call waiting, through with love, ain't got you, shaking it off, hurtin' bad, never loved a man, used to love a man, brown skin brotha to sleep; and I thank them for the company.

At my apartment, I unlocked the door and was no sooner over the threshold when I made a beeline to the computer desk near the kitchen. The computer was still on from my earlier use in the day but in sleep mode. A mere tap of the mouse and it was alive again.

I logged onto the site I used for cruising—the same site I met Tony on. Sometimes I resented being a man, the little power we seem to exercise over our sexual desires. I used to think this was common only of gay men, but I heard far too many conversations at work and abroad of men who were cheating, have cheated, or considered cheating on girlfriends, fiancés, or wives. I wondered if it was just in our nature. I didn't want to live like that, nor did I want to have to worry whether or not my future partner was sticking it to anything that moved.

Most of the time, I wasn't sure if I was actually looking for sex on the all too popular hook-up site. I think, more than likely, I was looking for love, but in most instances it's strictly sex being served up. Make no mistake, there were days when I just wanted sex. Those were days when I wasn't equipped to deal with the emotional side of human interaction. I know its ridiculous, but I dreamed of the day when a one-night stand would flourish into a happily ever after. I know it doesn't sound very logical, but many gay men work backwards. If we first hit it off sexually, then there is a chance we may want to pursue more. What's the point of dating someone for a couple of months then finding out you're not sexually compatible? Maybe working backwards was how it should be.

I was looking through pictures of other members who were also logged on when I got an e-mail alert. I opened my mailbox. I had a message from *Daddy4play.* "Daddy" could mean any number of things on a cruising site, such as a sugar daddy, an aggressive guy, or someone with a leather fetish. I opened his message and picture. In this particular instance, it meant a sixtysomething—a *sex*agenarian—trying to pass himself as a fortysomething. I deleted the e-mail with no reply. In the world of online cruising, it was my belief that no reply was perfectly acceptable when you were not interested. I had certainly received my share of no replies. Besides, the last time I had told someone he was out of my age range, I found myself in a twenty-minute instant message debate. He was trying to convince me that my generation was pushing aside the older gay community. He argued that was wrong of us since his generation had made great strides for the community. I agreed and merely tried to explain to him that I appreciate such endeavors, but I wasn't looking to have sex with him. I didn't get a response when I finally asked him, "When was the last time you slept with someone your age?"

I received a second email alert. This one was from *MascJock34.* I opened his profile. The picture revealed an attractive, athletic, shirtless guy with his arm cocked just as he was about to release a football, or at least posing like such. His profile stated he was of white and Latin mix, thirty four years old, five-ten, and 170 lbs. The email message simply read, *"Wassup?"* At least he had a way with words.

I clicked on the option to talk with him in a private chat and sent him a message.

"How's it going?" I typed.

"Horny and u?"

Well, he was by no means shy. *"Same."*

"Where do u live?"

"North Park, u?"

"University Heights." University Heights was the neighborhood just north of my own. Both North Park and University Heights are neighboring communities of Hillcrest, which is San Diego's gay Mecca, or what many refer to as "the gayborhood."

"*What u into?*" I asked.

"Let's meet and see what happens."

I hated vague responses, but it was late and I was horny or lonely. I guess one could be a little shy asking for a stiff dick from a complete stranger. Although, I have had my share of people who were simply looking for a big black dick and had no problem asking for it—as if to say that was the *only* thing black men had to offer.

I chatted with *MascJock34* several more minutes and learned his name was Troy. Troy was in the Navy, and he claimed not to be too experienced since he was recently divorced. That could be fun, but I wasn't buying the whole "inexperienced" line. It was probably his experiences that got him divorced. I gave Troy my address. He responded that he would arrive within twenty minutes.

It was almost 3:00 a.m. when I freshened up and threw on a fresh V-neck T-shirt. My bedroom overlooked the street where I instructed him to park. I peered down from my second floor apartment awaiting his arrival. It wasn't long before a black sport utility vehicle parked in front of the building. Even from a distance I could see a short, chubby, fortysomething looking guy get out of the SUV. This couldn't have been *MascJock34*! If it was him, he would have to use the call box, which was out of my view, to gain entry into the complex. I knew if the phone rang in the next minute, it was mostly likely him. I waited for the call…. A couple minutes went by, then I heard a knock at the door.

Damn it!

Either I or someone else had left the door to the courtyard ajar because he was now knocking directly on my apartment door. *MascJock34* wasn't using his own picture, which was starting to be a common occurrence with online hook-ups. My first reaction was not to answer the door, but then I thought, "Why let him off that easy?"

I opened the door. Troy was obviously the alter ego to the Danny Devito look alike at my door. He had a receding hairline and more wrinkles than the average thirty-four year old he claimed to be. A belly protruded from his black T-shirt and over the band of his boardshorts.

"Yes—?" I said.

"I'm Troy," he said, as he stuffed his hands into his pockets.

"You're Troy," I said. "You don't look anything like the picture on your profile."

He looked downward. "Well, it's a few years old."

"Look. This isn't going to work Troy. You're obviously using someone else's picture."

"But I came all the way over here…. Just let me suck your dick."

I said, "Bye Troy," before closing the door. I'm pretty sure I heard him mumble "asshole."

Maybe I was. But he had been dishonest with me.

I again peered out of my bedroom window and watched Troy get into the black SUV. I started to feel pity for Troy, or whoever he was. We were a community that thrived on physical appearance. When our looks are gone, it seems we no longer exist. At what age would I have to resort to using someone else's picture, or old pictures, in the hope that I could at least give a cancellation blow job after arriving at an unsuspecting young man's home?

After I watched him drive away, I began to peel out of my clothes as I walked out of the bedroom. I let articles of clothes land wherever. By the time I reached the bathroom I was completely naked. I turned on the shower and stood in front of the mirror. I studied my body. I looked at my shaved head, my brown skin, clean shaven face, and thought, "Handsome. I'm a catch."

Then why am I single?

I was educated, had a good job, and carried a gun. Gun carrying had to be good for a few butch points and adding to my sex appeal. Ah, the difficulties of the homosexual lifestyle. I couldn't help but think that if I were straight, I would be happily married with a kid or two, or miserable, maybe even divorced, but I wouldn't have to deal with the drama that is the gay lifestyle.

I got in the shower and closed the sliding glass door behind me. For a moment, I thought about relieving my sexual frustrations single-handedly. The feeling quickly passed. My own touch wasn't going to satisfy my desires tonight.

I squeezed liquid body wash into the palm of my hand and began to lather my body while my mind drifted. I wondered what Pablo and Tony were doing at that very moment. I probably didn't actually want to know the answer to that question, but I was sure they weren't sleeping. As if I wasn't depressed enough, I had to dive into imaginary sexual escapades of Tony and Pablo.

When I was done showering, I toweled dry, brushed my teeth, and climbed into bed—naked and alone. I missed him! Countless times, I'd told myself I was over him. I missed how our bodies fit together like puzzle pieces as we slept through the night. I missed his cold feet against my own. I missed how his snoring told me he was there even when we weren't touching. I missed the occasional late-night, surprise lovemaking session. I missed his funky-ass morning breath. I missed him.

I reached for the other side of the queen size bed and allowed my hand to circle on a spot that had been vacant for months. The sensation of the Egyptian cotton sheets against my finger tips created a tingly sensation, but it was nothing compared to a warm body. I curled up next to the body pillow I bought to replace Tony and hoped to be in dreamland soon. I wanted to fall asleep before the tears came.

4

I was holding my usual morning wood when I looked over at the alarm clock. The display read 10:23 a.m. I tossed around the idea of going to the 11:00 a.m. church service. Over the years I had developed a dislike for organized religion, though I occasionally did go to church.

San Diego offered plenty of gay and gay-friendly services, but it wasn't the same to me. I wondered why should I have to seek a congregation's acceptance of who I am. Besides, being seated next to the porn star who hosted last night's wet underwear contest at *Bourbon Street*—one of the local bars—didn't appeal to me.

I guess you could say I grew up with religion; however, we didn't attend church regularly. My father was raised Advent Lutheran, while my mother was Pentecostal—

though divorced, how they ever got together was beyond me.

Imagine as a child going to a Pentecostal service one week and a Lutheran service the next; I was more than a little confused. I often wondered why was it that we went to both churches for the same reasons, but each worshiped so differently. The Pentecostal service had vibrant singing, shouting, and dancing. But wait, Pentecostals weren't allowed to dance. I later learned it wasn't dancing, but the Holy Spirit. Call it what you like, but the Holy Spirit at *Prince of Peace Pentecostal Church* had some moves. I can still remember Sister Jackson doing *The Running Man*. The Holy Spirit occasionally allowed Brother Wells to do *The Snake*. I was certain on some Sundays the Holy Spirit had to be exhausted with all the nonstop dancing he was doing. None of this went on at my father's church. I wasn't sure if the Holy Spirit attended my father's church. It was always so much more serene. The geriatric choir actually had robes and song books. Even as a child and with no musical experience, I knew they were out of tune. Worship was also on a schedule at my fathers church; worship promptly ended at noon. Restless husbands and children seemed to be the only ones concerned with time when we attended *Prince of Peace Pentecostal Church*.

After my parents separated, my siblings and I mainly

attended *Prince of Peace* with mom. After I received my driver's license, I volunteered to drive my younger brother, my sister, and myself to Sunday school, even when my mom didn't attend church. We were introduced to religion at a young age but were not inundated with it, which is why I think my siblings and I clung to it. Much like the cliché pastor's kids, if it was forced upon us, we would have probably rebelled.

I had actually enjoyed going to Sunday school. I guess it simply made me feel good. I looked forward to discussing the weekly lessons and sharing what I got out of the scriptures. At sixteen, I was in class with adults who listened to my opinions. Even outside of church, I listened to gospel music and read inspirational books. I thought I was God's right hand man. It wasn't long before I learned differently.

We were both seated in the living room. She was in the recliner; we referred to it as her throne. No one sat in mom's chair—at least when she was home we didn't.

She was home from work less than a half an hour and already in her house dress.

"You look like something botherin' you. What's on your mind?" she asked.

Not sure of myself, I said, "I need to tell you something."

"Well, go ahead! Tell me!"

My hands were shaking, my throat went dry, and I seemed to have lost my breath. I didn't know what a panic attack felt like, but I was sure I was going to have one.

"First, promise me that this is between you and me," I said. My mother told my aunt, her eldest sister, everything. In saying "between you and me," it was my silent plea for her not to tell my Aunt Ellen. I believed that was one of many reasons my parents were divorced. You weren't just married to Dolly Wallace, but her sister also. It was a package deal. Aunt Ellen advised my mother on everything; Aunt Ellen was the religious guide of the family. She had attended Prince of Peace Pentecostal Church for over three decades. Early on, my mother had once explained to me that Aunt Ellen was a prophet, a messenger from God. She could see and know things about you only God could reveal to her.

"Of course it's between you and me. Who would I tell?"

With clenched fists, I stammered, "This … this is hard."

"Talk to me boy," she said, losing patience. "I've always told you that you could tell me anything." Her tone said otherwise.

I was plagued with cotton mouth. I could feel beads of sweat forming on my forehead. I thought about not going through with it. I thought about keeping my secret to myself. Then, suddenly, it was like a surge of courage coursed through my body, like I was struck by lighting. Before I knew what happened, I blurted out, "Mom, I'm gay."

Her expression changed. Her normally beautiful face seemed stressed. I'm not sure what she was expecting,, but this wasn't it. This wasn't something that could be fixed from her throne. A teen pregnancy maybe she could handle, which seemed rather normal and acceptable in our extended family.

I repeated myself. "I'm ... gay." The surge was gone and the words were much harder to form the second time around. They came out flat and unsure.

She was trying her best to conceal her anger, but I saw how the corner of her lip began to rise like it sometimes did when she was upset. "What makes you think you're gay?"

My fists were still clenched, and I hadn't moved. "I'm attracted to men."

She closed her eyes briefly as if she was studying her eyelids for direction. "Who else have you told?"

"Nobody."

"Keep it that way!" She began to stare out the window from her chair. I assumed she was wondering where she went wrong. "You were raised better than this, Devon," she said, out of nowhere.

We weren't a family of communicators, so I can't say I remember conversations around the dinner table concerning homosexuality, much less being told it wouldn't be tolerated.

She carried her gaze from the window over to me. I could feel the disgust she now had for me radiating from her eyes. "Have you slept with a girl?"

"Yes," I lied. I knew that if I said no, that was always going to be ammunition. She would say, "How could you make a decision like that without trying it first?"

"You know you can catch the AIDS."

"I know about AIDS."

She shook her head. "This is just disgusting."

"I didn't want to be like this," I said.

"Have you prayed about it?" she asked. I found this slightly insulting; after all, I was God's right hand man.

"Yes. Yes, I prayed so much. I didn't want this, I—"

"You don't know how to pray," she interrupted.

I could deal with the look of disgust, but to tell me I wasn't capable of praying, because I was gay. That hurt. I loved the church. I couldn't begin to tell her how many times I had asked God to take this burden from me.

"Wait here," she said. She got up from her chair, retreated into her bedroom, and closed the door behind her. The walls deceived her. It wasn't long before I heard her on the phone. I may not have been able to make out what she was saying, but I didn't have to. I knew who she was talking to and what about.

A few minutes passed when she reappeared out of her

bedroom and out of her housedress, now wearing blue jeans, a pink polo, sandals, and her purse slung over her shoulder.

"Well, let's go," she said. She didn't have to tell me; I knew where we were going.

We climbed into my mother's Buick. Neither of us spoke the entire ride. Soon we were in the driveway of my Aunt Ellen's two-story brick home. I followed my mother up the steps onto the porch. I felt like a condemned man taking his last walk. My mother knocked on the screen door. My Aunt appeared from the shadows of the living room wearing a housedress similar to my mother's. She was a petite, gray-haired woman. There were almost twenty years between my aunt and my mother.

"Well, come on in," my Aunt invited, holding the screen door open. She acted as if the visit was a complete surprise.

"We come by for some prayer," my mother explained.

Aunt Ellen closed the door behind us. "Well, nothin' wrong with a little prayer."

"I don't know what's wrong with these kids nowadays."

"Nothing prayer can't fix," Aunt Ellen responded. She shouted to the back of the house, "Kenya!" Kenya was one of my many cousins.

"Yes ma'am," a tiny voice responded.

"Get grandma her oil," she said, referring to herself in the third person. Olive oil is the oil she was referring to. "Ya'll go upstairs. I'll be there in a minute."

46

My mother and I took the stairs to Aunt Ellen's bedroom. I sat in a chair in the corner while my mother sat on the bed. We said nothing to each other; the only sound that could be heard was a ticking wall clock. A few moments passed when my Aunt Ellen entered with her olive oil

"Ok, I'm ready," she said.

I didn't need direction; we all knew the routine. We all held hands at the foot of the bed, but not before she rubbed olive oil on my mother's forehead, then mine. The olive oil was to symbolize purity. It would be years later that I learned you could actually cook with it, because up to that point, I had only seen it used in prayer.

Aunt Ellen held both our hands and started to pray.

"Yes, Jesus.... Thank you, Jesus.... Say 'Thank you, Jesus.' Give him his praise," she commanded.

My mother and I repeated in unison, "Thank you, Jesus."

Like all the times before, Aunt Ellen was soon speaking in tongues as she broke the circle and laid hands on me. I awaited my message. It was always a message of hope, but this time I knew I wasn't going to be so lucky.

"Yes, yes ... destruction! You're heading down the path of destruction my son! Don't let the Devil lead you astray! He is a liar, a cheat, and a thief! He's out to kill, steal, and destroy! He wants your soul!" she shouted, with the brimstone and fiery tone of a preacher.

I felt numb. She went on for several minutes with the same message. I felt unworthy of God's love, or of anyone's for that matter.

Aunt Ellen turned to my mother, laid her hands on her forehead, and gave her a different message. "Stay encouraged my child, I am with you," she said. "Keep your head up to Me and you'll make it through."

I don't know how long we were in the bedroom praying, but by no means was it a short period of time. When it was all over with, I was drained, confused, and despite having just been prayed for, I felt more hopeless than when we started. There was a moment when I thought just maybe I could be cleansed of this sin, but I felt no less attracted to men than when we began.

My mother and Aunt Ellen whispered privately in the bedroom while I waited in the living room. There was no doubt that they were talking about me.

When they were out of counsel, Aunt Ellen pulled me aside. "If you have any unnatural urges, call on Jesus three times. He will be there," she consoled. I just nodded in despair. "Is that all it takes," I thought? It seemed a little too simplistic. The next time I felt unnatural urges, all I had to do was call on Jesus. Well, He was going to be sick of me.

"Remember, there is no victory in suicide," she continued.

At the time, I didn't know why she would say such a

thing. Sure, it was a troubling time in my life, but I wasn't contemplating suicide. Years later, it occurred to me that it is said that the number-one reason for suicide among teens is due to issues with their sexuality. Maybe God did tell Aunt Ellen I was a faggot; I'll never know, but I was sure my mom told her also.

I was feeling down, and church was probably exactly what I needed, but I decided not to go to the service. I got up out of bed and headed to the bathroom. After washing up, I walked to the living room window that overlooked the courtyard. As I suspected, it was another beautiful day in Southern California. I went down the hall into the guest bedroom and removed a T-shirt and running shorts from a pile of folded laundry on the futon. I decided to go for a run.

I only had one drink the night before, so I wasn't suffering from a hangover, though I have gone to the gym or gone running when hung-over on many other occasions. Vanity usually won out over the suffering. After I threw on my clothes and running shoes, I grabbed a towel, bottled water, my keys, and I drove over to Balboa Park.

Balboa Park sits on over 1,200 acres of city property. It is home to the world renowned San Diego Zoo, fifteen museums, The Old Globe Theater, and eight botanical gardens. The park offers several paved paths for running or walking. It overflows with culture—seniors practicing tai chi, musicians playing for tips, palm readers with makeshift stands, festivals throughout the year, and those who just appreciate the beauty of it all.

I parked on Sixth Street, which runs parallel to the park on its most western end. I was getting out of my truck when I realized I'd forgotten my iPod. I loved to run, but it was more of a chore if I didn't have my tunes. For a moment, I debated on returning home to retrieve it but decided not to. I crossed the sidewalk into a grassy area where I sat down and stretched for several minutes.

When I was stretched and ready, I began to run north, up Sixth Street, along the sidewalk that skirted the park. Eventually, I rounded the park at the north end. I continued to follow the sidewalk, which began to snake its way south. It was there, after the playground, that I approached my favorite area. The sprinklers that watered the manicured grass placed a light mist on my calves as I ran by. Exotic palms soon lined the walkway; I looked up to see where the fronds met the sky. It wasn't unusual for this scene to be interrupted by a low-flying aircraft headed into nearby Lindbergh Field Airport. It was a picturesque scene that said to me, "This is Southern California."

When I reached the end of the paved trail, I headed north, back up Sixth Street, to start a new lap. By my guess, one lap, which began where I'd parked my truck on the street, was approximately one mile. I would attempt four laps, but without my music the fourth lap would most likely not happen. I always made three laps my minimum; it made it worth the drive to the park.

I was into my second lap when I realized this run was different—I was more in tune with my surroundings. I wasn't hiding behind my iPod. I could hear everyday vehicle traffic to the west, children laughing as they conquered playground equipment, the rumbles of the jet engines descending into the airport, and the thud of running shoes on the pavement approaching me from behind.

I moved to the right of the sidewalk so the approaching runner could pass me if he needed to. I hated being passed. I may not have been the fastest runner in the park, but I could hold my own. Whenever I saw someone in front of me I paced myself to catch them. It would be my goal to not only catch up with them but to pass them. If I couldn't, I was more than ready to admit that they were faster than me. It was a just a little friendly competition.

Whoever was trailing me made no attempt to pass me. His or her steps were soon in sync with my own. They held their position behind me. Maybe they knew any attempt to pass me would be futile.

A few yards ahead would be the turn in the sidewalk

that would send me back, southbound, into the park. It would be there where I would get a look at my competition.

Rounding the corner, the stranger still on my tail, I casually glanced over my shoulder to get a look at him or her.

Damn, he's fine!

As far as runners go, not only did he have excellent form, but he had the physique to go with it. He looked to be a little taller than me, about 5'11" and not overly muscular. He was Latin, with golden skin. The color in his skin looked natural, not achieved by sun worship. He was clean-shaven with a tight buzzcut. He resembled the actor Jay Hernandez, who starred in the movie *Hostel*. I noticed his royal blue shorts that stopped just above his knees. He opted for no shirt on his run, and I couldn't help but admire his beautiful torso.

He was nice to look at, but probably trouble. He was one of the "gym people." *You know the type.* They spend countless hours at the gym, taking any drug they can get their hands on whether for recreation or to achieve physical strides that would have otherwise been unattainable. They made me sick. They made me sick because I wanted to be one of them. They travel in packs at the gym and the bars. They think they're *hot shit* in their tank tops and low-rider jeans laughing, drinking, and having a good time. He was more than likely bad news.

Shit!

He saw me looking.

The stranger began to smile. He had perfect teeth too and a radiant smile. During all my gawking, I nearly tripped on a segment of the sidewalk that jutted up slightly higher than the rest. There was no hiding this blunder. I was lucky not to have fallen face first. I heard him chuckle. I wasn't surprised that he took pleasure in my embarrassment. That's how they are, the gym people, they laugh at those who are less than perfect.

I tried to recover and began to pick up my pace. He did the same. I didn't dare look back again. I didn't have to—for the moment, his flawless face seemed etched into my brain. With the stranger still following me, I tried a new approach. I began to slow down to give him room to pass, but he declined the invitation.

Okay, I only had one more lap; I'd just put on the afterburners and take off, leave him in the dust. On the other hand, he was probably on some performance-enhancing drug, and I would just run myself into the ground trying to lose him. I gained more speed, well above my normal pace. I could still hear him following. He was matching me step for step. We sounded like a small army as our feet hit the pavement. *Who the hell is this guy?* I was headed northbound toward my truck, so I began to sprint. He sprinted too, right on my heels. *Damn!* After a few yards, I could feel the burn in my glutes. I gave it all I had, and he was with me every step of the way. This stranger was no fool. By now, he knew I was trying to lose him, but he wasn't having it. He was going to make sure I knew he was just as fast as—if not faster than—me. Thirty yards shy of my truck, I gradually slowed to a walk. The usual sensation of my thumping heart was now more of a pounding. The stranger sprinted passed me and slowed to a walk also. I was now behind him and admiring his backside. We were both breathing heavily.

I walked by him, pretending I didn't notice him. He said, "Good run." He was still panting.

"Thanks," I said between breaths. I grew excited by the fact that he had spoken to me. I continued walking toward the area where I had stretched out earlier.

I walked in circles for a few moments trying to catch my breath, I sat in the grass with my legs extended in front of me and stretched my hamstrings by touching my toes. He was walking over to me, and I started to feel the transformation to schoolgirl occur. I prayed I wouldn't start to giggle.

Bent over, hands resting on his thighs, the Latin stranger asked, "You mind if I stretch here next to you?"

Rivulets of sweat ran down his handsome face and dripped into the grass.

"No, go ahead."

He sat and mimicked my stretch. "I was pacing myself with you. You're kinda fast."

"I don't like to be passed. My competitive nature I guess." I said, while I sat up and released my stretch.

"I thought I was going to lose you for a minute."

I grinned. "Lose me? You were the one keeping pace behind me the whole time."

"No, I meant when you tripped," he explained. "I thought you were going to fall flat on ya face."

Embarrassed, I said casually, "Oh, that was nothing."

He gazed at me seductively before saying, "Hey, do you mind stretching my hamstrings?"

I swallowed the lump that formed in my throat. His request sounded like it involved touching. "Yeah ... I can do that."

He lay on his back while I took hold of his right leg and raised it off the ground. I took a knee and rested his foot on my right shoulder and began to push his leg forward. I placed my hand on his thigh to support his leg. The hairs on the back of my neck began to stand. His legs were long, lean, and slightly hairy. Unlike his legs, his chest was smooth and hairless. *I bet he is a shaver.* His long shorts fell to his groin during the stretch. It took all the willpower I had not to look directly down, and then I found myself looking into his eyes. I quickly searched for something to look at that wasn't him.

Without saying a word, he nodded and motioned for me to stretch the other leg. I repeated the process with his left leg. He signaled me to stop when his leg was extended as far as it would go. We held the stretch for what seemed like hours.

"So, you run here a lot?" he asked.

Looking off into the distance, I responded, "A couple times a week. I like it out here. Nice scenery."

"Yeah, I certainly had a nice view."

It wasn't original, but I still couldn't help but grin. I released his leg. He sat up. I took my place back in the grass a few feet from him.

"You want me to stretch you out?" he asked.

I grinned again. "No, thank you. I'll be fine."

"So, do you have a boyfriend?"

I was caught by surprise with his forwardness. "Wow, straight to the point. What makes you think I'm gay?"

"The way you were all trippin' when you saw me; besides, I'm never wrong about these things."

I couldn't decide if he was funny or full of himself. Either way, I was falling for it. "No. I don't have a boyfriend. Do you?"

"Do I what?"

"Have a boyfriend?"

"No, I'm not gay."

"Shit!" I said, before attempting to stand.

"Wait, I'm just fuckin' with ya," he laughed, reaching for my arm and pulling me back down. "No, I don't have a boyfriend, and yes I am gay."

I settled back into the grass trying to conceal my giddiness. "You're an ass, you know that?"

He showcased his pearly whites. They were perfectly aligned like a white picket fence. "I'm just having a little fun wit ya."

"So is this what you do?" I asked.

"What do you mean?"

"Pick up boys in the park?"

"Forgive me for saying so, but you look like you're past being a boy. What are you twenty-five … twenty-six?"

I sighed. His sarcasm was wearing on me, though he made up for it with his guess of twenty-five. "Twenty-nine, thank you, and you know what I mean."

"Damn. You're almost thirty."

"Yes, it tends to come after twenty-nine."

He smiled. "I just meant I wouldn't have guessed ya for thirty."

"I'm not, I'm twenty-nine."

"I guess I'm not picking up boys in the park anymore. I'm getting the old men now."

"Funny," I said, not looking the least bit amused. "How old are you?"

"Twenty-four."

A youngin'.

He pointed to a four-story apartment building across the street. "I live in that apartment complex, so I run here a lot—but no, it's not often I strike up a conversation with boys in the park," he said.

His hazel eyes pierced mine as my gaze left the apartment building. I felt like his stare could levitate me off the ground. There was a silence that made me feel awkward. Finally, I said, "I live in North Park." It was my lame attempt to keep the conversation moving.

He stretched out on his side in the grass and got comfortable. "What's your name?" he asked. With all the running and stretching, we never introduced ourselves. Up until now he was simply the stranger.

"Devon, and you?"

"Javier. Javier Cruz."

"Nice to meet you, Javier."

"Oh, the pleasure is mine," he said. "Look, I'm going to cut to the chase. I think you're fine. We should go out sometime."

If my skin tone would have allowed it, I would have

blushed. "Look at you, going for what you want."

"Life is too short. Wouldn't want to look back and have regrets."

"Aren't we mature?"

"Don't let the age fool ya," he said. "I'm on top of my game."

"I bet you are."

Javier stood up. "Look, I have to finish a paper before I head into work tonight. I'm bartending at *The Ritz* tonight. You should stop in for a drink."

A job and he goes to college; he could have potential.

I followed his lead and got up also. "I may do that." I wasn't one to pass up free drinks. "There's my truck. Come on over and we can exchange numbers."

With that charming grin, Javier shook his head. "No," he replied.

"No?" I echoed. "You *do* have a phone … don't you?"

Javier laughed. "I have a phone."

"Then, what's the problem?"

"Well, I figured if you're serious, you will take me up on that drink, and when you do, I'll give you my number."

"Oh, I get it. You have a wife."

Javier laughed. "I told you I'm not married."

"No, you said you didn't have a boyfriend, which is

different."

"I don't have a girlfriend, wife, or boyfriend. Has anyone ever told you that you're cynical?"

"Not without just cause."

"He must have hurt ya bad."

His presumption left me standing there with my mouth open. Was I carrying my Louis Vuitton baggage around in plain view?

Before he started walking away, Javier said, "Just come by." When there was a break in traffic, he trotted across the street.

"Maybe," I mumbled to myself.

I stood in awe as I watched the stranger, Javier, cross Sixth Avenue. His divine body glistened with perspiration in the afternoon sun. I couldn't help but smile. It wasn't until he disappeared into the foyer of his building that I got into my truck and drove away. I was sure he was aware of me watching him.

5

Back at home, I was just out of the shower when my cell began ringing. I quickly wrapped myself in a towel and grabbed the phone from the nightstand in the bedroom. Part of me grew slightly excited about the possibility that it may be Javier, but I reminded myself that we hadn't exchange numbers.

It was my dad. I took a deep breath and mentally prepared myself for the conversation.

Still dripping, I sat on the bed. "Hey, Pop."

"Hey, Devon. How's it going?"

"It's going good, Dad. How about you?"

"You know me, working hard. How are things on the border? Any action lately?"

I always felt pressured to come up with these great

cat and mouse stories about working the border. People always asked melodramatic questions: Have you had to use your gun? Ever get in any car chases? Have you ever been shot at? Some of the tackier ones were: Frisk any hot guys? Ever make out with anyone you arrested? Do you let the cute ones pass?

"Same ol' stuff, Dad."

Telephone conversations with my dad usually didn't last over five minutes, and that included speaking with my stepmom. The line of questioning usually didn't vary from conversation to conversation.

"Have you talked with your brother or sisters?" he asked. That was always question number two after asking about life on the border. I'm the oldest of three. I have a younger brother, Martin, and my sister, Kim, is the youngest at twenty-two. Dad remarried after the divorce. His second wife, Priscilla, has a daughter, Sasha, from a previous marriage. Sasha is older than me by a few months. This made up our happy nuclear family, not including my mother who probably wanted no part of it anyway.

"I talked to everyone this week except Sasha. She didn't return my call."

"You kids aren't big on keeping in touch. Anyway, you off today?"

"Yeah, I'm off. I just got in from a run."

"Any plans today?" he inquired.

I wanted to say, "I'm going to start drinking in a few hours and go dancing with Michael and Rafael later, but first I'm going to go and get the number of the beautiful stranger I met in the park." It seemed that both of my parents were fine with my sexuality as long as we didn't talk about it. Maybe they wanted to believe that I was living a devoted life of celibacy, or else they secretly cringed at the thought of my clandestine life of sex parties, drugs, and alcohol.

"No, Dad. No plans."

"Well, I'm not going to hold you up. I just wanted to see how you're doing."

"Ok, Dad. Good talking to you."

"Bye."

"Bye, Dad." I closed my cell phone and placed it back on the nightstand. In the past, my relationship with my dad had been rocky at best. Coming out to him was only an added strain.

Just days after coming out to my mom, I still went forward with telling my dad.

"You tellin' me you're a fuckin' faggot?" he shouted.

I was beyond scared. I had never heard my father talk like that. Hearing those words made me seriously reconsider my answer. With a quaver in my voice, I replied, "Yes."

He began pacing in the small bedroom I then occupied

in his home. I had never been more afraid of my dad. If I could have taken back what I said, I would have—hell, if I had the choice of being straight at that moment, I would have.

"Has someone abused you?"

I almost wished someone had. It would have been a reasonable explanation for what I was feeling and apparently a reasonable explanation for my father.

With my head hung at its lowest, I again replied, "No."

He still hadn't stopped pacing. "What about that fruity-ass cousin of yours?"

I just sat on the bed still not able to look at him. "No, no one has done anything to me." Apparently, he viewed homosexuality as a communicable disease, a learned behavior, or the result of trauma from being on the receiving end of sexual abuse.

He stopped pacing and towered directly in front of me. I stared down at his dirty work boots. "Look at me," he commanded. I slowly raised my head half expecting a blow to the face. He placed his index finger just inches from my nose, "You know better than this." He enunciated the words firmly, in a tone that was nearly threatening. For the second time, I tried to recall anytime when we as a family had talked about homosexuality. "What could you possibly enjoy about being with another man?" His eyes glared a fiery red.

"I don't know." I was sure he didn't really want me to explain it to him.

"This is what we're going to do. First of all, you're going to keep your mouth shut about this. Secondly, we are going to get you some professional help. From now on, you're on punishment. You go to work and school, that's it. We are going to nip this shit in the bud."

It was at that moment that I realized how our family functioned. We were a family of secrets. It was the same when my siblings and I had been ordered to tell no one when our parents divorced—one of the most trying things a child could go through, and we weren't even allowed to talk about it with anyone.

I was eighteen years old, attending junior college, and for the first time in my life I was grounded. Since I was eighteen, I guess it was more of a house arrest. What could I do?

I left my bedroom only once that night to use the bathroom. I couldn't bear to see my dad or anyone, for that matter. I must have fallen asleep just after 9:00 p.m., shortly before lights-out at the "Wallace Penitentiary." It was shortly after 11:00 p.m. when I heard my bedroom door open, and I could see a silhouette that could have only belonged to my father enter the room. Before I knew what was happening, I was being yanked out of bed by my T-shirt and flung clear across the room. The momentum hurled me into the bookshelves in the corner. My back received much of the impact, and I fell to the floor disoriented and confused. At any moment, I expected to wake from this strange dream before it turned to a nightmare. The silhouette was coming at me again. This time, the escaping moonlight from the blinds put a face to the silhouette. It appeared to be my father, but my father wouldn't treat me like this. This man—the one who was now grabbing me by the throat with one hand, his free hand cocked back and fisted—appeared to be a man out of control. I closed my eyes and anticipated the blow. Fighting back didn't seem like an option. I thought maybe I deserved this, maybe I brought this upon myself; after all, I was taught to keep things to myself. If only I had kept it to myself.

I heard a familiar voice from the doorway. "John, stop!" she cried. It was my stepmom, Priscilla.

"He's a fuckin' faggot!" my dad shouted.

She began to sob. "He's also your son."

He was still holding me by the neck as he dropped his fist. He was breathing heavily. Slowly, he let go his grasp from around my neck. He sank to the floor, drawing his hands to his face. I wasn't taking any chances; I made a run for it with nothing more than the clothes on my back. I nearly ran my stepmother down as I bolted through the bedroom's doorway. Her sobs echoed down the hallway as I fled. By the time I reached the backdoor, I heard her call my name. Although she had probably saved me from the ass-whipping of a lifetime, I wasn't about to stick around for round two or to thank her.

When I hit the pavement, I just ran. I ended up at the corner liquor store, which was closed at the time. I hid behind the dumpsters out back feeling like some kind of fugitive on the run. I sat there crying. It seemed I had no where to turn. Soon the excitement and adrenaline wore off. Shoeless, I noticed my right foot was throbbing; I must have stepped on something during my escape because it was swollen and painful. I finally got up and limped to a payphone to make a collect call. Not having many friends in a culture that was new to me, I had to call Steve, a guy I had only been dating two weeks.

I snapped out of my trance and reached for my cell phone. I maneuvered my way through the phone book until I came across Michael's number, and I hit send.

"Hello," he answered.

"What's up?"

"Nothing. Playing around online."

"You're always online. You need human contact," I teased.

"Well, that's my ultimate goal," he replied.

"True. Anyway, are we on for tonight?"

"Well, if you're going to twist my arm, I guess I can go out for a couple of drinks."

I thought about telling Michael about my encounter

in the park but decided to keep it to myself. "You don't need much convincing when alcohol is involved," I joked.

"And you should talk, Ms. Four Drink Minimum," he shot back.

"Hey, I'm big boned."

"Liking big bones isn't the same thing."

"Shut up," I said. I hated that he was so quick-witted, even more so than the average catty queen. "Did you talk to Rafael today?"

"No, but I'm sure that slut will be there with bells on."

"Alright, I need to grab a bite to eat. I'll see you tonight."

"Bye, Puta."

"Later."

I got up from my bed, and walked over to my dresser, and pulled out a pair of plaid pajama bottoms to wear. After my run and shower, I felt refreshed but hungry. I went into the kitchen and made some whole wheat toast, lightly buttered, and scrambled some eggs. It was a late breakfast. Finished with eating and after putting the dirty dishes into the dishwasher, I sat on the couch in the living room. For a moment, I just appreciated the silence and stillness of a Sunday afternoon. I thought about calling my mother. By this time in Chicago—where she lived—

she was either still in church or having a post-service meal with some of the members of her congregation. There were times I would purposely call during those hours so I could simply leave a message.

It wasn't long before my mind drifted back to Javier, the stranger in the park. I thought about how his skin glistened in the sun, his full lips, and his cocky attitude. I closed my eyes and stretched out on the couch. I allowed myself to imagine that we were in an embrace as I drifted off to sleep.

When I awoke, it was 5:40 p.m. I didn't plan it, but I had slept for over four hours. The late nights were catching up with me. I went into the kitchen to make myself a vodka cranberry before calling my mother. I figured I would get it over with before watching a couple episodes of *Noah's Ark* that I had TiVo'd earlier in the week. Back on the couch, armed with my cocktail and cell phone, I dialed her number. After several rings, she picked up.

"Hello."

"Hey, Ma. It's me, Devon."

"I was just thinking about you," she said. She sounded out of breath.

"Are you okay?"

"Yeah. I'm just having one of those days."

At fifty-two and suffering from complications from

Lupus, my mother was on oxygen. It had been eleven years since I'd left Chicago for the Air Force; the same year my mother collapsed at work. She was rushed into surgery, and all we were told by Aunt Ellen, or my mother, was that she had a cyst on her ovaries that had to be removed. I never believed that to be the whole story, but as I have said before, we were a family of secrets. The day of her collapse, it had been six years since she had been diagnosed with Lupus. Sadly, her health has declined slowly every since.

From research I had done, I learned Lupus is an autoimmune disease that turns against the body's own vital organs and tissues. There are treatments, but no cures. In her case, Lupus mostly affected her lungs, inflaming the pleura, the tissue that lines the lungs. That caused her shortness of breath and coughing. Her doctor prescribed Prednisone, a steroid commonly used for the treatment of Lupus. Some of the side effects of Prednisone are high blood pressure, aggravated diabetes, and weight gain. She suffers from all three and swears it was the Prednisone that was the actual onset of her diabetes.

"You're doing okay, aren't you?"

"Yeah. I'm just having a little tough time breathing today, so I didn't go to church. I didn't want to wheel around the oxygen with me, so I just stayed home."

I took a sip from my drink. "How's everything else?"

"I can't complain. I'm blessed, especially since they finally cleared up this disability stuff."

I admired her outlook on things but often found myself wondering if it was all a facade. It wasn't that I detected any deception, but how can someone who has been through what she has endured continue to have such a positive outlook? I would have been angry. She was divorced, strapped for cash, and her body was failing her. I hoped that one day I would find the peace to rise above my own trivial concerns.

The illness and the rat race had gotten to be more than she could handle. She didn't qualify for disability while she was still working. She simply had to quit her job when her body could take no more. So, last year she did just that, she quit. Initially, she depended on family, friends, and a modest savings to keep her afloat. It wasn't until a couple months ago when she had finally qualified for disability.

Since I was living in California and she in Chicago, I saw her only a couple times out of the year. At times, I felt helpless. I wanted to ease her pain and her financial burdens. I helped her out when I could, but it never seemed enough. I dreamed of one day buying her a house, one in a beautiful neighborhood and more accommodating to her needs. I thought a single-level home would be best, since stairs were becoming a challenge.

I could hear my nephew running around in the background. "Is that Mason?"

"Yeah, that's his little, bad behind making all that noise. Your sister says he is supposed to keep me company while she is at work, but it seems to me I'm watching him while she at work." My mother constantly complained about having to watch Mason, but we all knew she loved doing it. It was just her way of not making things too convenient for my sister. Her favorite phrase before Mason came along was "I ain't raising nobody's babies."

Little did she know.

"What is he doing?"

"Now, he is playing with his toys since we aren't watching the cartoon network anymore. I watched enough cartoons today to last me a lifetime. This little boy has somehow programmed the cable box so that when you turn the television on, it automatically flips to the cartoon network."

"Really," I laughed. "Well, maybe he can program your VCR." Yes, she still had one. It was fully functioning, so there was no need to "move on to that DVD thing," as she puts it.

Mason was five. My sister, Kim, had him when she was seventeen. I was shocked, but I guess all you can do is be supportive. I figured, if I supported her in this, then when the day arrives that I come out to her, she would support me. I was stationed in Germany with the Air Force when Mason found his way into the world, so I guess, in a sense, I depended on my mother's little anecdotes to give me some kind of connection with him, just like she made sure he knew who I was.

"Now that you mention it, your sister bought me one of those DVD players, and yes, the boy knows how to use it. He has a small fortune in Disney cartoons." My mother seemed to be more lighthearted, not like the woman I grew up with. "Enough about me and Mason. How you doing?"

I looked at the condensation forming on my glass. "I'm doing good." I wanted to say, "I miss Tony, and why does it still hurt?," but she knew nothing of him.

" 'Doing good.' That's your answer every time. I worry about you living out there all alone. I don't know *why* you don't move back to Chicago."

I forced a laugh. "I told you, Chicago is too cold and my job is here." She was right about one thing: No matter what I was going through—whether I was upset, depressed, or even on top of the world—when I talked to either of my parents, I was "doing good." I had confided in them once, and that was one time too many.

As much as I would have loved to be closer to my family emotionally and geographically, I truly believed for my sanity I could never move back home. A simple visit could stress me out. It would take me weeks to recover. Hence my early return last visit.

"You *sure* you okay?"

"I'm fine, mom. You don't need to worry about me."

"Well, I do. It's my job."

I figured this was a good place to end the conversation. With my mother—unlike my father—I was always the one who needed to end the conversation before it went someplace I didn't want to go. Occasionally, she felt the need to ask me, as she puts it, if I "still like boys?" The answer was always yes, and that was usually followed by her giving her own telephone sermon.

"Mom, I better go. I have to watch my phone minutes."

"Boy! You just got on the phone."

"I know, but my phone bill last month was outrageous," I lied.

"Alright boy ... I love you."

"I love you too."

I closed my cell phone and placed it on the table. I grabbed my glass, titled it up, and finished it off. I turned on the television and started an episode of *Noah's Ark*.

After catching up on Noah's drama, it was time to rejoin the real world. I spent the next hour and a half at my closet trying to decide what to wear. I guess sometime after my second vodka cranberry, I decided that I was going to *The Ritz*. Javier's first sighting of me, I was wearing sweaty running clothes, so I was determined to leave a lasting impression this time around.

I took a quick shower once again for good measure, applied baby oil to my skin, toweled dry, and sprayed on some *Light Blue* by Dolce Gabbana. Finally, I put on a fresh pair of Diesel jeans and a Guess T-shirt.

6

I parked on the street two blocks from *The Ritz* and sat in my truck wondering what I was doing there. I was suddenly nervous and again found myself going into another situation without backup. I probably would have felt more at ease if Michael and Rafael were with me. What was I so nervous about? After all, he came on to me. There was something about me he liked. *I'll just go in, have a drink or two, see what he's about, and go on my way.*

I finally gathered up my nerve, walked the two blocks to the bar ... and paused in front of the large wooden doors. This was ridiculous. I took in a deep breath of the stale evening air and entered.

The Ritz was somewhat of a dive but not without

its own charm. A jukebox sat in the far right corner playing *It's Raining Men*, though only about eight were in attendance. Most of the eight looked as if they had been in their prime when the original version by *The Weather Girls* topped the charts in 1982. *The Ritz* wasn't very large; there were only three tables along with several booths lining the back and right walls. The bar was to the left. It featured elegant hand-carved pillars on each end and a lacquer finish. When my eyes finally drifted from the detailed workmanship, I spotted two guys behind the bar—one was Javier. His eyes were already on me.

Javier was now in blue jeans and a form-fitting T-shirt bearing the name of the bar. He waved me over. As I approached, I watched as he leaned forward, his forearms resting on the bar's lacquered finish.

"What, no kiss?" he laughed.

I laughed too. "See, I knew the drinks came at a price." I leaned in and our lips briefly met, while a shiver danced down my spine. I barely knew him and we were being too familiar, but it wasn't like I hadn't done more with guys I'd known less.

"I see it's quite busy in here," I joked.

"Our busier days are actually during the week. Tuesdays are amateur strip night and Thursdays are Karaoke."

"Sounds like fun."

Javier leaned back against the beer cooler and crossed his arms. He reminded me of a model posing for a spread. "You know, you should come in here on Tuesday and shake yo ass. There's never really much competition, and you could walk away with one hundred dollars."

I took a seat on a barstool. "Oh well, as long as there is no competition," I said sarcastically.

"I guess that didn't exactly come out right."

"If you were alluding to the fact that I could only win an amateur strip contest if the other contestants were slobs, it did."

"Oh, I see. You're one of *those*."

"One of what?" I asked.

Javier leaned in towards me. "One of those who constantly needs to be reminded of how sexy you are. It's a job I wouldn't mind having," he whispered.

I suddenly felt hot. "You think I can get that drink?" Oh, he was a major playa. I needed to be on my toes with him.

"No comment, huh. What's ya drink?"

"Vodka cranberry, please."

"I figured you were a vodka drinker."

"Oh, really?"

"Really."

"So, what's your drink of choice?" I asked.

"I don't drink."

I suddenly felt like a lush. "Really?"

"Really!" He must have read my look. "Don't worry no judgment here."

"So, what happens when an old-timer wants to buy you a drink?"

"I know how to say no. I have self control."

"That's refreshing."

Javier noticed that we were being watched by the other bartender. "Oh, let me introduce you to Scott." Javier motioned for the other bartender to come over. Scott was a tall, muscular, white guy, and unlike Javier, he wore no shirt bearing the *The Ritz*—in fact, Scott wore no shirt *at all*. "Scott, this is Devon. If you ever see him in here, take care of him."

"Nice to meet you, Devon,"

We shook hands. "Likewise."

"Scott's new," Javier explained. "He's been with us about a week now. On Sunday nights there is usually one bartender, but Scott's still in training."

"Yeah, talk about overprotective. I got this down." Scott said.

"What can I say? The boss has his ways, especially when it concerns his business."

One of the patrons walked over to the far end of the bar. "Excuse me," Scott said before returning to his post.

Javier began to make my drink. "Okay. I owe you a

vodka cranberry."

"You know, I kind of like his uniform a little more than yours. You might want to consider a uniform change," I joked.

Javier added cranberry and vodka, mostly vodka, to the ice in the glass and placed the drink before me. "We really don't have uniforms, but for you, I'll change." He gave me another mischievous grin like the one in the park. "Bartenders think it will help their tips if they show a little skin. They're right, but sometimes the guys like to get a little too touchy, so I try not to give them a reason to."

I removed the straw and took a sip. "Come on … I bet you like it."

Javier pulled his shirt off over his head and tossed it casually behind the bar. "Yeah, I do—from the right person."

The temperature seemed to rise again; I took a longer sip to compensate. "I was joking … you really didn't need to take your shirt off."

"You weren't joking."

He was right. I wasn't joking, but I didn't think he would call my bluff. My eyes gazed over his bare torso. I saw his lips moving, but I was too distracted.

"What?" I asked. I found myself snapping out of a daze. His new uniform had my *full* attention.

"I said, 'What are you doing tonight?'"

"Oh, I'm meeting some friends at *Urban Mo's* in a bit. Maybe *Rich's* later."

"Did you tell them about me?"

I was surprised by his question. "What do you mean 'Did I tell them about you?' We just met; what is there to tell?"

"Well, I guess I have to give you something to talk about." Javier looked at me seductively. I nearly stopped breathing. I was lusting after the young man in a big way.

"Relax, I'm not going to bite," he assured me.

"What are you talking about? I'm plenty relaxed." I drew another sip from my glass. It was strong. I suddenly realized I hadn't eaten since brunch, and again I was drinking on an empty stomach. This was beginning to be a habit. "This is strong. Are you trying to get me drunk?"

"No, besides I have a feeling you will do whatever I want you to do sober."

He was right. "Oh, so now I'm easy," I said, pretending to be offended.

"I'm not saying you're easy. I'm just saying I know you're into me. That's why you're so nervous. It's cool. I'm into you too."

He was onto me. I tried to sound cool and in control.

"Maybe I'm just into the free drink."

"Maybe you're into who's serving you the drink...."

"So, you're here until closing?"

"Do you do that often?"

"What?" I asked.

"Change the subject when the conversation gets to be a little much for you."

"I do not."

"You did, and I haven't decided yet."

"What do you mean you haven't decided?"

"I might have better things to do," he replied.

"Like what?"

"Hang out with you."

I figured this was the perfect time to gain back some ground. "I don't remember extending an invitation," I said.

"You didn't have to. Its written all over ya face."

"Who's going to close the bar?"

"Scott can handle that."

"Well, maybe I'm busy." I turned my glass up before realizing it contained only ice.

"See, you *are* nervous. You're drinking fast," he remarked. "Want another?"

"No, I better head out."

Javier sighed and his lips puckered slightly.

Maybe it was my imagination, but he seemed

disappointed. It *had* to be my imagination. I'm sure he had plenty of guys he could hook up with, although maybe not exactly in this place and time. "I have to meet up with my friends," I said while I stood. The floor seemed to shift under my feet.

"Well, let me give you my number." He began to head over to the cash register. I assumed he was going for a pen and pad.

I played his game. "No, it's not necessary. You know where I'll be tonight. You can give it to me then."

Javier stopped just short of the cash register. All he could do was laugh. "Sounds like a test," he said.

"I know, doesn't it?" I let my eyes slowly gaze over his body. I drank him in just in case it was the final time. Consumed with lust, I shook my head and backed towards the door. I turned and made my exit.

With vodka coursing through my veins, I left my truck parked and walked the few blocks to *Urban Mo's*.

Javier intrigued me. Was he looking for sex or looking to date seriously? I guess time would tell. If I slept with him, I would have to be prepared for the possibility that I would never see him again. I was definitely attracted to him and probably willing to take that chance. On the dating front, I wasn't sure if I was up for another round of the dating game. At twenty-four, Javier couldn't be ready to settle down and date seriously—not that he was that much younger than me, but the maturity level between twenty-four and twenty-nine can be a world of difference. He seemed mature enough for his age though, working his way through school unlike some of the guys out there with no goals at all. Anyway, we had just met. I was overthinking the situation. Besides, at what point did I stop believing in soulmates, romance, and happily ever after? I was examining the situation like a business venture. I guess I needed to minimize risk; after all, I was already working with a damaged heart. I needed to proceed with caution.

7

I soon arrived at the patio entrance to *Urban Mo's,* a restaurant that is comparable to *The Abbey* in West Hollywood, only smaller, not as upscale, and maybe a third less pretentious. I guess they're alike for the simple fact that you can get food, music, and martinis at both, and they're each the Sunday night hot spot. *Mo's* has an outdoor covered patio, a large dance floor in back, and several bars throughout. Throw a few tables in the mix, and there you have it. The food is good—mostly hamburgers, salads, and appetizers—though no one went to *Urban Mo's* for the food. On Sunday nights, *Mo's* is more of a bar and less of a restaurant. Among the people trying to dine on the patio were the smokers and crowds of people drinking.

I like the vibe *Mo's* has on Sunday evenings. The dance floor plays good dance music in back, but mostly, I like having drinks on the patio with friends. That is, of course, while checking out every guy who goes by.

When I reached the front of the line, I pulled out my ID and a twenty dollar bill from my wallet. There was a cover charge after 6:00 p.m. My cell phone began to vibrate in my pocket. I discovered it was a text message from Rafael: *Where are you?* I figured he was already inside, so I didn't bother replying. I attempted to show the bouncer my ID, but he waved me through as if to say, *I've seen you way too many times.* After paying the cover, I went straight to the back bar, which was usually less crowded than the others, and ordered another vodka cranberry, and proceeded to look for Rafael.

After five minutes of searching for Rafael with no luck, I stepped onto a semi-crowded dance floor and danced with my drink in hand.

Note: dancing alone may be a sign that I'm drunk or at least well on my way.

I was grooving to a gay classic, Amber's *Sexual*, when I saw Rafael. Not wanting to leave the dance floor, I gave him a wave to get his attention. He made his way through the crowd and greeted me with a hug.

"Hey, wassup?" I said.

Rafael fell right into the mix, and began dancing too.

"Nothing much, Papi."

"Here," I said, offering Rafael my drink. He took a couple of sips and returned it back to me.

"Are you fucked up already?" Rafael asked, giving me a disapproving look.

"Who me? No, not at all. I only had my vodka meal-replacement smoothie."

"Oh, yes. I must try that diet sometime."

"You don't know what you're missing."

Rafael looked around the dance floor. "Where's Michael?"

"I don't know," I said, still dancing. "I thought he was with you."

"I'll text him."

"Do you ever actually talk to people?"

"This is just convenient." he argued. "Besides, who can carry on a conversation with all this noise?"

All the while moving to the music Rafael pulled out his cell phone and with a few key strokes sent a text message to Michael. "He's probably on the patio smoking," Rafael added. "Oh, listen to this."

"What?"

"I met the cutest guy last night."

I took a long sip. "Imagine that."

"I was walking to my car, and he was waiting for his friend in the parking lot."

"Say it ain't so!"

"What?" Rafael asked with a look of bewilderment.

"You picked up parking lot trade?"

"He was not parking lot trade. He was waiting for his friend."

"So, did you take him home?"

"No. We talked and exchanged numbers. His name is Trevor. He's a Navy boy."

"How exciting. You exchanged numbers."

"Just because I don't fuck em and dump em like others I know…."

"I don't think Michael would appreciate you talking about him since he's not here to defend himself."

"You know very well I am talking about you."

"Well, you should try it sometime. No muss, no fuss." I walked off the dance floor slightly agitated and for no good reason. Rafael followed.

"Don't you want someone to hold at night?" Rafael asked.

I stopped and turned to Rafael. "What?"

"Someone to hold…. Don't you want someone to hold at night?"

"Take a look around Rafael. Does anyone here look as if they are looking to build a happy home? They are just looking for the next fuck. The sooner you realize that, the better off you'll be." I was even taken aback by the words spewing out of my mouth. I could be an angry drunk. "Why are we talking about this anyway? Let's just have a good time."

"Did you drink a whole pitcher of lemonade?"

"What are you talking about?"

"It's just that you seem a little bitter."

"I'm not bitter. I'm just a realist." I wasn't sure if I was buying any of it, but I felt that if I kept telling myself those things, then I wouldn't be disappointed. If I just accepted my reality, I could be at peace. If I knew there was no Prince Charming, then I could stop looking for him.

"You don't believe that."

I didn't respond. I just stared out onto the dance floor. Our conversation was soon interrupted by Michael's arrival.

"Hey, bitches," Rafael said.

I must have still had a blank look on my face from my exchange of words with Rafael because Michael noticed.

"Is she drunk already?" Michael asked Rafael.

"Yes, and preachin' the gospel," Rafael replied throwing his hands up in mock praise.

"Yes, I'm drunk, but I'm merely telling the young one here not to expect too much in the terms of happily ever after," I responded.

"That's a bad attitude." Michael interjected. "I mean,

that's why we're all here, right? Looking for the *one*. Besides, I have to find someone, because when this Angel retires she's not giving it up to become a Golden Girl with you two old maids."

We all laughed. Michael always knew how to lighten the mood. We spent the next two hours drinking and dancing, some of us doing a little more drinking than dancing. It was after 11:00 p.m. when Rafael suggested going to *Rich's*.

"I agree," said Michael, "It's dying out here."

"Then, let's go," said Rafael.

This was our usual routine, but I was reluctant to leave. I was hoping Javier would show up. I had spent the last couple hours looking for him out of the corner of my eye. I didn't even notice that Rafael and Michael had started to walk off the dance floor.

"Hello ... we're leaving ... you coming?" Michael shouted.

"Yeah, let's go," I said.

Rafael, the sober one of the group, drove us to *Rich's*. Upon entering, we notice most of the people looked familiar. That's because half the patrons at *Rich's* had also migrated from *Mo's*.

There was a modest-sized crowd. We bypassed the more luminous front bar for the darker back bar and dance floor. The dj was spinning some techno-type mixes.

Not exactly my favorite, but I was inebriated enough that it didn't matter. We took our places alongside the dance floor.

"Let's dance," Rafael suggested.

"You two go. I'm going to get a drink," I said.

"Come dance, you've had plenty to drink," Michael admonished.

"I don't like the music," I said, "and I forgot my glow sticks."

"Fake it."

Against my will, I danced alongside Rafael and Michael.

I was plotting my escape from the dance floor when I saw him. Javier was standing on the edge of the dance floor and looking directly at me. I smiled. Suddenly, the music seemed to have gotten better.

Javier pierced the crowded dance floor and made his way over to me.

"So, you found me," I said.

"What makes you think I was looking for you?"

"I'm never wrong about these things," I said, borrowing his line from the park. "You were supposed to meet me at *Mo's*; how did you know I would be here?"

"I did go by *Mo's,* but you already took off, so I figured the next logical place was *Rich's*—not to mention you told me you would be here."

"So, you're stalking me," I said.

"No, I just came to where I was being drawn by your lustful magnetism."

I laughed. "Just shut up and dance."

As if on cue, the dj creatively launched into a reggaeton beat—a beat Javier's hips were quite familiar with. His movement was smooth and fluid. Some people say you can tell how good a man is in bed by how he dances. So far, I was impressed. Javier was a natural on the dance floor, showing off his Latin rhythm.

Javier placed his hands on my waist to guide me. "Put your hips into it, Papa," he instructed.

The moment he placed his hands on my hips, I felt weightless. *Did he call me Papa?* Not quite the same effect when Rafael called me Papi. Rafael used it as a nickname. The way Javier used it sounded flirty and sexual.

"You're not a bad dancer," he said.

"Would you have expected anything less?"

"No, no I wouldn't."

The bass was beginning to move me. It was like an aphrodisiac. Before I knew what was happening, Javier spun me around. I followed his lead. He stopped me so that my back was to him. He wrapped his arms around me, and his hips dictated our movement. Rafael and Michael stood just a few feet away not knowing what to make of the situation. I was feeling good. Javier's right hand was slowly making its way up my abdomen underneath my *Guess* T-shirt. I began to feel an erection swelling in his jeans.

"Now it's my turn to check you out," he said. He pulled my T-shirt off over my head—I didn't fight him.

I began to wonder how far we were from having sex on the dance floor as he tried to move a hand down the waistband of my jeans. I too was now stiff with excitement. I turned to face him to counteract his move.

I felt a tap on my shoulder.

"Whore! Who is this?" Michael shouted in my ear.

"I guess I better introduce you to my friends," I said to Javier. "These two guys, with bad timing, are Michael and Rafael."

Michael and Rafael exchanged handshakes with Javier. "Nice to meet you. I'm Javier."

In the middle of the dance floor, our dancing ceased.

"So, how do you two know each other?" Rafael asked. I wouldn't have been surprised if he had pulled out a notepad and pencil for further questioning.

"Devon picked me up in the park this morning," Javier replied.

"You're turning tricks in the park now?" Michael asked.

"No, I was jogging in the park and he picked me up,"

I said.

"Actually, it was kind of mutual. Kind of a love at first sight type of thing," Javier said, looking like he meant it.

"Since we're no longer dancing, maybe we should move off the dance floor," I suggested.

"Maybe we should move to the patio so we can get to know Javier," Rafael said.

Javier led the way off the dance floor with Rafael and Michael on either side, and I followed behind.

"You know, today actually wasn't the first time we met. I met Dee about a year ago. He had his way with me and dumped me. I've been looking for baby Carlos' daddy every since," Javier joked.

"I believe it," Rafael responded.

"She can be a little fast," Michael said.

The three of them laughed. He met them less than five minutes ago and already he had won them over with his charm; and winning Michael over so fast was no easy feat. At least I wasn't the only one vulnerable to it. Rafael turned to me and mouthed the words, *I like him*.

On the patio, the questioning didn't stop. Rafael and Michael could be overwhelming. I thought I would help Javier out.

"I'm going to the bathroom," I said, my eyes fixed on Javier. It was more than obvious that I was trying to rescue him.

"Oh, I have to escort Devon to the bathroom," Javier said. "He just can't get enough of me," he said in a loud whisper to Rafael and Michael.

I led as we left the patio. Javier was trailing behind me. He pulled me by the arm. As I turned around to see why we were stopping, he kissed me. It wasn't a peck like earlier in the day, but a full kiss. I hoped my breath wasn't too foul after all the drinking I was doing.

"I wanted to do that all day," he said.

He tasted every bit as good as he looked.

"Let's go," he said.

We weren't going towards the bathrooms, but towards the front door.

"I need to tell Rafael and Michael I'm leaving," I protested.

He pulled me by the hand and continued for the door. "I think they will understand."

"I think they like you, but stealing me away like this could work against you."

Javier pushed through the crowd. "I'll take my chances. Besides, it's you I want to impress, not them."

When we reached the sidewalk outside the door, I pulled out my cell phone and sent a text message to Rafael and Michael. *Tired. Going home.* Like they were going to believe that for a minute.

8

Javier took my hand as we walked down the street—something I only felt comfortable doing here in Hillcrest.

"You think I can have my shirt back?" I asked. The breeze *did* feel good on my bare skin, but I wanted to look respectable.

"I guess so," Javier said reluctantly, while handing over my T-shirt. "Some friend you are, dumping your friends for some guy you just met."

"You're the one who dragged me out of the club like some Neanderthal."

"I didn't exactly have to club ya over the head did I?" he commented.

"No, you didn't," I laughed. "Where did you park?"

"I walked."

"Oh … you don't have a car?"

"Yes, I have a car. Where did you park?"

"I left my truck at *The Ritz*," I said.

"Well, I guess we'll walk. It's a nice night. You can't drive anyway."

"I've been drinking, and you just want to take me home and take advantage of me." I teased.

"I don't need to get you drunk to have my way with you."

I shook my head. "You're full of yourself."

From *Rich's,* Javier's apartment was about ten blocks. I resisted the urge to flag down a cab. We proceeded up University Avenue hand in hand. I pretended for a moment that he was mine. I noticed he turned heads too. On more than one occasion, I wanted to say to some onlookers, "Back off he's mine." At least for the night he was mine; I had to remind myself of that.

"What if I didn't have a car?" he asked.

"Well, it can make things a little difficult at times, but I guess if you had a bus pass or some form of transportation it wouldn't be a big deal," I said. "See, I *knew* you didn't have a car."

"I have a car. It was just a question."

"Did you get the answer you were looking for?"

"Well, you're a snob, but I think I could work with

you."

"I am *not* a snob," I protested.

"Please … if you had your way, we would be in a cab now, but we wouldn't have this moment."

"What moment is that?"

"The first time we held hands and walked down the street."

I stopped and withdrew my hand from his. "What's up with you? Why are you laying it on so thick? Are you a playa or something?"

"I forgot you're cynical." He paused and simply held out his hand. "You coming?"

I reluctantly latched back onto him. "Yeah. Just so you know, I'm watching you."

I hardly knew him and he was picking me apart. He already had a sense of my pains and weaknesses. His directness and arrogance could be overbearing and exciting at the same time. Those were the very things that attracted me to him, besides his body and looks.

We soon arrived at his building without further incident. Before we entered the foyer of the four-story building, I checked my phone for messages from Rafael and Michael. There was one text message from Michael: *You slut.* Not as harsh as I expected.

We passed the elevator and took a flight of stairs to the second floor. Four doors occupied the hallway, each leading to an apartment. Javier proceeded to unlock the first door on the right. He entered and turned on a light, and I followed. To the right was a small kitchen with two bar stools and counter which served as his dining area. In the center of the room was a neatly-made, full-size bed. A love seat occupied the foot of the bed across from the television. An office area with a computer was to the left of the room.

"It's not the *Four Seasons*, but welcome to my home," he said.

I knew the *Four Seasons* remark was a dig at me being a snob, as he put it, but I let it go—partly because I never used the bathroom before we left *Rich's,* and I had to go badly. "Bathroom?"

He pointed to the left. It was actually a rather large walk-in closet with the bathroom on the far end. After I relieved myself, I looked through the medicine cabinet for mouthwash. I was relieved to find some under the sink, because I was sure a kiss from me would have been fatal.

With minty-fresh breath, I exited the bathroom. The cozy studio was no longer lit by overhead lighting but by three vanilla-scented candles placed in various spots throughout the room. The candles were accompanied by smooth jazz music. *What did this twenty-four year old know about Jazz?* He was trying to impress me. Javier was near the bed removing his pants; his shirt was already off. I was paralyzed by the site of his nearly-naked body. The flames from the candles projected shadows that danced over his golden skin. I just stood and watched the flickering glow caress his skin. When he was down to just his fitted boxers, he held his hand out to me.

"Come here," he enticed, the tone of his voice low and sensuous.

I slowly walked over to him, carefully taking him in with my eyes. When I reached him, my reward was a kiss. This one was longer, deeper, and more intoxicating than before. Again, for the second time tonight, he pulled off my T-shirt. I kicked off my shoes and slid out of my pants.

"Lie down," he breathed. I did exactly that. "Under the covers…." He followed.

We kissed.

And kissed.

And kissed….

Each kiss seemed more satisfying than the last until, finally, he wrapped his arms around me. I turned to lie with my back to him, and I could feel the throbbing in his boxers that we both seemed to ignore but were fully aware of. Before I knew it, we drifted off to sleep.

Not exactly the story I had hoped to brief Rafael and Michael on, but that's what happened. Maybe I would embellish it a little; besides, they wouldn't believe I didn't do *anything* with him. I felt so safe drifting asleep in his arms, so much better than I had imagined earlier in the day.

When I awoke in the morning, there was no music, no candle light, and no Javier. I propped myself up in bed. The studio apartment was now lit by natural sunlight streaming through the window. The wall clock displayed 8:45 a.m. Maybe he was in the bathroom.

"Javier!... Javier!" No answer. *Did he ditch me in his own apartment?*

It was when I got up to investigate that I noticed the note on the counter.

Morning Sexy,

I had to go to class. I won't be done until about noon. Feel free to sleep in. There are some croissants in the kitchen and OJ in the fridge.

Javier

I smiled and placed the note back on the counter, then I crawled back into bed. I was a little surprised that he had left me alone in his apartment. I guessed we wouldn't be finishing what we started the night before.

I could have slept until noon, but I didn't want to be there when Javier returned. I figured I would have looked very lazy if I was in still bed, since he had been up since Lord knows when attending classes. Needy wasn't a look

I was going for either.

It was 10:30 a.m. when I got out of bed and dressed. I scribbled my number on the note he left for me. Locking the door behind me, I started the long walk back to my truck. I was grinning like I was starring in my own toothpaste commercial. I pulled out my cell phone to see if I had any messages. The night before, I had silenced the ringer so Javier and I wouldn't be disturbed. The only message I had received was from Michael. He first chastised me for ditching him and Rafael, and then he demanded details.

I had just reached my truck when my cell phone rang. The caller ID displayed Michael. I figured I would just get it over with.

"Hello," I answered.

"Spill it ho."

"Sorry to disappoint you, but nothing happened. You saw how much I had to drink. I just passed out."

"You had all that in your bed and nothing happened?"

"No—he had all of *this* in his bed and nothing happened."

"Boring!"

"Get a life."

"You know I live for your meaningless encounters."

"Well, I promise I will do better next time. There will

be others."

"Not like him."

"Are you saying I can't pull anyone like him again?"

"All I'm saying is there will never be another Javier."

Thanks to Michael's remark, the thought that I may never see Javier again suddenly entered my head. "I have to go, I'm just getting to the gym," I lied.

"You spend way too much time at that gym."

"We all can't be bears comfortable with our plus sizes. Besides, if I don't stay in shape, then boys like Javier won't look my way."

"I am not a bear."

"Byeeee!"

"Bye, Bitch."

No sooner had I closed my cell phone than it rang again. "Javier" showed up on the caller ID. This confused me, since I hadn't added his number to my phone yet and didn't know any other Javier.

"Hello."

"Morning, sleeping beauty."

I was back, center stage, in that toothpaste commercial—grinning. "How did you get my personal line? Fans usually contact my answering service."

"Oh, I'm a fan."

"You said it, not me."

"I put my number in your phone this morning. Then

I just dialed my cell phone from yours."

"Well, that was pretty bold of you."

"Well, I'm a bold type of guy."

"Speaking of bold…, do you often leave strange men in your apartment?"

"I didn't realize you were strange, but no I don't."

"Well, to be perfectly honest, I cleaned you out. I pulled my truck up and took everything. I am on my way to the flea market now to sell it all. Then I'm leaving the country."

"Someplace nice I hope."

"Yep, being a fugitive and all, I can't exactly tell you where I'm going."

"That's too bad. I was going to invite you to dinner this week."

"I may be able to return for dinner…."

"When are you off this week?" he asked.

I was free that night, but I didn't want to appear anxious. I remembered that on Thursday I would be at the gun range qualifying during the day which would leave my evening free. "How about Thursday?"

"Let's see, today is Monday. Thursday is so far away, but I guess I'll have to wait. I'm off too, so that works out."

"Patience is a virtue," I said. "Give me a call later in the week. You have my number right?… That's right …

you confiscated my cell phone."

"No, I didn't. It's still in your possession; besides some people might call that romantic."

"Some might call it psychotic, but I won't hold it against you."

"Well, I need to get to class. I'm looking forward to Thursday."

"Study hard."

"Bye, Dee."

He was right. I did find the intrusion on my cell phone slightly romantic—but just because I did, I didn't have to let him know it.

9

Thursday came in its own sweet time. Not only did I have a dinner date with Javier later in the evening—he confirmed the day before—but I also had my weekly appointment with Dr. Lindale.

Normally, this appointment was in the morning; but this time, I had to reschedule it to late afternoon because of my day at the gun range. Dr. Lindale was my therapist. The truth was that I never had a psychotic episode, never heard voices, or ever tried to harm myself. I had thought that because I'd been single for so long, maybe something was wrong with me, and I figured maybe I should examine that. Sure, I was only twenty-nine, and I can't say I was looking to protest on the steps of City

Hall with my longtime, imaginary boyfriend, Diego, for the right to marry. It just seemed that I had no significant relationships prior to Tony. It was in my twenties when I was supposed to make all my mistakes, learn from them, eventually meet Diego, and live happily ever after. So, I found myself in therapy. I had been seeing Dr. Lindale for a year and a half. Shortly after starting therapy was when I'd met Tony. I continued to go; besides, I felt a symbolic raise in social status by having a therapist. It was the equivalent of having a nanny. It was like saying that my life is so hectic I can't possibly handle it all on my own. Today, I felt on the verge of taking little Mateo's Ritalin before going to Dr. Lindale. Mateo would have been Diego's and my adopted baby boy from Guatemala.

At each appointment, Dr. Lindale and I talked about anything and everything going on in my life. I wasn't entirely sure if I felt any different, but I guess I was learning a lot about myself.

I was a few minutes early for my four o'clock with Dr. Lindale. She shared a suite with two other colleagues, as far as I could tell, though I didn't think they were therapists as they rarely seemed to be in the office. Like most days when I arrived for my appointment, I was the only person in the waiting room. Nothing on the magazine rack was of interest to me. I was always a little anxious before an appointment. As much as I liked talking about my favorite subject—me—sometimes it was hard to fill an entire hour if I had an uneventful week. Some days I didn't feel like going.

On my first visit, she gave me some literature on her philosophies, procedures, and general guidelines. One bit of information stated that when a patient didn't want to go to sessions, it was probably when the patient was making the most progress. I didn't feel like I was on the verge of some tremendous breakthrough, but simply put, some days I didn't want to go.

Dr. Lindale emerged from her office. "Good afternoon. Come in, Devon."

"Good afternoon."

I guessed Dr. Lindale to be in her late forties. Her black shoulder-length hair was always meticulously styled. She carried a few extra pounds on her frame, but it just added to her curve appeal. She was attractive and somewhat of a fashion diva. Her cream-colored pantsuit complimented her brown skin.

As I walked into Dr. Lindale's office, her familiar, but not overbearing, flower-scented perfume tickled my nose. I sat on the sofa opposite her black leather chair. She closed the door behind me and took her seat. She always kept the office a little too warm for my taste. It gave new meaning to being in the hot seat.

She took her seat. "What's new?" she inquired, getting right down to business.

I've heard that given the opportunity most people can go on and on … and on … talking about themselves. On first dates, it is said that you should get the other person to talk about themselves. It's a subject they won't get tired of. It also prevents you from monopolizing the conversation, and you appear to be a good listener. I have to admit, to some degree I felt a slight bit of self-centeredness sitting down talking about myself for a whole hour in therapy. After eight months I knew nothing about this woman except the names of the schools she had attended, and that's only because her degrees were hanging on the wall.

I got over my initial jitters and proceeded to tell Dr. Lindale about my running into Tony.

"How did it feel to see him?"

"Well, when I learned he was at *Numbers*, I felt kind of panicky, but when I saw him, I was just glad to see him. I have to admit I was crushed to see him there with someone else."

Dr. Lindale took down a few notes on her legal pad. "Do you still have feelings for him?" she asked.

"I guess I do."

"Are you still in love with him?"

I was taken aback by her question. Hesitantly, I said, "I'm not sure … I mean, no."

More notes. "Hmmm ... I see," she said. "What did you hope would happen Saturday night when you saw Tony?"

I sighed. "Not that I'd thought about it, but when he saw me, I hoped it would have stirred up some emotion in him ... you know. He would of thought about the good times we had. We would have talked and caught up on things, and all the while he'd be thinking, *what have I done? I had such a good thing and threw it away.* He would tell me that he wants to try again, and he'd hope that I'm willing. Of course, I would have to think about it, but in the meantime, we'd go home, have great sex, and live happily ever after."

Why, all of a sudden, was the phrase "happily ever after" in heavy rotation within my internal and verbal dialogue?

Dr. Lindale smiled. "Sounds like a lot of thought went into that."

"Yeah, kind of sad isn't it?"

She laid the legal pad on her desk. "I wouldn't call it 'sad,' Devon. There is no shame in loving someone. It's not always reciprocated. Unfortunately, this situation is part of the whole dating process. It didn't work out this time," she encouraged, "but, who knows what the future holds?"

"It's not like I'm sitting at home waiting for him to call. I'm realistic about the situation. I know we will never have what we once had. I guess my heart just hasn't caught up with my head yet," I said. Then I added, "I have a date tonight."

"Really? Tell me about him."

I told Dr. Lindale how Javier and I met, and how we spent the night together. I was always pretty open with Dr. Lindale about my sex life, sparing details of course. I didn't know if she had heard worse, but she never seemed shocked over my tawdry affairs.

"That sounds promising."

"We'll see."

"May I offer a piece of advice?"

"Sure," I said. I wanted to say, *Isn't that the reason I come here?* Though, in actuality, I know it's not a therapist's job to make decisions or lead a patient.

"Be careful not to let your past with Tony taint anything that might be in your future. I would hate for you to let a good guy get away because you're still holding this torch for Tony."

"I hear you, but I would say it's more of a match now."

She gave me a look that I interpreted as, "Who do you think you're fooling?"

"I think I'm cynical,… a jaded queen," I said, thinking

about the conversation I had with Rafael at *Mo's* as well as conversations with Javier.

"How so?"

"Well, when I was in my early twenties, anything was possible. Prince Charming was going to ride up on a white horse and rescue me, but that's the stuff movies and dreams are made of. The truth is, most guys don't really want to marry and spend the rest of their lives with someone. They think they do, but they're just sticking around until something better comes along. It's hard to find a guy to date, not to mention one who believes in monogamy. Life is just one big party to gay men —"

"Do you really believe that, or are you just blowing off some steam?" she interrupted.

"I don't know *what* to believe anymore. All I know is all my friends are single, and supposedly we're all looking for Mr. Right. We all can't be overlooking him, can we? I know the Internet is crawling with guys in long-term relationships looking for a little fun on the side or single guys looking for one-night stands. What I'm starting to believe is that two men in a relationship is a joke. Being heterosexual would be so much easier."

"Well, let's examine that. The divorce rate in this country is over fifty percent. Men cheat on their wives. Wives cheat on their husbands. There are women much older than yourself looking for Mr. Right too. Do you honestly think heterosexuals have it any easier than you?"

I sighed deeply and reluctantly agreed. "I guess not."

"We're out of time. We will pick this up next week."

"Next week," I echoed.

10

It was almost 6:30 p.m., and Javier had insisted on picking me up at my apartment at 7:00 p.m. Paranoia told me he wanted to pick me up so he could see how I lived. You can tell a lot about a person by their home, so I did an apartment walk-through a couple hours earlier. There were no dirty dishes in the sink, no scary prescriptions or creams in the medicine cabinet, no condom wrappers in the wastebasket (can't appear easy), and plenty of condoms bedside just in case. With the apartment clean, and with compromising evidence out of sight, I was standing in front of the closet in nothing but a pair of briefs trying to decide what to wear.

After several minutes of looking through the shirts and jeans in my closet, like it was the clearance rack at the Nordstrom, I decided on a pair of Express jeans, a blue polo, and a pair of black Italian loafers. After I was done dressing, I sat on the couch anticipating the arrival of my date. I began wondering what I was thinking going out with someone so young. This guy was twenty-four years old. He was still wet behind the ears, as they say. I'd always been drawn to the older, more mature guy—of course, that always got me nowhere fast. Javier was too young to settle down. His hormones were just peaking at twenty-four. Just months away from thirty, I couldn't say that mine had calmed down any, but regardless, he was a little young. That's why it had to be only about sex.

My thoughts were interrupted by the telephone. I picked the receiver up off the end table.

"Hello," I answered.

"Hey, it's me," Javier said.

I hated that I suddenly felt giddy. "Where are you?" I asked. It was a stupid question considering Javier didn't have my home number, so he could only be calling from the call box downstairs. Of course, a few days ago, I didn't think he had my cell phone number either.

"I'm at the door downstairs."

"I'll buzz you in."

I hit the corresponding number on the phone's keypad to unlock the security door. Javier was on his way up. I quickly went to the full-length mirror in the bedroom to look myself over again: nothing stuck in my teeth, shaved head (no hairs out of place), and clothes wrinkle-free. With everything to my satisfaction, I went to the door.

Within seconds he knocked. I patiently waited for the second knock then opened the door.

I smiled. "Hi."

"Why didn't you open the door?" he blurted out. He looked rather nice in a black, deep V-neck short sleeve shirt.

"What are you talking about?"

"You were standing in front of the door, but you waited before you opened it."

"No, I didn't."

"I could see your shadow in the peephole."

I was dumbfounded. "I don't know what you're talking about," I said. "Couldn't you have just walked in and kissed me like a normal person?"

He did exactly that. I could have gotten used to his lips on mine.

"I think that's cute," he said as our lips drifted apart.

"What's cute?"

"That you've been waiting for me by the door all evening," he said, with a chuckle.

"You're crazy," I said as I began to walk away.

Javier pulled me back by my arm. "Okay, don't admit it—but remember, I waited *three days* to see you again, and I admit I couldn't wait."

I was moved by what he said. "I didn't realize you were counting."

"Believe it."

He kissed me again.

"Okay, you got me. I was by the door," I admitted. "I let you knock twice because I didn't want to appear anxious."

"Yeah, you're busted. Just be real wit' me, and I'll be real wit' you. Now, was it so hard to admit you couldn't wait to see me? No need for false pretenses."

I searched his eyes, his big, beautiful, hazel eyes. I didn't know what I was looking for, maybe the neon sign that flashed *playa*. He seemed too good to be true. "I was looking forward to seeing you, but I wouldn't go as far to say I couldn't wait."

"That's a start," he said. "Now show me ya place."

I gave Javier a tour of my apartment that ended—not by coincidence—in my bedroom.

This time, it was me who headed in for another lip session.

"You keep that up and we might not make dinner," Javier joked, playfully.

"That's fine with me. We have some unfinished business anyway."

With my arms wrapped around him, he smiled. "You

have to buy me some ice cream or something before you get the good stuff," he teased. "I'm not *that* easy."

"Is that right?"

"That's right."

"Then tell me, where are we going for dinner?" I asked.

"That's a surprise," he said. "You ready?"

"Let's go."

Once outside, I followed Javier to an early model two-door Honda Civic Coupe parked on the street. The Honda was black with custom wheels and tires, aftermarket head and tail lights, racing stripes, and a spoiler. It looked like a car straight from the movie *Too Fast Too Furious*. The only thing I didn't see was a nitrous tank, which it may have had somewhere out of sight.

Standing by the passenger door, I said, "This is quite a fancy car for a college student."

"Yep."

I knew his lack of response was intentional. I let it pass; I wasn't going to fall for it.

We both got in the car.

"I have to tell you something, so don't freak out," he said.

"What?" I asked, noticing quite a difference in his tone of voice. I knew this was when he would tell me that he is actually married, is on parole, has kids, or is really sixteen.

"I think it's only fair I tell you this. I mean … if we continue to see each other." His voice grew quiet, nearly somber.

"What?" I repeated with some urgency.

He hesitated. "I sell drugs to get myself through college."

Heat began to radiate from my face. My body tensed, and I could feel perspiration building on my forehead. "Well, that's just great," I said with a hint of demoralized sarcasm.

Javier broke into a broad grin.

"And you're obviously joking." I felt quite gullible. "You can be a real ass, you know that?"

Javier pulled away from the curb. "You love that about me."

"Whatever." I looked out the window to hide the smirk forming on my face.

"You'll be surprised how many people think you're a gang banger or drug dealer by the car you drive."

"Like I don't know about stereotypes."

"It was my mom's car. When I decided to come down here for school, she gave it to me," he explained.

"This used to be your mom's car?"

"Well, it didn't look quite like this when she owned it," he said. "Slowly, over the last couple of years, I added a little flava to it."

"Oh, *flava*," I mocked. "So, where are we going anyway, a street race?"

With the same tone he used when he claimed to sell drugs, Javier said, "I quit racing after the accident."

I quickly turned to look him in the eye to detect any deceit. That was hard to do, since he was driving and concentrating on the road. He noticed me looking at him.

"Okay, you got me. There was no accident," he admitted. "I don't race, but I'm not going to pretend I don't like a little speed now and then on an open highway. I'm not reckless. For me, how my car looks is just an expression of who I am—"

"What? Flashy, fast, and dangerous?" I interjected.

"If that's how you want to see it. I see it as bold, sporty, and different."

"Different, huh?" I secretly hoped he *was* different.

After a few minutes, we pulled up to Javier's apartment building. "This doesn't look like a restaurant," I commented.

"This is better than a restaurant," he said. "You'll see."

As we got to the second floor, I began to smell a pleasant aroma. Definitely tomato based. I couldn't tell exactly what it was, but something told me it was dinner.

We entered Javier's apartment, and he went directly for the kitchen. The smell was more powerful and definitely coming from his kitchen. I watched as he used oven mitts to pull a casserole dish from the oven.

"Need any help?" I offered.

"You just relax. I have it all under control."

I did exactly that, making myself comfortable on the love seat. Sitting there, I couldn't help but play back Sunday night in my head.

I noticed Javier placing food into storage containers, and there was a picnic basket sitting on the counter. "For some reason I wouldn't have guessed you owned a picnic basket," I said. "Are we having a picnic in the park?"

"I don't; it's borrowed. And we're having dinner someplace better than the park."

What could be better than having a picnic in the park?

"Okay, 'looks like everything is ready to go," he said. Javier finished putting a few more items in the picnic basket before carrying it to the door. "Vámonos."

I followed Javier out the door and down the hall. We took the stairs to the fourth floor. Once on the fourth floor, we walked down a short hallway, turned a corner, and came to a final set of stairs that took us up to the rooftop.

On the roof, we were greeted by a slight coastal breeze that cooled the evening perfectly. I was sure I could smell the saltwater from the Pacific Ocean just a few miles away. The sun's trip across the Southern California sky was nearing an end.

Javier extended his free arm with a flourish, "Welcome to Javi's."

"I can't say I've been here before."

"I know you haven't; it's our grand opening."

Javier's building was only four stories, but we had a great view of the place where we had first met—the park. The view of downtown was limited in almost every direction by new high-rise condos. Anyone from the two larger condominium buildings on either side of us could look down onto our semiprivate dinner.

I followed Javier over to the patio table, which was covered with a red table cloth adorned with a fresh floral centerpiece and two candles.

Javier placed the picnic basket next to the table. "Now, if you direct your attention to the west, in about forty-five minutes you will witness an unforgettable sunset," he enthused. "Do you know why it will be unforgettable?"

"I suspect you will tell me."

"It will be our first."

I searched his eyes again. Whatever I was looking for, I couldn't find it, not a clue. My intuition was of no help either; I was already too caught up to come up with a rational impression of him.

"Are there going to be more?" I inquired as we sat down.

"I have a feelin' there will be."

I was beginning to think he wanted more than a booty call. Who would go through all this trouble for a booty call? He already knew from Sunday that I was pretty much at his beck and call.

"I took a chance not knowing what type of food you like. I should have asked you over the phone. I hope you're not a vegetarian or anything."

"Cute *and* you can cook."

"To be perfectly honest, my mother cooked this meal," he confessed, "but make no mistake, I can throw down in da kitchen. I'm a mama's boy, so I used to help her out in the kitchen a lot."

"So, your family lives here?"

"No, she and my sister live in L.A. She drives down every once in a while to check on me. I don't like for her to drive down here, but she does sometimes."

"That's nice of her, checking on her baby boy.... So, what did *she* cook?" I asked.

"Tonight's theme is Italian. I told her, 'No Mexican food.'"

"Why no Mexican food?" I asked. "I love Mexican food."

"Because once you taste my mom's Mexican food,

you'll be ready to marry me."

"It's that good, huh?"

"Her food and me as your husband, it doesn't get any better. Of course, *me* being the major bargaining chip in dat deal."

I grinned. "Of course."

Javier leaned over to open up the basket and began to pull out the contents. "First we have a nice bottle of red, a Caesar salad, mom's famous lasagna, breadsticks, and Tiramisu. The breadsticks are store bought, and the Tiramisu is from *Extraordinary Desserts.* We can't take credit for those."

"You mean *your mom* can't take credit, and I love *Extraordinary Desserts.*"

I couldn't help seeking a little revenge for Javier's earlier mischief. "I'm assuming there is cheese in the lasagna ... and the salad"

"Yeah—is that a problem?"

"Well, I'm lactose intolerant."

Disappointment riddled his face. "I *knew* I should have asked," he said. "We can order some take-out; it's not a problem."

"Yeah, you should have asked," I said, but not before losing control and laughing.

"Your messin' with me, aren't you?"

"Well, you started it with the whole 'drug dealer'

thing," I said. "Now, open up that bottle of wine and fix me a plate. I'm starving."

We were halfway through dinner when we stopped to admire the sunset. Three quarters of the sun had already disappeared behind the skyline. Orange hues peered from behind buildings and distant palms. Red-orange light danced on a sliver of ocean that could barely be seen from the rooftop. It wasn't long before the sky dimmed to purple, which eventually faded to dark.

When the sunset was over, Javier poured the remainder of the wine between the two of us. The rest of the meal was eaten almost entirely in silence, but not the uncomfortable type.

"I thought you said you didn't drink," I noted.

"I don't normally, but this was a special occasion," he explained. "It's our first date."

Jaded me couldn't help but wonder if that was the first of many lies to come.

"Well, you have to tell your mother how much I enjoyed the lasagna," I said.

Javier looked intently off in the distance, in the direction where the sun was already laid to rest. Candles and ambient city lights illuminated our rooftop scene. Something about him seemed seductive to me under candlelight. I was sure he didn't strive for that look, but it came naturally.

"So, does mom know her boy ... likes boys?" I asked.

Javier smiled, still not drawing his attention away from the scene of the already-set sun. "She knows. That woman is like my best friend."

"Really," I said, wondering what that must feel like.

"Yeah, she never gave me a hard time about it. When she was down today, I told her I had a date and was wondering where I should go. You know what she told me?"

"What?"

"She said, 'I'll cook you two a nice meal, mijo. Have him over for dinner.' She went to the grocery store, bought all the ingredients, and spent most of the day in the kitchen."

"So, this was all mom's idea?"

Javier turned towards me. "Well, it was her idea to cook, but the rooftop theme was my idea."

"What about your dad?"

"I don't know him," he said rather quickly.

"I see," I said. I didn't want to push the issue. I would let anything more on that subject be voluntary.

"What about your family?" he asked. "You haven't told me much about yours or yourself for that matter."

I took a sip of wine as if buying myself time. "Well, there's not much to tell. My parents are divorced, and me being gay ... well we just don't talk about it."

"Does that work for you?"

It sounded like a question Dr. Lindale would have asked. "No. Not really. I mean, for once I would like to have a real conversation with them ... you know. I don't want to talk about the superficial bullshit like the weather. And my dad with his 'How are things on the border?' routine—"

"What do you mean 'border'?" Even with the lack of light, I could see how Javier's face suddenly became flushed.

It was then that I realized I had never mentioned my line of work to Javier. This was our first date, and we hadn't talked much since our initial meeting. "Oh ... I'm a Border Patrol Agent. I guess that never came up, huh?"

He swallowed the remainder of the wine in his glass. "I see. How do you like that?"

A lot of agents pride themselves on being able to pick an illegal out of the crowd. Often, the agents detect a particular look or attitude, a way in which the illegals carry themselves, or their refusal to assimilate to life in the United States. In actuality, I guess this is more of a stereotype—one I didn't think fit Javier at all, but his sudden nervousness was apparent to me.

"It's okay. It's a job."

"So, you arrest a lot of immigrants?"

"Yeah, on the border.... That's sort of the job."

"Do you feel guilty about it?"

"Guilty? I don't think 'guilty' is the word. Compassionate maybe, but not guilty."

"Wow, that's interesting."

"Not a supporter, huh?"

"It is what it is."

"I don't want to kill the mood with an immigration debate."

"You haven't killed the mood, Papa," he said as he pulled my hand to his mouth and kissed it. Even with the attempt at affection, something about him felt withdrawn— maybe because he was no longer looking me in the eye.

Javier gave me that mischievous grin again. "Since you wanted to change the subject, I've got a question for you," he said.

Almost afraid to ask, I ventured, "What's that?"

"What do you like to do in bed?" he inquired.

"I'm assuming you want to know if I'm a 'top' or 'bottom'."

"That's a start."

Suddenly he was like Barbara Walters, but it was a valid question. It was why I believed in sex on the first date. It addressed the compatibility factor.

Without hesitation, I responded, "I'm versatile."

"That wasn't the question," he said. "Your choice was, 'Top or bottom?'"

"Like I—"

"There are only two answers to this question. Top or bottom?"

The conversation was getting aggressive, and it was turning me on. "What's with the labels?"

"If you and I were butt-naked on my bed right now, what would you want to do? Fuck or be fucked?"

Hearing those words come out his mouth excited me. The vision played out in my head. Before I knew what I was saying I heard myself say, "Fuck me."

What was I saying? I couldn't be a bottom-bitch to this mere twenty-four year old.

"Was that so hard to say, that you want me to fuck you?"

Suddenly my fitted boxers lacked the space to contain their contents. It was like phone sex without the phones, and we were right in front of each other. The romantic dinner had taken a turn.

"No it wasn't," I said. "What about you? What do you like?"

"To fuck you."

Damn. I was ready to do it right there on the rooftop.

"Congratulations, by the way."

"For what?" I asked.

"You've just come out. You're a 'bottom'," he said, following up with a kiss.

"I really don't like you at times, and I'm not a 'bottom.' Such a question is subjective; besides, that's just what I feel at the moment."

We were interrupted by my ringing cell phone. Normally, during a date I would have put it on vibrate, but I must had forgotten. The display showed Rafael. I placed the phone on vibrate and placed it back in my pocket.

"Sorry about that. Where were we?"

"You were telling me how wonderful dinner was, and trying to figure out how you could return the favor."

"The wine must be going to my head, because I don't remember any of that," I said.

"Let me refresh you memory," he said. "You said you were going to give me a massage and whatever else I wanted."

"Really?"

"Yup!"

Now my cell phone began to vibrate. I pulled it out; this time Rafael had sent a text message: *Need help 911.*

"Damn it ... I'm sorry. I better call him and see what

he wants. It's Rafael, he says it's important." It better be, I thought. The last 911 text I got from him was to TiVo an episode of *American Idol*, which I TiVo anyway.

I dialed Rafael's cell phone. He answered on the second ring.

"Are you working?" he slurred.

"No, I'm not working. What's the problem?"

"The fucker took my wallet," he said.

Confused, I asked, "Who took your wallet, Rafael?" Javier looked concerned.

"I had a date with that guy Trevor."

"The one from last weekend."

"Right. We go to *Aladdin's* for dinner. Everything is going well. After dinner I go to the bathroom, and when I come back, he's gone. I wait about twenty minutes, thinking maybe he stepped outside. Tired of waiting, I go for my wallet and it's gone. I think I left it in my jacket at the table."

"Please tell me you didn't have your badge and credentials on you." It would be hard enough going to work and telling superiors you lost your badge and credentials, but I would have hated to see Rafael try to explain the circumstances through which he lost them.

"No, thank God they're at home," he said. "I hate to ask you this, but could you come and pay the bill? I'll reimburse you. The restaurant won't let me leave, since I have no identification. They think I'm trying to run a game on them. If I can't get anyone to come down and bail me out, they're going to call the cops."

"Yes, okay," I said with a sigh. "What did he get away with?"

"Eighty dollars in cash, two credit cards, and my ATM card."

"You should call the police."

"Are you kidding? No. I'm too embarrassed."

"You should consider it. Anyway, I'm on my way."

"Thanks, Devon."

"Bye."

I closed my cell phone.

"Is this where a friend calls with some emergency to end a boring date?" Javier asked.

"Apparently so, but this wasn't premeditated nor a boring date," I said. "I'm sorry, but I have to cut it short. Rafael got his wallet stolen, and he needs me to pick him up."

"Where is he?"

"He's at *Aladdin's*."

"I can drive you."

"You sure it's not a problem?" I asked. I was glad he offered to take me to *Aladdin's* instead of returning me to my apartment to get my truck. I wanted him to see that this wasn't some lame attempt to get out of the date.

"It's no problem," he said. "So, um, both Rafael and Michael—"

"Yes, they're agents too."

11

Within half an hour, after cleaning up the remains of our rooftop dinner, we were at the restaurant. Javier and I walked in and immediately spotted Rafael near the hostess. He was seated on a bench that was usually occupied by patrons waiting for tables, not by suspected dine-n-dashers.

Rafael jumped up. "Devon, you came!" he exclaimed, rather loudly, and attempted to hug me.

I held him at bay by placing my hand on his chest. "Keep your voice down. Are you drunk?" I whispered.

"Well, when he left, I finished off the bottle of wine," he confessed, with less enthusiasm but loud enough to draw onlookers from the dining room.

"Sit down," I said. "How much is his bill?" I asked

the hostess.

"His bill is $83.54," she replied. Her tone suggested that she had better things to do than talk to some friend of a suspected dine-n-dasher. She looked more like a blonde centerfold than hostess. I asked myself, *where did a hostess get the money for fake boobs anyway?* Maybe it was a part-time job to pay for the new enhancements.

I pulled my debit card out to pay for the bill.

"Do you have an ID?" the blonde asked.

I handed her my driver's license, and she was off to the back of the restaurant. I looked at Javier waiting patiently by the entrance. His cocky grin told me that he was slightly amused by the whole situation … or maybe he was thinking about getting me back to his place after bailing out Rafael.

"Wait till I see him again," Rafael threatened from the bench. "I'm going down to that naval base first thing in the morning and find him."

"Rafael, I tend to doubt he was really in the Navy," I said. I knew I was starting to sound a little annoyed, but he *did* interrupt my date with Javier. We still hadn't gotten down to business yet.

"You mean you think he lied?"

"He stole your wallet. I'm sure lying wouldn't be out of character for him."

"Shit!" he slurred. "I think he set me up."

"It wasn't much of a setup. You left your wallet in your jacket at the table. It couldn't have gotten any easier for him than if you'd left him an invite."

"It was a sports jacket. You're supposed to leave your wallet in the inside pocket. It's *very* classy looking," Raphael slurred, "and the less likely to be pickpocketed too."

"That worked well for you," I commented dryly.

The hostess returned with my debit card and the receipt to sign. I wondered if I was required to leave a tip, since technically, I didn't eat there. I left fifteen percent anyway and mentally tallied it to Rafael's "You owe me big" bill.

Javier approached. "Maybe we should take him home," he suggested.

I agreed. "That's probably best."

Rafael walked out of the restaurant leaning on my shoulder and didn't acknowledge Javier. In his condition he probably wouldn't. Rafael poured himself into the backseat of Javier's car.

I gave Javier directions to Rafael's apartment. I couldn't help but think, "What a first date *this* turned out to be." If nothing else, it would be memorable.

"I'm sorry about all this," I said to Javier.

"No need to apologize. You're helping a friend in need."

"I just feel like maybe I ruined our first—"

"You know you're right, Devon," Rafael chimed in from the backseat.

"Right about what, Rafael?"

"Men out here are just good for a lay. What was it you said? 'Fuck em and dump em.'"

"Rafael! Shut up!"

"You were *so* right. Fuck em and dump em. If I would have done that, I wouldn't be in this position now."

Javier glanced towards me. It was hard to read the expression on his face with so little light in the car. I wondered if hearing what was said changed any perception he may have had of me. I could have denied it or explained that I said those things out of anger … but I let it go. Maybe he would just believe it to be the rants of a drunken Rafael.

Other than me giving directions, most of the drive was in silence. I was too embarrassed to bring it up, and Rafael was now drifting to sleep. I looked back and could see where a few tears had streamed down Rafael's face. I knew those tears weren't about stolen money or credit cards—but about Trevor. Not that he was in love with Trevor, but Trevor was another disappointment to Rafael—one he could add to a growing list. A list many of us had.

When we reached Rafael's apartment, I walked him

in. I wouldn't have blamed Javier if he wasn't there when I returned. I led Rafael up the stairs to the door of the building. He fumbled with the keys but eventually got the security door opened. At least Trevor was nice enough to have left him his keys. He was probably just some crystal meth freak looking for his next hit. All he needed was the fast cash to get him through. The dinner was a bonus. He probably had intended to take Rafael's wallet later in the night, perhaps after a romantic encounter. Rafael just made it easier for him by leaving his wallet at the table.

We walked the hallway to Rafael's first-floor apartment. He opened his door with a little more ease. "I'll be fine," he said. "You can go." He seemed to be slowly shaking off the effects of the wine.

"You sure? I can stay."

"Yeah, go."

"I'll call you tomorrow and check on you."

"Okay."

I hugged Rafael and began to walk down the hall when he started to enter his apartment and stopped.

"Devon!—" he shouted.

"Yeah?"

"I hope I didn't ruin your evening."

"It's fine. Maybe next time you will listen when I tell you not to pick up trade in the parking lot," I chastised. "And, Rafael—"

"Yes?"

"Don't let this guy.... Don't stop believing in the things you want."

"Okay," he said, grinning.

Fortunately, Javier was still waiting when I returned. I took a deep breath and approached the car. When I got in, Javier began to drive without a word.

"I want to apologize. You put together this incredible evening, and here we are playing 'designated driver' to my buddy," I said. I waited for a response.... Nothing. "Say something. Please."

Javier was driving with a little more speed than before and creeping through stop signs. "Maybe we shouldn't do this," he said.

"We've only know each other for four days. What exactly are we doing?" I asked.

"I guess that's a plus; neither one of us wasted too much time," he mumbled.

"Okay, we both know what this is about. Yes, I said those things, but I was in the same frame of mind as Rafael when he repeated them. I was drunk and upset."

"Is that how you feel? You just want to fuck and move on? We can do that if you want. I'll be more than happy to fuck you and never call you again."

I thought his response to the matter was overdramatic—but flattering. I wondered if this is how it would be dating Javier? Drama. "I get it! It sounds horrible. I just don't know what I believe anymore when it comes to relationships."

"Well, that's the difference between you and me. I know there is someone out there for me. There is more to life than waiting for the next fuck," he said, while going through an intersection without any regard for the stop sign…. Luckily, we were in a residential area and there was no traffic in sight.

"I believed that too, when I was your age—and do you mind paying a little more attention to the road?"

"I see … now I'm young and inexperienced."

"I didn't mean it like that. I just meant that when you get a little older you become a little more—"

"Cynical."

"Well, yeah."

"I will never be like that. And you're not that much older than me."

I couldn't help but think that maybe he was just naive. "Javier, we met just a few days ago. We shouldn't be having this conversation now. Let's just see where things go. I mean, we haven't even had sex."

"I'm not looking to see where things go. I'm looking for someone who wants something a little more serious than a fuck, buddy. Now, I thought we had a connection, but I guess I was wrong. Do you think everything I did tonight was for a piece of ass?"

"This is too much."

"It's fine. At least we didn't waste each other's time."

Javier dropped me off in front of my apartment with not even as much as a goodbye. I was sure I made Javier's list tonight. When I got in my apartment, I turned off my cell phone, undressed, and crawled into bed. It was after 10:00 p.m. and I was drained. At dinner I was on a euphoric high and now a desolate low. How did an evening take a turn for the worse so quickly?

12

The following Saturday—after my disastrous date with Javier—I was seated in my Jeep at work when Michael phoned.

"Hello," I answered.

"Hey, Puta! You going to meet us out tonight or what?"

"I don't think so. I am kinda tired."

"You are so full of shit! You're still moping over that busboy aren't you?"

"He is a bartender, not a busboy," I said, before realizing I walked right into his trap.

"So you *are* moping," Michael said, with an air of self-righteousness.

"No."

"Then meet us out."

"I told you, I'm tired."

"The only thing wrong with you is that your *dick*stracted," Michael said.

"You're foul."

"If you're so into the busboy, why not give him a call?"

"He hates me."

"Stop being such a little bitch. The worst he could say is, 'fuck off.'"

At that moment, a voice blasted through my service radio. I knew more than likely it could be heard by Michael as well. I used it for my escape. "I have to go, that's for me," I said.

"You are so full of shit, but I'll let you go this time. Like, I don't know that trick; I taught you the 'fake radio traffic' trick."

"Goodbye, Michael."

"Call him."

"Bye," I said, and closed my phone.

I did want to call. Although I appreciated Michael's advice, I also knew that he didn't have all the facts about Javier. I didn't have all the facts. I had my suspicions about him.

It was 10:23 Sunday morning when I awoke tangled in sheets with my old friend, self-pity. I knew it was a long shot, but I had an idea. It was exactly one week ago when I met Javier running in the park. There might be a chance he would be there again. I didn't know exactly what I would say to him, but at least there was a chance I would see him.

When I arrived at the park, I parked my truck as close as I could to where I had parked it a week ago. I was like some mad man trying to retrace my steps exactly as they were a week prior, looking for something I had lost. I stretched and surveyed the park looking for any runners that resembled Javier.

Almost out of hope, I began my run.

It wasn't until the end of my second lap that I spotted him. He moved steadily along, again with no shirt. He ran poised and full of confidence. I would have to pick up my speed to catch up to him.

Several minutes later, I was directly behind him. He never looked back. I knew he was aware of my presence when he began to speed up. I was growing tired; I should have figured it wouldn't be easy. Suddenly, a phone call seemed more of the sensible approach, but it was too late. Before long, we were sprinting. He was dishing out much worse of a serving than I had a week before, but I held my ground. I wasn't sure how much longer I was going to be able to go at this pace; after all, I had nearly exhausted myself simply trying to catch up to him. He was punishing me. My chest and legs began to feel as if they were on fire, but I kept moving as fast as my legs would take me. Out of nowhere, I felt a tight pinch in my right hamstring that seemed to burn with an intense fury. It was a cramp.

"Shit!" I yelled.

My sprint slowed into a light jog and then a limp.

"Javier!" I yelled, not entirely sure he would stop. I collapsed onto the grass on my side panting. He stopped and turned back. I must have looked pathetic enough, because he jogged over to me.

"What happened?" he panted, also out of breath.

"Cramp!"

"Where?"

"Right hamstring," I said, wincing. I lay out on my left side to expose the cramped leg. "I wasn't that hard on you," I said.

"Well, you deserve it," he replied, before kneeling beside me. He was beginning to massage my hamstring.

"Maybe," I said. I looked into his eyes. "I want to go out again."

With both hands he continued to work on my hamstring. It felt good and painful all at the same time. If I wasn't so distracted by the throbbing muscle, his touch would have produced an erection.

"Why should I go out with you again?" he asked.

"Because I'm twitching on the ground, in the middle of the park, like a little girl."

"Yes, you are," he laughed.

"Can we do that? Go out again?"

The smiled slowly left his face. "I don't think that's a good idea."

It wasn't until I was no longer panting that I took hold of his arm and said, "I don't care, Javier."

"What are you talking about?"

I pulled him close. "I don't care if you're illegal."

He resisted me. Javier's mouth fell slightly open, and he hesitated while he searched for the right words. The massaging stopped. "I don't know what you're talking about."

"Look, I want to see you again, but I need to know the truth. No lies. I saw how you reacted when I told you what I did for a living."

Javier stood. He was peering down at me, yet his eyes looked everywhere but at me. "You're mistaken. You seem to be ok now, so—"

"The other day you told me to be real with you, and now I'm asking the same."

He took a moment. "Okay. What *if* I am illegal?" he asked, finally looking me in the eye.

"It wouldn't make any difference to me."

"And how would that work? You're a Border Patrol

146

Agent."

"Why wouldn't it work?"

"Well, in theory, you could have me deported if things got ugly."

"First, I'm not vindictive. If I can let my ex walk around unharmed with some of the things he has done to me, then I think you'll be safe. Second, turning you in would only implicate me as aiding and abetting illegals. All you would have to do is talk."

"I guess we both have a lot to lose."

I adjusted my position so that I could sit up and look up at him. "The patrol is just my job. I'm not looking for illegals on my days off. I met a nice guy who just happens to be illegal."

"So you're assuming."

"Let's just see where it goes."

Javier frowned.

"Hear me out, Javier. I like you, but we're just getting to know each other. I can't make any promises that three years from now we'll be exchanging rings on some beach in Hawaii.... Let's just take it slow."

The smiled returned just as slowly as it had left. "I never said I wanted to marry you. But I do feel a connection with you."

"I feel it too, but it will still be there if we take our time."

"And what about your 'fuck em and dump em' code of conduct?" he asked.

"Honestly, I think it was an attitude I adopted to protect my heart. You've called me cynical, but I wouldn't be here if that were true. I haven't completely given up on finding someone."

"I need to say one thing."

"What?" I asked.

"This 'damsel in distress' routine is way overdone.

"Shut up and help me up."

Javier helped me over to a nearby bench where we sat.

"So we're dating now?" I asked.

"Slow down. I'm just giving you a second chance."

"Oh, are you?"

"That's right."

"Be honest. You missed me?"

For the first time, I made him blush. "Maybe a little."

"Damn, I got you whipped."

"Hardly. You might get me there though."

Javier took my hand and squeezed it. In the distance, we could see a game of volleyball in action.

"Where are you from, Javier?"

"I was born in Tijuana."

"How did you—"

"Let's not go there just yet. It's too soon. From the time I was a child, I was trained not to tell anyone I was born in Mexico. Very few people know I'm illegal, and you come and pick me apart in a day. It's a little unnerving."

This time it was me squeezing his hand. "I understand. You will talk about it with me one day … won't you?"

"I will. I promise."

The thought of Javier going through some of the things that I witnessed other illegal immigrants going through to enter the United States saddened me. We weren't in love, at least not yet, but I still didn't want to picture him going through the extremes of hiding in drainage pipes, crossing polluted waters or deserts, climbing fences, or running from the likes of me. Javier had just a hint of an accent. I suspected he had been in the United States for quite some time. Maybe he didn't even remember his crossing; he could have been a child. I hoped, for his sake, that he didn't remember.

13

Javier and I had been dating two months, and everything was going well. Much to the disappointment of Rafael and Michael, we celebrated my thirtieth birthday with a quiet evening at home—just the two of us. Javier cooked rice, beans, chicken enchiladas, and flan for desert. He remembered how much I loved authentic Mexican food. He wasn't lying when he said he could throw down in the kitchen. We watched one of my favorite DVDs, *Latter Days*, which he had never seen. He made me model the underwear he bought me, although I felt bloated as hell after our large dinner. From there, the underwear came off, and the party moved to the bedroom—not ending until the wee hours. Afterglow and pillow talk followed.

We were still in the blissful new beginnings. Michael

and Rafael said it was like Javier and I were joined at the hip. In reality, we didn't get to spend that much time together—I worked second shift, and Javier was in school during the day, plus he worked weekends, because that's where the money is in the service industry. We both arranged our work schedules to have Wednesdays and Thursdays off. I guess you could say that on Wednesdays and Thursdays we were joined at the hip, and there was no other hip I wanted to be joined to.

We managed to fall into a predictable routine. Every week, we alternated whose place we spent our days off at. Not sure how we came up with that, but it worked. Wednesday mornings we would get up and go to the gym to work out or go for a run in the park, which was followed by breakfast. Breakfast was followed by a shower, sex, and another shower. At this point, I would be content on lounging in bed the rest of the day, but Javier was always adamant about doing something with our days off, whether it was a movie, the zoo, or one of San Diego's many museums. I saw more of San Diego in two months than I had seen in the entire three years I'd lived in San Diego.

I'm not sure why, but I didn't tell Javier about my meetings with Dr. Lindale. After switching my days off, I switched my appointment with Dr. Lindale to Tuesdays mornings. Somehow, over the last couple months, I managed to make my appointments without really explaining to Javier what I did every Tuesday morning, since he was usually in school anyway. He respected my privacy; not that I went out of my way to conceal my appointments.

One Thursday afternoon, Javier and I were in bed at his studio lounging around in our boxers after one of our rounds of sex. I was channel-surfing, and Javier was looking over some notes for an exam when my cell phone rang.

"Don't answer it," Javier said, without looking up from his notes. I liked how when we were together, he didn't want to share me with anyone else.

"I won't, but I want to see who's calling," I said. I reached for my cell phone in my jeans pocket on the floor.

"You're afraid you're going to miss something?"

I flipped open the phone. It was Tony. Suddenly I felt flushed. I closed the phone and placed it back in my pocket.

"Who was it?"

"Rafael," I said.

I lay back against the pillows. *Why did I lie?* I didn't do anything wrong. I had told Javier all about Tony. I may have left out the fact that I still had feelings for him, but that was a couple of months ago. I *did* have feelings for him. *Do I still have feelings for him?* I hadn't thought about it in some time. I hadn't seen Tony since that night at *Numbers*. Now, I was dating Javier, and everything was going great. *Let's not mess it up.*

Shortly after the phone call, Javier went to the bathroom. I quickly grabbed the phone to check my message. There was one new message that had to have been left by Tony.

"Hey, Devon, it's Tony. It's been a while—just calling to see what's new. Actually, I know what's new. Rumor has it you've been seeing some young, hot Latino boy. Anyway, give me a call so we can catch up. Bye."

I didn't hear Javier return. "You couldn't wait to get on the phone could you?"

I was startled by his stealthy entrance, nearly dropping my phone. "Just checking my messages."

Javier crawled back into bed and resumed his studying. I continued to watch television, trying to appear unfazed by the message, but my heart raced—and why, I didn't know.

"Oh, I almost forgot. My mom is coming down tomorrow. Do you think you could meet us for lunch before you go to work?" Javier asked.

I repositioned myself on the bed. "You want me to meet your mother?"

"Yeah! She's already heard so much about you, I figured

it's time you two met. I mean, you *are* my boyfriend."

I know I should have felt honored, but for some reason I felt smothered. I wished he would have given me more than a day's notice—and when did I become his boyfriend? Yes, he was the only guy I had been with in the last couple of months, and I never asked him if he was seeing or having sex with any other people, but we had never talked about being exclusive. What happened to taking things slow?

"I don't know ... I need to go to the gym and—"

Javier closed his notebook. "I am asking you to meet my mother, and you're putting us off for the gym?"

Note to self: Going to the gym is *not* a good reason not to meet your boyfriend's mother. *Did I just refer to him as my boyfriend?*

"Well, that is my usual routine."

"How about you make an exception....You know what?—forget it. I shouldn't have to beg you to do this."

"Alright, I will meet you and your mother for lunch tomorrow. Now lay off!"

"Lay off? You don't get it, do you?"

"What is there to get? You're close with your mom. We all don't have that. Why is it so important to you that I meet her?" I asked. "To rub it in my face?"

Javier got out of bed and began collecting articles of clothing off the floor. I first thought he was beginning to clean in some kind of mad rage, but I suddenly realized he was picking up *my* clothes. He tossed them at me on the bed.

"If you think I would do something like that. You should leave."

"What?!"

"You heard me. I want you to leave," Javier ordered.

"You're kidding me? One little disagreement, and you're throwing me out?!"

"Yep."

"Fine!" I got out of bed and pulled on my pants. "You 'mama's boy.'"

"It's not my fault you hate your fuckin' family."

"Whatever. You're crazy." No longer wanting to stick around for anything more he had to say, I left wearing only my jeans and carrying the rest of my clothes and backpack. He slammed the door behind me. I finished dressing in the hallway, all the while wondering what had just happened.

Later that night, after several failed attempts at calling Javier, I sat on the couch watching television with a vodka cranberry. I don't remember how I arrived at the channel, but I was watching the Home Shopping Network. Some D-list celebrity was pushing her new clothing line. It seemed everyone in Hollywood had a line of clothing nowadays.

It may have been best that Javier didn't answer. I didn't have an apology ready. I couldn't begin to explain my actions to him. I had no answers. I was partly convinced I did nothing wrong.

My cell phone began to ring. I went for it, almost knocking over the drink on the coffee table. It was Rafael.

"Yeah," I answered.

Rafael must have sensed my sour mood instantly. "What's going on?" Rafael inquired, with an air of concern in his voice.

I didn't have the energy to pretend everything was okay. "We had a fight."

"What happened?"

I took a sip from the glass on the table and placed it back down. "It was too much. I kind of freaked out."

"You lost me."

"There we were lying in bed watching television when guess who calls?"

"Tony."

"Yep."

"What did he say?"

"I didn't answer the phone, but basically, he heard I was seeing someone, so I guess he had to call and fuck with me. Man, he has great timing."

"That sounds innocent enough."

"Please. There's a motive behind everything he does; besides, you know how I felt about him."

"I still don't understand how that started a fight between you and Javier."

"That was compounded by Javier asking me, just minutes later, to meet his mother ... I guess I just freaked out. It was too much."

"He asked you to meet his mother?" Rafael said excitedly. Even over the phone, I was sure he was smiling.

"That's how I should have reacted. But no; I told him I had to go to the gym."

"No ... you didn't ...!"

"Yes, I did, and it gets worse. I called him a 'mama's boy.'"

"Ouch! Devon, that's a lot of candy and flowers."

"Maybe even some foot rubs."

I heard the cellphone tone indicating I had another call. I hoped it was Javier, but it was Tony.

"Rafael, I need to take this call," I explained. "I'll call you later."

"Okay, I'm here if you need anything."

"Bye."

I hit the flash button.

"Hello," I answered.

"You're not returning calls anymore?"

"I've been busy," I said, harshly.

"From what I hear you've been getting busy."

"You believe everything you hear?" I asked.

"Is it true? You have a man?"

"Why does it matter, and how is um ... Pablo?" I inquired with pure disdain.

"That was just a fling," he said. "Devon, I need to talk to you. I messed up."

"What are you talking about?"

"Can I come by? I would really like to talk to you in person. Are you alone?"

"Yes, I'm—"

"Good, I'll swing by," he said.

"Look Tony. I don't think so. It's not a good time."

"Is he coming by?"

"No, look—"

"Then I'm coming by. I swear, I won't take up too much of your time. I really need to talk to you."

"Fine. Once you get here, you've got ten minutes to say what you need to say."

"I can live with that. I'll see you in an hour."

I know what you're thinking. Maybe this wasn't such a good idea, and maybe I wasn't thinking clearly, but I needed to see him. I think part of the reason I flipped out on Javier had a whole lot to do with Tony. I figured if I got some closure, then maybe I could move on.

I knew exactly why Tony was coming over, and that gave me a little leverage. He wanted what he couldn't have. I prayed I didn't give it to him either. Tony knew I was happily dating, so he was going to come over and proclaim his love for me.

It was 7:50 p.m. when I buzzed the front gate to let Tony in. I was in baggy sweatpants and a T-shirt; I was over the idea of trying to impress him. I opened the door. "Hey," I said, rather dryly. I quickly retreated so I wouldn't have to hug him. Tony closed the door behind him, crossed the room, and immediately sat on the couch. "Why don't you make yourself comfortable?" I mumbled. "So, what's this about?"

He wore a black and red designer track jacket with nothing but a wifebeater underneath to show off his body. To my surprise, I was no longer moved by his nearly flawless body.

"Alright, I guess I'll just get to the point. Devon, when we broke up, I was going through some rough times emotionally—some things that really didn't have anything to do with you. I just needed some time to find myself."

I took a seat on the love seat, purposely sitting nowhere near Tony. "It seems you were finding other people when you were trying to find yourself," I said, sarcastically. "So, what do you want from me?"

"I want another chance with you, if I'm not too late," he said. On the heels of messing up with Pablo, Tony was apparently desperate enough to overlook my sarcasm. "Are you happy with him?"

Tony's question hit me like a revelation. A smile erupted. "Yes. Yes, I am."

"The way your face lit up, I guess you are," Tony said. "I guess I don't have a chance, huh?"

Before I could reply, there was another knock at the door. I wondered who it could be. I returned to the door to answer it.

It was Javier.

I had given him the manual code weeks ago so he wouldn't have to call up to gain access to the building.

"Can I come in?"

The visit was obliviously a surprise, since up until now he hadn't returned my phone calls. "I—"

"I don't want to fight about this," he pleaded. "If it's too soon to meet my mom that's cool.... Are you going to let me in?"

The door was only half open. Javier had no view of Tony on the couch. I stepped aside without a word to allow Javier in.

"Who's this?" Javier asked me, upon entering.

"This is Tony."

"Tony?!" Javier repeated. "We had one fight just a

few hours ago, and already you go running back to him. The same guy who treated you like shit!"

"Javier, calm down."

"I hope you two are happy together," he said, storming out the door.

Immediately, I followed him. "Wait, Javier! Nothing is going on." I caught up to Javier and grabbed him by the arm. "Will you wait a minute?"

He stopped and looked me in the eye. "If I were you, I would think twice about grabbing me."

I didn't want a confrontation, so I released him. I had never seen him upset before. I thought it would be best if I let him leave. I hoped that once he calmed down, I could explain to him what had happened.

I watched Javier walk angrily away, down the stairs and out of the courtyard.

"You want me to go explain to him what I'm doing here?" Tony asked.

I didn't realize Tony had followed us out of the apartment. "I really don't think that's a good idea. Why don't you wait a couple minutes before you leave?" Javier never struck me as violent, but I didn't want to risk a scene. I started back to my apartment. Javier's outburst had drawn the attention of a few neighbors. I could see a couple people peering through their blinds.

I collapsed on the couch on the verge of tears.

"I'm sorry, Devon. I feel partly responsible," Tony said. Just when I thought maybe he wasn't the asshole I'd figured him to be, he spoke again. "I guess you're single now."

"Get the hell out!"

The evening had unfolded like a bad sitcom. Guy walks in to find his girlfriend in a compromising position with her ex. Guy is furious and leaves in a jealous rage. Only guy doesn't know the ex only came over to deliver some items left by the girlfriend at the ex's apartment. Guy also doesn't know the girlfriend only fell into the arms of the ex after tripping over her Prada shoes left in the middle of the floor.

Okay, it didn't exactly happen like that, and no girl was involved, but you get the picture—besides, we weren't in a compromising position, and I don't own a pair of Prada shoes. Javier had let his imagination get the best of him and he came up with his own elaborate explanation of why Tony was at my place.

At the same time, I couldn't help but think about the pain I'd felt after walking in on Tony when I caught him cheating. No, Tony and I weren't cheating. And no, Javier didn't physically catch us in the act. But if he believes it to be true, he was probably *very* hurt. I was sorry to put him through even a fraction of the pain that I had known so well.

It was almost midnight when I left the third message on Javier's voicemail. I thought about going by his place, but didn't want to risk starring in another episode of *Three's Company*. Although, I was sure Javier wasn't the type to go out and have revenge sex.

14

On Tuesday morning, I was seated on the love seat in Dr. Lindale's office explaining what had happened between Javier and me.

"And you haven't heard from him since last week?" she asked.

"No. I've called, and I stopped by his apartment a couple times. I think he's avoiding me."

"He's obviously upset. You can understand that," Dr. Lindale said, all the while taking notes. She directed her attention back to me. "So, why do you think you panicked, Devon?"

"I don't know."

"Come on, Devon. You have to have some clue."

I took a moment and considered my answer. "Hearing

from Tony didn't help, but then Javier asked me to meet his mother ... and within the same conversation, he referred to me as his boyfriend—"

"You wanted a boyfriend," Dr. Lindale interjected.

"Well, yes."

"Then what's really the problem?"

I think the answer was always there, but I chose to ignore it, or didn't believe it to be true. Slowly, I said, "I got scared."

"Scared of what?"

"Trusting him."

"Care to elaborate?"

"I put my trust in Tony, and not only did he disappoint me ... he hurt me. I don't want to go through that again."

"Javier isn't Tony."

"It's not just that."

"What do you mean?"

"I left home when I was eighteen, and I didn't leave under the best circumstances as far as my relationship with my parents. Being gay in the military wasn't easy either. I learned to hide who I was at a time when I was just learning about myself. I felt like a fraud pretending to be like everyone else. I didn't have gay friends, relationships, or anyone to talk to about it.... I've gotten so used to being on my own that it's hard to let people in sometimes.

My parents disappointed me, and then Tony."

Dr. Lindale looked over her wire-framed glasses. "So you wanted to push Javier away before he does it to you?"

I thought about the night Tony asked me if I was happy with Javier and how my face lit up. I felt recharged. "No, I don't want to lose him. I want us to work out." I was then plagued by a question of my own. "Why didn't I run from Tony or push him away when we dated?" I asked.

Dr. Lindale removed her glasses. "Honey, Tony didn't love you," she said, as if stepping out of character from "good doctor" to "good girlfriend." "That's why you didn't feel compelled to run. Sure, you two dated, but what is there to run from if someone doesn't truly love you? There was nothing to fear, because there was no real love. Now, that's not to say that you didn't love him. If he loved you, he wouldn't have put you through what he has."

My mouth went dry. I felt a certain doom. I was the trailer park trash—not a nice trailer park either—who only fell for the bad boys. I would do the talk show circuit vowing my love for the asshole who is also sleeping with my sister. I would lunge at her, attempting to pull out her hair weave, saying, "He's mine bitch!" with a Southern twang, while he just sits there smug and content.

The session with Dr. Lindale gave me a lot to think about. Was I so desperately in love with Tony that I was almost willing to put up with anything? I no longer wanted to be the victim to all the perpetual "bad boys" out there. Javier—so far—hadn't given me any indication that he was one of them. I had to fix things with Javier.

15

By Saturday night, I'd had enough of being ignored. It had been over a week with no word from him. Not even a "Fuck off; it's over," or a "Die and go to hell." It was more of a last resort, but I was going to confront Javier at his job. I needed to know if I should move on or if this was worth fighting for. I didn't want to end up like the trailer park trash running from true love because drama was so much more exciting.

When I walked into *The Ritz*, I immediately spotted Scott and Luis, a new hire, behind the bar. By now, I was familiar with the staff, since I would stop in after work occasionally to see Javier—but now, he was nowhere in sight. The bar was moderately busy on Saturdays, and they usually ran two bartenders. Tonight, it appeared to be Scott and Luis. So, where was Javier?

I approached Scott. "Hey, Scott."

Lines shot across Scott's forehead, and his lips tightened. Javier obviously told him I was some kind of two-timing ho. "Hey, Dee. How's it going?"

"Alright," I said, casually. "Is Javier working tonight?"

Scott's eyes widened. "No ... no he isn't. You haven't heard, have you?"

My heart began to pound on my rib cage. I quickly prayed nothing happened to him. "Heard what?" I nearly shouted. "We had a fight. I haven't spoken with Javier in days."

"Oh.... Well ... his mom passed away last week. He's in L.A.... The funeral was Wednesday. I don't know when he's returning to work. I'm sorry I'm the one to break it to you...."

I slowly sat on the nearest stool. "He must be devastated. He is so close to her."

"Yeah, you and his mom is all he talks about."

I took a certain comfort being held in the same class as Javier's mom, but I was sure I was no longer in that class. "How did she ... die?"

"Last word I got, it sounded like a heart attack."

"Oh, God."

I felt horrible. I could only imagine what Javier was

going through. I just wished he would return my calls. For him not to call me and share this—he must really hate me. I thought about hopping in my truck and driving there. I was sure someone had the address; Don, the owner of *The Ritz*, would probably have sent flowers. Although, the way we left things, I'm not sure it would have been a warm reception, and the last thing I wanted to do was to cause a scene in front of his family just days after the funeral.

"Have you spoken with him, Scott?"

"No, but Don has spoken with him a couple times. He says he's about as well as can be expected at a time like this."

I got up from the stool. "Thanks for the information, Scott." I headed for the door.

"No problem. When you hear from him, tell him we're thinking about him."

It was more like *if* I hear from him. I got in my truck and drove home. I made one final attempt at calling him and again reached his voicemail. I decided not to leave another message. Anything I felt I now needed to say, I didn't want to leave on voicemail.

I grabbed a pen and some paper, and sat down at my dinette table to write.

Dear Javier,

After not hearing from you for over a week, I finally

went down to the Ritz on Saturday to speak with you. I was informed of your loss. I am truly sorry. My first instinct was to drive to LA and see you, but I wasn't so sure that was a good idea. All I can say about last week is, nothing happened or was going to happen. You have to trust me. I don't want to dwell on that, because it's not the pressing issue right now. No matter what happens between us, I care about you deeply. I'm just really concerned about your well-being. Please, just let me know how you're doing and if you need anything. I'm here for you.

Love, Devon

The next morning—with very little sleep—I put on my running gear and took the letter along. I slid it under Javier's door before my run. It was the first time I came to the park to run without him since we met. I couldn't find the motivation. Everything there reminded me of him. His studio was right across the street. And the park was where we had first met and where we made up. I just sat in the grass, in the same area as when I had touched his leg for the first time to stretch him out. I missed him, but most of all, I was worried. I wondered how he made it through the Border Patrol checkpoint in San Clemente on his way to Los Angeles. I assumed he made it to L.A. without incident, since Don had spoken with him. I suddenly realized how difficult life could be here as an illegal. Just traveling two hours north to visit his family could pose a problem for him.

Later that afternoon—after a not-so-successful run—I was lying on the couch, while Alicia Keys vocals filled the room, when Michael called.

"Hello," I answered.

"Okay, Bitch. You've been avoiding us the last few days. I *know* you're going to spend some quality time with us tonight," he demanded.

"I think I'm going to stay in."

"What's going on with you?"

"It's Javier."

"Have you heard from him?"

"No, but last night I found out his mother passed away."

"Oh, shit! How did you find out?" he asked.

"One of his co-workers," I said. "I'm worried about him."

"That's natural."

"There's something else," I said.

"What?"

"He's illegal. He drove to L.A. I mean, what if he got caught or something?"

"Damn! You certainly know how to pick'em."

"Yeah!"

There was a moment of silence on the line. Michael was trying to find the right words to comfort me. "It's not his first trip to L.A. I'm sure he knows what he's doing."

"I hope you're right."

"He's okay."

"Anyway, I'm just going to get some sleep. You guys go out and have a good time."

"Are you sure? I could come bring Gee Gee and we could have a threesome."

"Gee Gee? A threesome?"

"You wish. I'm talking picking up a bottle of Grey Goose and trash talkin' men."

Sometimes, I could hardly keep up with Michael's vocabulary of gay slang. "No, really, I'm fine."

"Ok, I'll have a drink for you."

"Do that."

"Ciao."

I wondered if Javier was sitting around doing some trash talking of his own. I wanted to be past this misunderstanding.

Alicia sang me to sleep.

16

Work was a bitch. My Jeep had a flat tire when I arrived at work, which I had to change since the garage was closed after hours. Then, later, I managed to lock my keys in my vehicle at the 7-Eleven during my break. Next, the group of six illegal immigrants I tracked and followed into the swamp managed to disappear into thin air. The one arrest I did make turned out to be a removal proceeding—many stacks of tedious paperwork. Through it all, my head was elsewhere the entire day.

I was glad to be home when I pulled into my assigned parking space, shut off the headlights, and killed the engine. I sat for a moment in my truck thinking about the recent chain of events. I began to think it was time to give up on Javier. Suddenly, the air in the cabin of the truck seemed stale. It wasn't any better once I was outside of the truck either. I was hot and sticky from an honest day's work, and my uniform trousers were still damp with swamp muck. I felt as if I was carrying the weight of the night's full moon, even though it hung high in the night sky.

I was unlocking the door to the courtyard, when I heard his voice. "Dee—" he called out. Could it really be Javier? I hoped I wasn't imagining it. I turned in the direction of the voice. Javier approached from the shadows of the parking lot, "Dee—"

"Javier! I've been so worried about you."

I approached, took hold of him, and hugged him tightly. Javier's arms clamped just as tightly around me. Considering the time of night, I doubt we had an audience, but to anyone looking on, it may have been a strange sight: two men holding onto each other at 3:00 a.m. as if for dear life, me still in uniform and muddy from the swamps and tire changing. But I didn't care if anyone was watching; I was wary of letting go. It nearly two weeks since I had laid eyes on Javier or heard his voice.

When I finally *did* let go, he asked, "Can I come up?"

"Yes, of course."

Once in my apartment, and in better light, I could easily see that he wore the pain of the last couple weeks. His eyes were bloodshot, his face sullen and thinner, and, judging by his stubble, he had not shaved in days

Somberly, he said, "I love to see you in uniform," as he ran his index finger along the top of my gun belt.

"Let me get out this uniform so we can talk," I said.

I hadn't taken two steps before he began sobbing. "I didn't know where else to go. I didn't want to be by myself. The longer I stayed in L.A., the worse I felt. Too many memories, I guess."

I took him in my arms again. "It's going to be okay, Javier."

"It hurts like hell."

"I know."

"I can't believe she's gone," he sobbed.

I didn't know what to say to him. Everything I wanted to say sounded like clichés: *Let it out. I'm here for you. Everything happens for a reason. Time will heal.*

I had never seen him cry before, let alone sob like a child. Watching him was putting me on the verge of tears. I knew that nothing I could say to him was going to be adequate or really help. I just held him for over an hour on the couch. He cried until he could cry no longer. He fell asleep in my arms, and I was there in my muddy, tear-stained uniform comforting him.

After a while, I managed to get up from the couch without disturbing him too much. I laid him out and placed a pillow under his head. I got a blanket from the closet to cover him.

In the bedroom, I removed my gun belt, placed it in my footlocker, and undressed. Placing my soiled uniform into the clothes hamper, I went into the bathroom for a long hot shower. I felt for Javier as I thought of him lying on the couch in so much pain. My mind was racing, wondering what I could do to help. I came to the conclusion that only time could heal. I could only be there for him, if he allowed me. He may still have been upset with me about our earlier argument and over Tony's unexpected appearance. Yet, I was the one he had turned to now.

After my shower, I exited the bathroom in my robe. I went to check on Javier one last time, but he was no longer on the couch. To my delight, he had made himself comfortable in my bed. His clothes were piled on the floor next to the bed. He was sound asleep. I dropped my robe, and crawled into bed next to him. His body quivered and shuddered, which he didn't normally do. I wondered if he was having a bad dream. He seemed to have stopped once I held him. I was exhausted, but I didn't want to fall asleep. I wanted to watch over him, and I was afraid he would be gone when I awoke.

The alarm clock went off at 8:30 a.m. An early appointment with Dr. Lindale is what forced me up after only a few hours of sleep. I rolled over to look at Javier. He hadn't left in the middle of the night like I had feared he might. His eyes were open. They appeared cold and distant.

"Is he your Tuesday hookup?" he asked. "Tony?"

The hurt, sensitive Javier from last night was gone. I awoke with the angry, hateful Javier. I guess it was understandable, since we hadn't exactly cleared the air about what had happened.

In fairness, I should have told Javier by now about Dr. Lindale. To him, I was always busy Tuesday mornings, without telling him exactly why—I appeared to be hiding something.

"Will you go somewhere with me this morning?" I asked.

"Where?" Javier's voice was flat and disinterested.

"I need to show you something."

"I guess," he said, reluctantly.

I got up and made French toast and fresh-squeezed orange juice. We ate in silence. Javier's eyes were red and puffy, and he avoided eye contact. What I wouldn't do to take away his pain.

After breakfast, Javier showered while I cleaned up

the dishes, then I drove us over to Dr. Lindale's office. We both took seats in the waiting room. I knew Javier was baffled as to why we were here.

"What's this about?" he asked, impatiently.

"I guess you have to wait and see," I said. I was trying to be understanding, but I was growing impatient with his attitude this morning. For the moment, this wasn't about his suffering. It was about Tony.

A few minutes passed, and Dr. Lindale entered the waiting area. She looked unusually casual in blue jeans and a white blouse.

"Good morning, Devon," she greeted.

"Good morning, Dr. Lindale." I stood and approached her. "I have a problem. I can't stay for my appointment today. Something unexpected came up. I know I will still be billed, but I just needed to come down and tell you."

Dr. Lindale looked over my shoulder.

"Oh," I said. "Dr. Lindale, this is my friend Javier. Javier, this is Dr. Lindale, my therapist."

Javier walked over and exchanged handshakes with her. "Nice to meet you," he said. His eyes suddenly seemed larger and brighter as they pierced Dr. Lindale with an undeniable curiosity.

"Likewise," she replied. "I suppose I can overlook it this time, but let's not make it a habit."

"You have my word."

"Bye now," she said as she retreated back into her office with a smile.

Javier and I walked up Park Avenue to no place in particular, since my truck was in the opposite direction. It was time to talk.

"You have a therapist," he commented.

"Yes."

"Are you crazy?" he chuckled.

"See, this is why I didn't tell you. It's really not a big deal."

"If it wasn't a big deal, why didn't you tell me? Why do you see her?"

"Well, I started going to her for one thing, but it seemed to have evolved. I used to think maybe something was wrong with me. I so badly wanted to be in a relationship, and it just never seemed to happen. I thought it had to be me. I don't think that's the case anymore. Now she's someone to talk to and help me think things out with."

Javier stopped and faced me. "You talk about me?"

"Yes."

"So, this is what you've been doing every Tuesday morning?"

"Yes."

"Why wouldn't you tell me this?" he asked.

"I don't know. I just kept it to myself. I thought it may freak you out."

"After that Sunday, seeing you with Tony, I thought maybe it was him you were seeing."

"Tony practically dropped by unannounced that night. He came by to tell me he was still in love with me and that he had made a mistake dumping me."

"What did you say?" Javier asked. His eyebrows rose in anticipation of my response.

"For a long time, I had waited for those words from Tony, but when I finally *did* hear them, it made me realize it was too late. I'm in love with *you* Javier." The declaration brought more tears to his eyes. He hugged me with such force that I thought we were both going to tumble to the ground.

"I'm sorry I didn't trust you. I love you too."

Two elderly men, walking hand in hand with their white miniature poodle, passed us by. They both looked on with smiles.

After a few moments, Javier released me. "I wanted to say that for so long."

"So, why didn't you?" I asked.

Javier let out a sigh. "I don't know. I guess my head was tellin' me it was too soon."

"I think mine was too."

"Dee—?"

"Yeah?"

"Promise me you won't leave me…. I just lost my

mom; I can't take losing anybody else right now."

"I'm not going anywhere. I promise."

Javier leaned in for a kiss. It was the happiest I'd seen him in the last few hours. I knew it was only temporary. Sooner or later the reality of losing his mother would find its way back into his head.

"I was so afraid to come see you last night," he confided.

"Why?" I asked.

"It had been days since I'd spoken with you. I was scared that maybe you wouldn't be alone."

"I wasn't getting over you *that* fast. You could have returned a call though."

"I know. I was hurt. I wanted to forget my *pinche migra* asshole boyfriend. I thought … well, you know what I thought."

"Well, let's just move past this. But you have to agree never to shut me out like that, at least not without hearing me out first."

"I promise, Papa," he said. He took my hand, and we continued down the street following the couple with the dog. "I need one more thing," Javier said.

"What's that?"

"Do you think I can stay with you for a few days? I don't want to be alone. I know you have to work, but

I'll feel a lot better knowing you were coming home at least."

"Of course, baby. After not seeing you for close to two weeks, just try to get rid of me."

17

Javier and I stopped at the mailbox in the foyer of his building to retrieve his mail. He wanted to grab some clothes before going back to my apartment. Upon entering his studio, he picked up the letter I had written him days ago. Apparently, he had not been home that entire time since leaving for L.A. I left him in the room while I used the bathroom and returned to find him reading my letter.

"I'm sorry, Papa. I should have called."

"It's over with now."

"It's good to know that you care so much. You signed 'With love.'"

I smiled. "I think we established I kinda like you."

Javier tucked the letter away in a kitchen drawer

and then sat down at his computer. I lay on the bed and stared at the ceiling thinking how nice it was to have him back. I regretted how silly I had acted about meeting his mother, and now I would never have the chance.

"Dee, look at this." I sat up from the bed. Javier's face was streaked with more tears. No sobs, but plenty of tears. I wondered what he had read on his computer that set him off. I got up for a look. It was an email from his mom.

Mijo,

Sorry I couldn't come down to visit. I'm not feeling all that well today. I was really looking forward to meeting Devon. He sounds good for you. You deserve someone special.

I just want you to know how proud of you I am. I couldn't have asked for a better son. I know growing up was hard, especially with me being a single parent. I was always grateful for how you stepped up to the role of being the man of the house and looked after your sister and me. I thank you for that.

I remember when you were having second thoughts about going to school in San Diego. You wanted to stay and look after me, but I wouldn't have it. You worry too much about me. You helped me in so many ways. It's your time now Mijo. I want you to go out and experience life. It's been one of my greatest joys, seeing you on your own, taking care of yourself.

And look, you're going to be graduating soon. I know you are going to make me proud.

Remember I love you.

Mama

I leaned over the back of the chair and held him. He was silent, but the tears were streaming down his copper-colored cheeks.

"That Friday morning she called to say she couldn't come down, but I didn't know she sent me an email. I haven't checked my email in days…. I really wanted you to meet her."

"I know Javier," I said, quietly. I fought the urge to cry, because an overwhelming feeling of helplessness was creeping in.

I called in sick to stay with Javier that night. We were on the sofa watching television, and I don't think either of us was paying much attention to that particular syndicated episode of *Will & Grace*.

Ring!

I pulled my cell phone from my pocket. The display showed "Mom." I hesitated. It seemed unfair to me that I could talk to my mother, but he could no longer talk to his. It had been about a week since I last spoke with her.

"I'm going to take this in the bedroom," I said.

Javier didn't respond or move as I left the room.

"Hello," I said. I anticipated the attack.

"You too busy to call?"

"No, it's just—"

"Well, it seems that way."

"Sorry I haven't called, Ma," I whispered.

"What's wrong? You sound funny."

I sat on the bed. "I have been busy. I have a friend staying here with me … he just lost his mother."

"I'm sorry to here that, but you would think it would at least make you remember to call yours."

"I'm sorry!" I said, again.

"So what's this young man's name?"

"Javier," I responded. I knew she was asking only to be nosy and not out of concern.

"Why is he staying with you? He don't have any family there?"

"Do you really want to go there?"

"I guess not," she said. "Well, I'll let you get back to your *friend*. I will say a prayer for him and you."

"Thank you. I'm sure he will appreciate that … and, Mom …"

"Yes."

"You know I love you. I know we say it at the end of every phone conversation, but I really love you."

Silence.

I thought the call was dropped by my sometimes-undependable cellphone provider, until she finally said, "I love you too." Her voice cracked in such a way that I knew she was becoming emotional.

"Bye, Mom."

"Night, baby."

I went back into the living room and rejoined Javier on the sofa, He nestled himself into my side, and I put my arm around him.

"How long are you going to do that?" he asked.

"Do what?"

"Leave the room when your mom calls."

"I don't know; it seemed—"

"You don't have to do that."

"Okay," I said, and kissed him on his forehead.

The closing credits to *Will & Grace* were running when Javier muted the television.

"My sister found her on the kitchen floor." His revelation caught me by surprise. I nearly forgot to breathe. "How fucked up is that? To die alone? Scared and alone. Someone should have been there. I should have been there."

I rubbed his shoulder consolingly. "Javier, things beyond our control sometimes happen. You can't put yourself through this. If you lived in L.A. chances are you would have been at school or work. It's not your fault.

There was nothing you could have done."

I wanted to tell him she probably experienced the symptoms of a heart attack earlier and ignored them. It sounded insensitive, so I didn't. I think she sensed something wasn't right, and that's why she sent Javier a final goodbye. An email.

Javier's chest noticeably began to rise and fall. The tears were coming again. "If I couldn't have saved her, I wish I could have at least held her hand. No one should die alone," he cried. "I think about how scared she probably was."

I held him tight, as I was learning to do, and said, "It'll be ok." It seems that had been my response every time he succumbed to tears. I was beginning to wonder if I was qualified for the task of consoling him. Then, it occurred to me—if I were in as much pain as Javier was, his arms are where I would want to be. It may not fix the problem or heal the pain, but it would certainly be a comfort to me.

"She made so many sacrifices for me and my sister."

"I know, Javier."

"No … you don't." Javier pulled away from me and looked me in the eye. "You don't…. You once asked me about my dad. My dad left for L.A. for work when I was two years old. My mom was pregnant with my sister, Maria. He was supposed to have gone to work with my uncle there. He was going to cross illegally, but he never made it to L.A. He never contacted my uncle. After a couple of months my mother decided she had to do something. She was living with his family, and she didn't want to be a burden." Javier's chest heaved again as he wiped away tears. "She wanted a better life for us, so she crossed illegally in the trunk of a car. She was pregnant with Maria and holding a two year old tryin' to keep me from crying in the trunk of a car."

I was dumbfounded. "Javier, I had no idea."

"It was three times before she made it over. At least that's how she told it." Javier managed to chuckle. "Maybe she added that to guilt us."

"Wow, I didn't know…. What about your dad?"

"We don't know. Mom always said she believed he died providing for his family. You know … tryin' to cross over here, but something went wrong. I hope she was right. I hate to think he was just some deadbeat who abandoned us."

I certainly wasn't around the border in the eighties, but I heard from the old-timers at work that there were even more dangers crossing the border back then. One of the greatest dangers was bandits. They preyed on the people attempting to cross into the United States. In some cases, bandits posed as foot guides, helping illegals cross into the United States for a fee. Once they were across the border it wasn't uncommon for the bandits to leave a group of people in the desert for dead after robbing them. If someone didn't have enough water, they could fall victim to the extreme temperatures.

Javier found his way back into my arms.

"Javier."

"Yes."

"Did you tell your mother what I do for a living?"

"Yeah."

"How did she react?"

"It was kind of weird, actually. I didn't tell her for awhile. I kinda avoided it. Finally, she said, 'Mijo, what does he do?' I said, he's La Migra. She just looked at me and started laughing. She thought I was joking."

"Then what?"

"She thought I was crazy. I explained to her that you had just as much to lose as I did. At first she didn't like it. She eventually came around though. She was nervous about meeting you. I told her to think of you as my boyfriend not *La Migra*."

"I'm sorry I didn't meet her, Javier."

"It's Okay," he said. "Dee …"

"Yeah?"

"I think she took you being black a lot better than the whole border patrol thing."

I laughed. "That's good to know."

18

It had been three weeks since Javier came to stay with me. Things were getting worse instead of better. We haven't had sex at all during his stay, which was understandable considering the circumstances, but I viewed our sex life as a gauge to his mental well-being. Some days he didn't even sleep in the bed with me. He would just fall asleep in front of the television. Neither of us had seen the inside of a gym lately either. I couldn't remember the last time I hung out with Michael and Rafael—luckily they had been understanding about my social sabbatical. I couldn't get Javier to carry on a conversation, and hygiene seemed to be out the window. I wondered what personal matters he let fall to the wayside also. I'm sure his rent was late, and he hadn't been back to school or work.

The only positive thing was there was no crying this week. Even that may not necessarily have been an indication of improvement; he could have just been emotionally numb or suppressing his feelings. My fear was coming true; I was failing him nearly as much as he was failing himself. I resolved to do better and make him do better.

As I opened the door to the apartment, I hoped I'd see some change in him. Some sign that he was getting better. No such luck. He was in the same track pants and T-shirt as when I had left for work. In fact, I believe he had worn them the last three days.

"Hi, Javier," I said.

"Hey," he responded, without removing his attention from the television.

I undressed in the bedroom. I felt like I was beginning to lose it. I didn't know what to do or how to help him. I even considered making an appointment for him with Dr. Lindale.

I went into the bathroom and ran the shower. Wearing only my boxers, I walked into the living room, and turned off the television.

In a stern voice, much like the one I used with someone I may have apprehended, I said, "Get up!"

"What?"

"You heard me. Get up!" I repeated.

"Where we going?" he asked. He still hadn't moved from his spot on the sofa.

"To get cleaned up," I said. "Get up!"

Javier slowly moved to his feet.

"Follow me," I commanded.

Javier followed me into the bathroom. I ran water over his toothbrush and applied toothpaste. "Here's your toothbrush. Now use it."

His eyes grew angry and defiant as he stared down at the brush in my hand. "I'm not your fuckin' child!" he shouted. "Don't treat me like a child."

"I'm treating you like someone I care about, and if you care about me you will do as I ask." Javier looked me in the eye and pondered my words. Slowly he took the toothbrush and leaned over the sink and began to brush. "I know you been through a lot baby, but I can't just watch you waste away. Your mother wouldn't want to see you like this. I know grieving can be a long process, but you have to get off that couch."

He stared at himself in the mirror and began to brush with more conviction and then closed his eyes to fight back the tears. Steam from the shower began to fill the bathroom.

"I'm not saying it has to happen today or tomorrow, but you have to go back to work and school. You have to go back to your life. This apartment is not an escape,

Javier. You have a degree program to finish." He nodded and continued to brush. Foam ran down the side of his mouth and dripped onto his T-shirt. "If you don't get it for yourself, then at least go get it for your mother."

I took his toothbrush and handed him a cap full of mouthwash. "Rinse." He gargled and spat in the sink.

I pulled his T-shirt off from over his head. As I continued to undress him he offered no resistance. I couldn't help but think how child like he did seem with his blank expression.

"Come on, baby," I said before removing my own boxers and ushering him into the shower. I directed him under the shower head. The water was hot, yet he was shaking. As the water ran over his body, I took a handful of liquid soap and began to lather him up.

"I don't know what you need me to do." Now I was crying. "I can't stand to see you like this. I want my Javier back. This ... this is not you." I scrubbed him from the top of his head down to his feet until he was entirely covered in a soapy lather. "I'm sorry.... I am *so* sorry you lost your mother, Javier, but I'm here. What about me...? I love you.... Can you pull out of this for me?"

Javier pulled me into his arms under the shower head and embraced me. He trembled violently and let out an anguished cry that startled me. "I'm sorry, Dee ... I'm sorry ... I'm so sorry ..." he apologized. "It just hurts so much … It just hurts *so* much … I'm so sorry …" he wept.

"Don't apologize baby. You've been through a lot. Just try for me," I pleaded.

"I will…. I will."

For a moment, we both just stood there locked in embrace, the hot shower water coursing down our bodies as our silent tears coursed down our cheeks.

I took a step back to look him in the eye and then placed a simple kiss on his lips as the water ran down his face. He pulled me close for something much longer and deeper than I expected at that moment. We hadn't kissed like that in weeks. I could feel him growing between us. I did as well. The soapy lather cascaded down our bodies while we continued to kiss under the hot running water.

Before I knew what was happening, we were out of the shower still dripping wet and headed for the bedroom. On the bed, I collapsed on top of him. Our wet bodies dampened the comforter making it cling to our skin. We thrashed around and grinded against each other for several minutes; all the while our lips never parted. It was both lustful and playful. Soon, the words "I love you" bounced off the walls repeatedly between passionate kisses. We seemed to be in a competition: who could say it the most and with the most feeling. We rolled around on the bed fighting for the top position. This was one time I wasn't going to relent. I had an overwhelming urge to be inside him and make him feel pleasure. I knew it was what he wanted and needed.

I was on a high when I entered him. It felt like forever since I'd heard him moan with pleasure, "Yes, Papa." We teetered between the line of fucking and making love. At times we were rough and other times slow and gentle. He wanted it while he was on his stomach and then begged me to roll him onto his back. He wanted to see my face and look into my eyes—both pain and pleasure filled his own. He shouted with joy as his own milky substance erupted on his chest and stomach. I followed suit having one of the most intense orgasms I had ever experienced. We were hot, sweaty, and spent. I fell on top of him, and he held me tightly.

The next morning I awoke to a letter on the nightstand.

Dear Dee,

Gone to the gym and need to take care of some loose ends. I'm going to talk to Don about going back to work also. I'll probably be pretty busy most of the day, so I will see you tonight. Thanks for last night

Love, Javier.

P.S. Don't you like the sound of that? "Love, Javier."

P.P.S. You might think about going to the gym also. You

looked liked you picked up a couple pounds in the last few weeks. Just kidding. You're beautiful.

I knew Javier was still going to be in for some tough days, but I was glad to see he had at least decided to take on the day. I was proud of him for that.

Later, while at work, I decided to give Javier a call. I hadn't heard from him all day and was wondering how he was doing. I called him from my Jeep.

"Hello," he answered.

"Hey, baby, how's it going?"

"I'm hanging in there. I just got to my apartment. It smells in here." After last night I didn't really expect him to be his normal self, and he wasn't, but I was glad he was trying. I could hear in his voice that getting on was a bit of a struggle. "I talked to Don about going back to work next week," he informed me.

"You ready for that?"

"I think it's about time," he said. "It looks like my professors are going to work with me also, but I'm really behind."

"If anyone can do it I know you can."

"Thanks, Dee."

"Well, I know you can."

"No, I mean thanks for everything. You really have been there for me. I don't know where I would be right now without you."

"I'm sure you would have managed," I protested.

"No.... You've really been there. I don't know how I can ever show you how much that means to me."

"It's what I'm here for," I said, trying not to get sentimental at work.

"I'm lucky."

"I think we both are, Javier."

"Well, I have a few more things to do here, like find out where that smell is coming from. I'll see you at home."

"Talk to you later, baby."

"Bye."

It wasn't until I was off the phone with Javier when I realized he said, "See you at home." I grinned.

When I did finally arrive home, I arrived to the unusual smell of something burning. Javier greeted me at the door in black slacks and a blue V-neck sweater exposing a considerable amount of man cleavage.

"I ruined dinner," he said to me as I entered. "I was going to surprise you with a candlelight dinner, and I fell asleep. I slept right through the timer and burned the pot roast." Javier was clearly upset beneath his squinted brow as he pushed his hands inside his pockets. The dinette table was set for two, with cloth napkins, candles, and wine glasses.

I smiled. "It's fine, Javier. I appreciate the thought."

"No, I fucked everything up."

"Come here," I said as I held out my arms. He buried his face into my chest so hard that I was sure the badge from my uniform was going to leave an imprint on his face.

"I missed you," he said.

"I missed you too. Don't worry about dinner. We'll figure something out."

"Okay, Papa."

We had burritos by candlelight from a local taco shop. It was still just as romantic.

Javier made me feel useful. He needed me—and to be honest, I needed him just as much. I've always heard that in a relationship there is always one person more in love than the other. I guess sometimes that is the case. I knew that Javier was definitely in a time and place that our relationship was a comfort, especially with all that was going on in his life. But I wouldn't say that one of us was any more in love than the other. We were just in love.

19

It had been six months since Javier moved in. We had never planned on living together. I'm not quite sure how it happened. It seemed that he just never went back to his apartment after the funeral. One drawer turned into several drawers, then eventually, half the closet. The second bedroom—that doubled as a guestroom and office—is where Javier did most of his studying. One day, he told me his lease was up and asked if he should renew it. I said no, and that was that. There was no long-drawn-out discussion, no contemplation. It wasn't really a question in my mind. Sure, it was quick, but it was just a natural progression. I guess dealing with his traumatic loss bonded us that much faster. We had slept in the same bed every night for several months. I don't know how I would have reacted if he ever told me he was going to stay at his place for a night. As far as I was concerned, he was where he belonged—with me.

We hadn't been without our challenges. There were times I didn't think Javier was ever going to shake off the depression. At one point, I suggested that maybe he should see Dr. Lindale—whom I had stopped seeing. I felt I was in a good place, and no longer needed to examine myself in therapy. Javier refused to see Dr. Lindale for even just one visit. Eventually, he did pull through on his own terms. I knew there wouldn't be a day that went by when something wouldn't remind him of his mother and how much he missed her.

Still ... it wasn't *all* bliss. I overlooked the dirty dishes in the sink, even though we had a dishwasher. I ignored the hairs left in the bathroom sink after he shaved. I pretended not to be bothered by clothes left on the floor next to the laundry hamper. Who cared if I seemed to be the only one in the house who knew how to do laundry or clean the bathroom? He apparently had me mistaken for a desperate housewife. Honestly, those things didn't bother me much. It was such a small price to pay when, in the end, I had him.

I'm sure he had his complaints about me; although, I couldn't possibly imagine what. He didn't express any. One day, he did utter something in Spanish when I asked him to make the bed for the third time. My Spanish was improving, so I understood him when he said, "You have become worse than a nagging wife," in his native tongue.

Remarkably, Javier graduated on time. I was so proud of him. His sister, Maria, and I were disappointed that Javier didn't want to participate in the graduation ceremony. He said he couldn't walk across the stage without his mom being there. We both understood. The three of us *did* go out to dinner to celebrate.

Javier was recruited on campus by Southern California Credit Union. He was worried he wouldn't get hired because he had used a counterfeit Social Security card during the hiring process, but they didn't detect any fraud. Employers do have the ability to verify if Social Security card numbers match the name on the card versus the name that the government has on record. The number was real but not his own, so all his adult life he's been paying into someone else's Social Security account. I learned that Javier uses three pieces of false documentation, all of which were purchased in L.A. from some of the best underground counterfeiters on the West Coast. First, there was the Social Security card; second, a BCC (Border Crossing Card); and lastly, a driver's license. I couldn't detect any flaws in any of the documents. The BCC card was useless for crossing the border, and he didn't use it for that purpose. He had never been back to Mexico. It would immediately be detected as a fake by any immigration agent once put through the system at a Port of Entry. Javier would only use the BCC card if by chance he was pulled over by the police or highway patrol, since they weren't trained in detecting fake immigration documents. It would be much easier to deal with the consequences of driving without a license than to try to regain entry into United States after being deported.

With every drive to L.A. he was taking a chance of being arrested at the San Clemente Border Patrol Checkpoint, nearly an hour north of San Diego. I was, of course, familiar with checkpoint operations. If Javier didn't appear nervous, look illegal, or profile as such, he could probably make it through the checkpoint without being sent into secondary for further questioning. He had been lucky so far, but every trip was a risk. A good driver's license fraud could possibly make it by a Border Patrol Agent since most of our training is for immigration documents. Most Border Patrol Agents, excluding checkpoint agents, deal with people who don't have documents, but a checkpoint agent sees documents and driver's licenses on a daily basis.

I didn't realize how much he juggled due to living in the United Stated illegally. Every time he left the house, a small part of me worried. I would make him promise to abide by all the speed limits and street signs. I would tell him not to talk on the cellphone while driving—even if it was with me. I tried to get him to limit his trips to L.A., but that he wouldn't listen to. That's where his sister, Maria, lived as well as some extended family; family was everything to him.

Javier's mother had a savings account that he and Maria were the beneficiaries of. He was surprised by the amount of money left to him. He said that while he was growing up, his mom worked two jobs most of the time, to make ends meet. I guess that didn't mean she didn't pay herself first, as they say, or know how to invest. Javier hadn't touched any of the money. He hadn't even disclosed any dollar amount to me. That was fine with me; it wasn't as if we were married with shared accounts. I think he felt a little guilty about having the money. To him it seemed like a tradeoff, although he much rather would have had his mom instead of the money.

The biggest challenge was spending time together. Javier worked days, banker's hours. I switched my days off back to Sundays and Mondays. That at least gave us a partial weekend together. When my workday began, his was nearing an end. Unless he waited up for me, it only gave us two nights a week—my days off—to spend any quality time together. I didn't have the option to change to day shift for a few months. I think maybe it was good we didn't spend that much time together; this way we wouldn't get sick of each other. It was nice to come home and find him waiting up for me. Usually, those were the nights he wanted sex, and you wouldn't hear me complain—but try getting sex out of him if he was already asleep; I was just out of luck. No matter how much I licked, or rubbed, he always slept like a rock. I was a happy participant if he woke me in the morning for a quickie before he was off to work. It was easier for him, since most mornings, I already had morning wood anyway. I guess I was just easy.

It was one of my nights off, and we had just finished watching a DVD, when Javier jumped up from the couch.

"You and me—John Madden football!" he shouted, like a boxing announcer. I had no idea he was such a video game junkie. I guess he didn't really play all *that* much, but it could seem like that when I wanted us to do other things, and I had to pry him away from a video game controller.

"I'm sick of that game," I protested. "I never win."

Javier settled beside me on the couch and handed me a controller. "You get better at things by practicing. Don't have such a defeatist attitude."

Leave it to Javier to take a video game so seriously and use it to try and teach me a lesson. "Fine," I relented.

I wasn't sure how much of a difference it was going to make, but I had spent a few nights during the last couple of weeks practicing while Javier slept. I think at least now I could probably give him a run for his money.

"You can be San Diego," he said, "and I'll be Oakland." Javier refused to jump on the San Diego bandwagon. Like many people from L.A., he was a diehard Raiders fan. We reenacted this rival every time we played together.

"Care to make a wager?" he asked.

He piqued my curiosity. "What do you have in mind?"

"Loser bottoms?" he smiled.

As far as I was concerned it was a win-win situation. "I'll take that bet."

Forty-five agonizing minutes later, the San Diego Chargers suffered another defeat to the Oakland Raiders. I'll save myself the embarrassment of revealing the final score.

"Two out of three," I said.

"No way. I think I'll take my winnings now."

I climbed onto Javier's lap and straddled him. "I guess I better pay up … huh?" I said before kissing his neck.

"Can I give you some advice?" he asked, while he

grabbed my ass.

"What's that?"

"When you're in here practicing at night against the computer, set it to 'expert.' You've been practicing under the novice setting."

So much for my little secret. I couldn't keep anything from him, even when I tried. "*Now* you tell me. You know one of these days, when you least expect it, I'm going to spank yo azz at this game."

"Well … you can dream …" he said, caressing my back and planting kisses on my neck. My skin began to tingle.

Javier pulled my T-shirt off over my head. He started working my nipples with his mouth. He knew that drove me crazy. A bulge rose to the occasion in his jeans.

"What's that, baby?" I asked.

"You know exactly what it is, Papa," he said. "You want it?"

"Yeah," I whispered.

"No, say it like you mean it!"

"Yeah, baby," I said, more sure of myself. He knew how to summon the freak in me.

A much more pleasurable forty five minutes later we were lying naked on the living room floor. The television still asked if we would like to start a new game.

"Damn … I love you," I said. We both stared at the

ceiling.

Javier grabbed my hand. "I love you too."

"Javier."

"Yeah, Papa?"

"Get us a towel."

"It's your turn," he responded.

"My turn? Since when have we taken turns? Besides, I washed and folded the towels. When was the last time you've done that? 'My turn—'"

Javier jumped to his feet. "I'll get the damn towel. Just shut up."

I laughed, "I love you."

Javier stopped and smiled. "I love you too, Papa."

That was another thing I loved about our relationship. We had been together all these months, and it was still like a first date—minus an interruption from Rafael. Suddenly, I realized we were soon coming up on a year. We were still newlyweds. I hoped we'd never lose that feeling.

That got me thinking further.

"When is our anniversary?" I asked Javier, when he returned. "I mean is it the day we met or when you moved in?"

"I don't know," Javier said, tossing me a towel. He lay back down next to me on the floor. "I never thought about it. When did we meet?"

I gave him the *you-should-know-the-answer* look. "July 22nd."

"You remember the exact date?"

"Well, yeah. And I see how important it is to you," I said, sarcastically. "I was just thinking maybe we should agree on an anniversary date. We will be hitting a year soon. Maybe I should come up with one since, obviously, you have no memory for these things."

"Is that right?" he said, with a chuckle.

"I'm just stating the facts."

Javier rolled onto his side so that he was facing me. He placed his hand on my chest and looked me in the eye. "July 22nd is when I first saw your bouncing bubble butt in the park—" I was just beginning to remind that him I'd already stated that fact when he placed his finger to my lips. "October 9th is when you told me you loved me, and I told you the same. It was October 9th—the same day—I came to stay with you for a while after my mom passed, and I never left. I think we should pick one of the two.

With his finger still on my lips I smiled. He was amazing. I thought I was something for remembering the date we'd met, yet he remembered every milestone in our relationship. I was soon embarrassed because my eyes began to well up with tears. He removed his finger from my lips as if he was now giving me permission to speak.

He stroked my cheek.

"Wow, I can't believe you remember all that. I guess July 22nd, the day we met, will be fine."

"Sounds good, Papa."

Later that same night, in bed after football, sex, and a shower, I was just about to drift off to sleep. Javier was lying next to me watching the nightly news.

"I've been thinking," he said.

"Uh-oh," I responded in my tired, hoarse, sleeping voice.

"No, really. I think we should buy a place together."

I rolled over to face him. "What?"

Javier muted the television. "This is your place, furnished with most of your things. I think we should buy a place together. Besides, it will be an investment."

He seemed to be so business-minded all of a sudden. I guess maybe it was from working at the credit union. "Who are you, Donald Trump now?" I joked. "How are you going to buy property anyway? You're illegal,... remember?"

I had never said that out loud to Javier before. The only person I had disclosed that information to was Michael. Saying it out loud made it all the more real. My boyfriend was illegal, a member of the very same group I was supposed to arrest and deport.

"There was an article in the *Union-Tribune* where

they were talking about how illegal immigrants have bought property here in California. Or we can put it all in your name with a contract on the side, sort of like a prenup. If something happens, we sell the place and split the proceeds."

I sensed I wasn't going to get any sleep anytime soon, so I sat up to better defend myself. I wasn't going to win with the illegal argument, so I tried a different approach. "Think about it, Javier. Do you really think we're ready for that? We've only been living together six months and known each other ... what ... ten? How did that happen so fast anyway?"

"You know a good thing when you see it," he teased.

"Do you mind getting that big head of yours out of my personal space?"

"Which one?" he replied.

"Seriously, Javier, I think it's too soon."

"I understand that. Everyone thought we were crazy for moving in together in the first place. We're making it work. We make up our own rules, Papa."

I hated that he resorted to calling me 'Papa' at that moment. He knew he was apt to get almost anything he wanted from me when that word rolled off his tongue with his trace of an accent, but now, I had to disagree. "I can't swing a down payment on a new place."

"We could get into a place for next to nothing, if you

use your VA home loan," he smiled.

"I still say it's too soon."

"We need to go bigger anyway," he said.

"Bigger? Why?"

"We can get a dog," he said. "Besides you ain't gettin' no younger. It's 'bout time ya gib me sum chil'ren," he said, with a southern twang.

Laughing, I said, "I'm only twenty-nine."

"Excuse me?" Javier said, looking at me intently.

"Alright, I'm thirty. You couldn't just let me have that moment."

"So, what do you say?"

"I think we should discuss it more in length when I'm not so tired."

"I can live with that."

"Javier?"

"Yeah, Papa."

"Do you really want kids?" I asked. "We never talked about kids before."

"Yeah. Yeah, I do…. What about you?"

I smiled. "Yes," I said, and stroked his chest. Suddenly the image of tiny people running around the apartment filled my head. And he was right, the apartment was too small. "For some reason I never really envisioned the day I would actually be talking about kids and buying property with my boyfriend."

"'Boyfriend'? That's dating shit. I think partner sounds better."

"Okay then, partner."

At that moment, I realized how caught up in love we were. We were just stumbling in the dark, and luckily, no one had gotten hurt. We still had so much to learn about each other. We seemed to want the same things, but Javier seemed to want them so much faster.

He was now twenty-five and wanted the American Dream. I was the thirty-year-old. I should have been the one pushing for the house, kids, and dog. I knew thirty wasn't old, but it was a reality check for me. According to statistics on black men, my life was already half over. I wondered how many years I would have before my body started to sag. Let's not even get into the issues of growing old in the gay community where youth and body reign.

Javier's mom was fifty-two when she fell victim to a heart attack. Sometimes, I wondered if he was trying to do everything now out of fear that he may not have much time left.

20

I maneuvered my Jeep down a narrow gravel road. It wasn't often that I was assigned a backup position allowing me to roam around freely. In this particular area, we depended more on sensors and infrared equipment to help with our mission of border security. It was hilly and more rural than most of our territory, unlike other areas which were becoming more industrialized. A lot of businesses were sprouting up near the border, bringing along factories and warehouses. Places where we once looked for illegal immigrants, in bushes and behind rock formations, were now being replaced with dumpsters, semitrailers, and 7-Elevens.

I slowed the Jeep to a stop on a plateau. Here, there was no fence because there was no need for one; the terrain was much too treacherous, and crossing through Border Patrol territory could take days on foot. The land itself was enough of a deterrent. With housing in Mexico visible from this area, it wasn't unusual for Mexican children to cross over and ask agents for candy, food, or money.

I turned my gaze toward houses south of the border that were perched along the hillsides. From the distance, you couldn't tell, but in actuality, they were probably more like shacks. I could hear children's laughter and screams of joy as they played games that could have only been powered by imagination. If I lived in one of those shacks and had children, I too would have probably attempted what so many have—illegal entry into the United States. Now, I wondered if this would be my lifelong career after all. It seemed that my once clear stance on immigration and border security was now muddy and murky. *Did Javier and the story of his family have an effect on me?* One thing was certain: not everyone crossing our borders are law abiding citizens looking for work. We have caught thieves, rapists, murders, con artists, pedophiles, wife beaters, and the list goes on. It was that side of the job that provided some sort of equilibrium for me. On the other side of the scale was the husband and his pregnant wife who simply wanted the American Dream…. Let's face it, it wasn't the American Dream they were after—they simply wanted a roof over their heads, three meals a day, running water, clean clothes, and the opportunity to earn it. Prisoners get those basic necessities, but I wouldn't call that the American Dream.

I diverted my attention to the sunset. It was funny to me how it took all day for the sun to cross the sky, but in just a few moments, the sun could set in the mere blink of an eye. The day was nearly depleted. The sun was a ball of red-orange molten lava slowly easing its way into the cool abyss of the Pacific Ocean. The farther it plunged, the cooler and darker the evening became. Without any light other than the headlights of my Jeep and the distant light from Tijuana, there would nearly be complete darkness when the sun's plunge was complete.

I picked up my cell phone and dialed Michael's number. It was probably the high elevation that allowed me to pick up an obscure Mexican cell tower and receive a telephone signal. I was probably on a roaming network.

"Hello," he answered.

"What's up? You working?"

"I'm on my way home. I was on day shift this week for that antiterrorist training."

"I'm not looking forward to going back to days, but I need to make the switch next rotation."

"I know … to spend time with ya man, so you better get used to it," he teased. "How is he anyway?"

I paused. "He wants us to buy a place together."

"And why don't you sound thrilled?"

"He's illegal. Besides, it's such a big commitment."

"I'll be the first to tell you I think it's too soon, but I think it's that whole commitment thing that has your panties in a bunch … not that you ever wear any…. I wouldn't worry about it. Like you said, the whole illegal thing works against him as far as buying property goes."

"Believe me, he has it all figured out…. He wants kids someday too."

"I'm going to stop you right there. You have a good man who seems to want the same things you want. I don't see the problem, besides the whole illegal thing."

"Okay. Yes, we know he's illegal, and you're right. I'm overreacting. It just seems he wants everything so soon."

"Relax, Bitch. At least you got a man."

The call waiting kicked in. Dad.

"Damn. I probably should take this. I'll call you later."

"Ciao, bitch."

I hit the flash button. "Hello," I answered.

"Devon, what's going on?"

"Nothing much. How about you, Dad?"

"Just trying to make a living. You catch anyone yet today?"

I sighed at hearing the same question, yet again. "No,

the sun just went down. I'll probably be pretty busy out here tonight though."

"I won't keep you then. I just wanted to let you know Pricilla and I are going to be at our place in Vegas for two weeks in May. We wanted to drive down for a weekend to visit. Can you get the time off?"

"Yeah, just get me the exact dates."

"Good. You have a spare bedroom too, right?"

Shit! That was exactly what I was afraid of. No one back home knew I was living with Javier. His name had come up, but I never told them the nature of our relationship, though I was pretty sure they knew.

"Yeah, you can stay with me."

"Good. I'll talk with you later about it and get you those dates. Be safe."

"Bye, Dad."

I had about a month to figure out how to handle the situation.

Like I suspected, I was quite busy for the rest of the evening. I apprehended a total of sixteen people throughout the shift. I had to do removal proceedings paperwork for two out of the sixteen.

I was in the processing and holding area when I excused myself to call Javier from outside to let him know I would be late—in case he was waiting up. I longed for the day I could make this phone call from inside like my colleagues, but I guess they weren't exactly ready for that. It was probably more that I wasn't ready for that. I dialed his cellphone.

"Que pasa, Papa?" he answered.

"Hey, baby."

"What's wrong?" he asked.

"Nothing. I'm going to be late, so don't wait up."

"You oppressing my people again, Papa?"

"Yeah, you take out your frustrations on me later if you like."

"How late?"

"One, maybe two at the latest."

"Yeah, I will most definitely be asleep."

"Oh, baby, before I forget. My dad and stepmom want to visit next month."

Javier must have heard the reservations in my voice. "What's wrong?... You haven't told your family about me, have you?"

"They know about you," I said, defensively.

"Let me guess. They don't know we live together, or at least not as partners.

So ... will I be your roommate?"

"Don't be like that."

"Are you ashamed?" he asked.

"Ashamed of what?"

"I don't know. Who you are.... Me?"

I looked around to see if anyone was in earshot of what I was about to say next. "Why do you think I have to broadcast my sexuality to be proud of who I am? I'm in law enforcement, Javier. People don't want to know that the guy backing them up is a faggot. It's not like I work at a fucking bank."

Click!

The line went dead.

Note to self: Don't insinuate your job is more difficult or more important than his.

I called back several times and got no answer. I absolutely hated it when he didn't answer the phone. It reminded me of the week he was in L.A. attending his mother's funeral, and I was home worried. Not to mention it was just childish. I went back inside to finish my paperwork.

I got home shortly after 2:00 a.m. Not a light was on in the apartment, and all was clear—at least it seemed that way. I could have been walking directly into an ambush, an angry confrontation about what I had said. I was hoping Javier was asleep; that way, I would sneak into bed after an already exhausting shift. I didn't have the energy to fight. If he indeed was asleep, I wouldn't see him until possibly the following night … if he waited up. Hopefully, it would have blown over by then, though not likely.

I hit the light switch. He wasn't sitting on the couch in the dark at least. Sounds crazy, but he had done it before. I took off my boots and gun belt in the living room. I wanted to make as little noise as possible once I was in the bedroom.

At the bedroom door, I discovered it locked. I wasn't even aware the bedroom door had a lock. I saw right through his plan. For me to gain entry into the bedroom I would have to knock and wake him in the process. Then he could start his assault. I could simply sleep in the guest room, but that would be an admission of guilt. Damn it! He had me.

I wasn't prepared to admit my guilt. Wincing, I lightly knocked on the door. "Javier, the door is locked." No reply. I knocked harder. "Javier, open the door."

"Why should I?" was his response. "You're ashamed to sleep with me."

"Stop it. This is stupid. Now open the door."

"Like my job…?"

He was certainly going to make me pay. "I'm sorry. I didn't mean that. I was upset."

"Well, you must have thought it before."

"No, Javier. I just simply meant our jobs are different. I think it's easier for you to be *out* than for me. At least as far as our jobs are concerned."

"Bullshit!"

I was growing annoyed. "Javier, open the damn door!"

"Sleep in the guestroom."

"How in the hell are you going to lock me out of my own bedroom?" I shouted. "Now open the door!"

The silence seemed to go on for hours. Then I heard the lock disengage. Somehow, I didn't think I wanted in anymore. The door swung open and I stepped back. Javier emerged out of the darkness.

"You see why I want a place for the both of us? You can have *your* bed, and I'll sleep in *your* guestroom," he said as he pushed pass me.

Oh, he fought dirty. Now, we were fighting over yesterday's conversation as well. I wouldn't have been surprised if he planned this whole thing with the lock just to make his point.

"Baby, I didn't mean it like that," I said following after him. I wasn't entirely sure what I didn't mean anymore: insulting his work or that it was my place and he merely resided here.

He plopped onto the futon in the guestroom. I sat on the floor beside him. "I'm sorry. I'm an asshole. You know the last thing I want is to hurt you. Now come on, let's go to bed."

"I'm sleeping here tonight," he protested. "You know what bugs me? You don't get it. I want to build a life with you. You want some college romance. Shack up and see where it goes."

"That's not true."

"Well, let's see. Your family doesn't know about me. You don't want to go and get something for the both of us. I'm not going to be yo fuckin' illegal houseboy."

"That's low Javier. I never thought of you like that. And no, I haven't told my family about you. There's a lot I don't tell them. I will in due time. As far as the place goes, we can start looking tomorrow if you want, but I still feel it's too soon … and as you mentioned, you *are* illegal which makes it a little difficult to buy property."

"So, now you're willing to do it to shut me up?"

"No."

"Let me ask you something. If you were straight and moved in with a girl, would your family know by now?"

His question hit me hard and unexpectedly. "I see your point."

Javier moved to the edge of the futon. "It was so hard for me to come out to my mom. I was afraid I would disappoint her. She told me, 'If I am being the best person I can be, there is no reason to be ashamed.' Too many of us play into the shame, Dee. We don't speak about our relationships to our families, and we hide by not coming out. It feeds into stereotypes and homophobia. I refuse to live like that."

Javier had voiced his opinion to me on coming out before, but I had no idea he felt so passionate about it. Frankly, it frightened me. I wasn't on that level and wasn't sure if I ever would be. I didn't know what to say. I simply got up and went to bed, and Javier didn't join me. I tossed and turned all night waiting for him.

Saturday morning, when I awoke, Javier was already gone—to where, I didn't know. On the futon sat the neatly folded blanket and pillow. I wanted to believe he was at the gym, which may have very well been the case. He didn't leave a note either. Javier always told me where he could be found. He was still mad. I hadn't heard from him or seen him by the time I left for work.

Saturday night, home from work and still no word from Javier, I was beyond upset. I hated how he reacted, or more like … overreacted. I didn't know if I should be worried or pissed.

It was after two in the morning, when he strolled in. I continued channel surfing. He sat next to me on the sofa. Neither one of us said a word. My first reaction was to lay into him, but I didn't want to make the situation worse.

I calmly said, "I was worried about you."

"I'm sorry. I should have called."

"Where were you all day, or do I want to know?"

"I went to L.A. to see Maria."

Now, I really wanted to curse him for driving to L.A.

"I was beginning to think you weren't coming home," I said. "You're that upset with me?"

"Yeah, but it's not completely your fault. I can't expect you to change and live your life according to my rules or standards."

"Hmmm....That must have been Maria's advice."

He smirked. "I can think for myself."

I finally turned to look at him. "I dream of the day I can take you home to visit my family, but they haven't been that accepting, and it may never happen. I was practically disowned and cast to the fires of hell when I came out to them. You have to believe me when I say I will tell them about you, but on my own time. As far as work, I don't know if I will ever be out at work. I hope you can live with that."

Javier took my hand. "It's okay, Papa. I shouldn't pressure you like I've been doing."

"What's your urgency with everything Javier? The bigger place ... wanting me to tell my family about you?"

"Come on, Dee. It's not if you don't already know, even if I haven't said it.... It's about my mom. I mean, she still had so much life to live. I know she had to have some dreams, even if it was just seeing me graduate. There is so much I want to experience. Her death has made me examine my own mortality. What if I'm gone before we get the chance to have a family?"

"Come here, Javier." I held him close in my arms. "You're right. Tomorrow isn't promised, but we can't live in fear either. If we're meant to have kids, a house with a dog, and a white picket fence, it will happen. Just let it happen. We can't escape our fate."

"I know …you're right," he said, resting his head on my shoulder. "I love you, Papa."

"I love you too…. I tell you what. How about we start looking for a place? I'm just talking about some window shopping for now, just to see what we like."

Javier managed to smile. "You're not just throwing me a bone are you?"

"I got another bone for you," I said.

By daybreak, the previous day seemed like a bad dream. We quickly got back into our Sunday routine. We rolled out of bed around 10:00 a.m. and went for a run in the park. Running in the park, for me, was like rejuvenating the relationship. It was where we had met and reconnected. It was our retreat.

On the way home, we picked up a Sunday paper and a couple of DVD's from Blockbuster. Javier drew us a bath. It was a tight fit with the two of us, but romantic. Javier reclined between my legs, resting his head on my chest. He was reading the real estate section of course.

"How does this sound? Two bedrooms, two baths,

two parking spaces, 1200 square feet, North Park."

I wrapped my arms around him and kissed his head. I remembered we were talking about real estate in Southern California, so I replied, "Expensive."

"We can afford it."

"You, maybe—"

"Let me worry about the money."

"If we do this it has to be together. Fifty-fifty. That's the point, right?"

"It's all pipe dreams now," he said.

"You sound pretty serious to me."

"Let's go look at it. They have an open house today."

I sighed. "Okay, but don't get any ideas."

"I know. We're just looking."

An hour later, we were standing in front of a five-story condo conversion. The building's exterior was finished in beige stucco with russet trim. The tropical landscaping featured a row of swaying palm trees and neatly manicured shrubbery. A sign in front read, "Casa Del Rey." House of the king.

"This is a condo. I thought you wanted to look at houses," I said.

"Have you seen the prices of houses here? It's unreal."

We walked into the lobby and were greeted by a tall, slender blonde woman who appeared to be anorexic.

Despite being so thin, she had pretty facial features. She was wearing a black skirt, heals, and a fitted white blouse.

She stood and greeted us, "Good Afternoon, I'm Cindy. Welcome to Casa Del Rey."

We both exchanged handshakes with Cindy. Her hand seemed fragile. I thought if I squeezed too hard, I would break it.

"I'm Devon, and this is Javier."

"So, who's in the market for a condo?"

"Well, actually both of us. I mean … we're just kind of looking now," I explained.

"I see. Are you a couple?" Cindy asked, while grabbing a brochure off her desk and handed it to me.

Javier grinned with pride. "Yes we are."

"This shows you our different floor plans. The last sheet tells you which units are available and the prices. All available units are open for viewing. Anything else is most likely occupied, so we ask that you don't bother the residents. That's about it, so feel free to look around, and I'll be here to answer any questions you may have."

"Thank you," Javier and I said, in unison.

We walked down the hall to the elevator. Javier hit the up button.

"She called you out," Javier said.

"Funny, that only happens when I'm with you," I

joked.

Javier studied the packet. "Let's start with 403."

The door to 403 was already propped open. A young Asian couple in their Sunday best exited while we approached. We exchanged pleasantries.

The condo's entry way led to a spacious living room. The kitchen, off to the right, featured black marble counter tops, stainless steel appliances, cherry oak cabinets, and a ceramic tile floor.

"Nice … huh, Papa?"

"I have to admit it's nice."

We walked into the living room, which had hardwood floors and a sliding glass door that lead out to a balcony that didn't offer much of a view. We mostly saw the backyards of surrounding houses, many which of appeared to house nothing but junk in their backyards.

"How much is this one?" I asked.

Javier looked over the paperwork. "This one is going for $380,000."

"Well, let's get it," I said, sarcastically. "I'll write them a check."

Ignoring me, Javier proceeded down the main hallway. I followed, muttering to myself, "No wonder it's called "Casa Del Rey"; it takes a king's ransom to buy it."

The master bedroom was a bit larger than our current

bedroom. The condo itself was bigger than our apartment by at least few hundred square feet.

"Papa, come here!" Javier yelled from the adjoining bathroom.

I found Javier in front of the sink.

"Look at this. Double vanities. I can leave all the hair I want in mine."

"Do you think just because you have your own, I wouldn't make you keep it clean?"

"That was the plan."

"Think again."

Aside from the view, I had to give it to him: the place was nice. It was equipped with a washer and dryer; we wouldn't have to haul everything to the laundry room like in our current place. There was substantial underground parking—no more lugging groceries in through the rain and hot sun. And, besides, Javier was just too excited.

"Thanks for coming," Javier said as we walked back to the car.

I took his hand. "There's no harm in looking."

21

With only my cardio left to do, I was nearing the end of my workout. I was making my way to the treadmills when I was stopped by a tall brotha with a caramel complexion. I had admired him from afar earlier. He had a goatee, his hair was freshly faded, and he stood well over six feet tall. He looked the part of a basketball player in his baggy shorts and fitted wifebeater.

"Can you spot me?" he asked from the flat bench.

"Sure, man."

I stood over him while he benched four forty-five pound plates—two on each end of the bar—with ease. "You got it," I said. "It's all you." I was beginning to wonder why I was spotting him as he easily did twelve reps with no assistance from me.

"Good set," I said.

The caramel brotha sat up on the bench. "Thanks man."

"No problem," I said as I began to walk away.

"Do you usually work out around this time?" he asked.

"Yeah, I work nights, so I'm usually here midmornings."

"Cool. My partner is in the Navy. I just moved here. I need to find a workout partner, not to mention a job."

His admission to having a partner reminded me of Javier, not giving a crap about what other people thought. Either that or I just screamed "gay" lately. "How long ya'll been together?" Seemed like a silly follow-up question for me to ask, as if I was the census bureau keeping tabs on the average length of gay relationships.

"Five years. I should have never gotten involved with a military man."

"Watch it now. I used to be in the military."

"Navy?"

"No, Air Force."

"Oh, that don't count," he said, sarcastically.

"Is that right?"

"No, I'm just giving you a hard time. It's just that he's Navy, and you know how that goes. Tour duty is a bitch.

Out of all the branches, I don't know why someone would choose the Navy. It seems to be the hardest, spending all that time on boats and shit."

"Yeah."

"So, what about you? Girlfriend? Boyfriend? Married?"

I looked around to see if anyone was listening before I said, "Boyfriend."

"I suspected."

"What did you suspect? That I had a boyfriend or that I was gay?"

"Both actually. You had a little hit on my gaydar, and after looking at you, I knew you wouldn't be single."

Like Javier, he had game. "Oh, really?"

"Really," he said. " … I'm all talkin' your ear off and shit. I better let you get back to your workout."

"Devon, by the way," I said, while extending my hand.

"Kenneth."

"Nice to meet you."

"It was my pleasure." He held my hand just a little too long.

I was thirteen minutes into my run on the treadmill, when Kenneth reappeared. He handed me a folded piece of paper. "Here's my number. Like I said befo I'm lookin' for a workout partner and some peeps to hang wit."

I took the paper. "Ok, sounds cool."

As I watched Kenneth walk away, I wondered if it was a good idea to call him. I was definitely attracted to him, which could pose a problem. I didn't think Javier would react well to me making a new friend either. I wasn't totally sure of Kenneth's intentions. I knew the fact that he had a partner didn't mean a damn thing to him.

I was contemplating the phone call for several days, but I knew it was something I had to do, especially if I wanted to keep the peace at home. I dialed the number and hit send.

"Hello," my dad answered.

"Hey, Dad, this is Devon."

"What's going on?"

"Nothing much …working."

"Catch anyone lately?"

I sighed deeply in response to his question. "No. Listen Dad, I need to talk to you about something."

"What's the problem?"

"It's about your visit next month."

"Can you get the time off?"

"That's not the problem," I said, with a slight quaver in my voice. "I think there is something you should know before you come down."

"What is it?"

"I don't live alone."

"You have a roommate?"

"No…. He's not a roommate. You heard me talk about Javier. Well, we've been living together for the past few months. We're a couple." I was shaking. It was like coming out all over again. I had to reassure myself I was an adult now, and if he didn't like it, he didn't have to deal with it.

"Oh, I see."

"Look Dad, we still have the room if you want to stay with us. I just wanted to be upfront with you. If you'd rather stay in a hotel I understand, but Javier will still be around. He's actually looking forward to meeting you."

"Okay."

"So, does this change anything?"

"I'll have to let you know later if we will still be staying with you or not."

"Okay. It's your call."

"Later."

I came home that night and found Javier playing— what else—John Madden football. I was glad he waited up.

I started to remove my boots by the door. "What are you still doing up?"

"Couldn't sleep."

"What's wrong? Horny?"

"Just wanted to see my baby."

I joined Javier on the sofa. "Well, that's funny, since you haven't looked up from your game since I came in." He did manage to briefly look my way for a kiss.

"How was your day?" I asked.

"It was alright. A typical Monday. Yours?"

Javier never really talked about work much, no matter how much I pressed him. When he was working at *The Ritz,* he always told me about his day.

"I talked to may dad today."

"Yeah, baby!" he shouted. Apparently, he scored a touchdown. I knew that degree of excitement wasn't because he couldn't wait to hear about my conversation with my dad.

"I told him about you. I mean about us."

Javier paused the game and set the controller on the coffee table. "How did he take it?"

"I'm not sure. He said he was going to get back with me on whether or not he was going to stay with us."

Javier looked confused. "Why would that change?"

It was almost cute to me how naive he could be at times. "Javier, this is kind of new to him. He may not be able to handle staying here."

"Well … I'm proud of you," he said. He planted

another kiss but with more attention to detail. "Now let me get you out of this uniform." He began to unbutton my shirt.

I laughed. "See, I knew you were horny."

22

I believe the song said, "Seems it never rains in Southern California ..." But it was the rain that kept Javier and me from our run in the park this Sunday. After leaving the gym, our casual conversation was interrupted by his ringing cell phone.

"Hey, what's up girl? ...What's going on? ... Just tell me....What? ... Get out of here!"

Even while I drove, I noticed how Javier suddenly became tense and rigid. His eyes darted back and forth between the road ahead and me.

"Liz, is this a fuckin' joke? ... Alright, I'll talk to you later about it. I have to go."

I never met Liz, but I knew she was Javier's high school sweetheart. He told me that she had spent a lot of time with his family after his mother passed away. He even took her along to help with some of the decisions for the funeral arrangements. Apparently, they had remained close friends since high school, so it seemed a bit odd that I had never met her.

It didn't take law enforcement training to know that whatever they were talking about just now, Javier preferred I wasn't around when they had the conversation. My first instinct was to tell him to lay it on the table. I had to believe that if nothing else, we had trust, so I took a different approach.

"Is everything okay, Javier?"

"Yeah ... her ... her um punk-ass boyfriend was beatin' up on her."

"What are you supposed to do about it?"

"I don't know what the fuck she wants me to do about it!" he shouted.

"Well, don't take it out on me."

"I'm sorry. I just don't understand how women let themselves get in these situations."

"They don't usually get there by themselves."

"What the hell is that supposed to mean?"

"This is obviously a touchy subject for you."

"Yeah."

Something was wrong. We didn't pickup the Sunday paper or any DVD's on the way home. Our usual Sunday flow was interrupted, and I had no idea why. For the rest of the day Javier was distant and short-tempered. He could barely sit still for ten minutes. I knew something was bothering him when I couldn't get him to play John Madden football. He didn't sleep well that night either. I knew this because he kept me up most of the night with his tossing and turning.

Instinctively, the next morning, I phoned Javier at work.

The female voice on the other end answered. "Southern California Credit Union. How may I help you?"

"Javier Cruz, please."

"I'm sorry sir, he isn't in the office today. Would you like his voicemail?"

I wasn't surprised. I knew his absence from work had everything to do with Liz. "No, thank you."

I tried his cell phone next; it went directly to voicemail. "Javier, I know you're not at work. What the hell is going on?"

Two hours later, and no word from Javier. I was letting my frustrations out on the treadmill at the gym. I was nearly drenched with sweat. I could see Kenneth approaching.

"Wassup?" he asked.

I looked down at the display on the treadmill. I had lost track of time and hadn't realized I'd been running for forty eight minutes. I slowed the treadmill to a walking pace.

"Hey, what's up?" I panted.

"How's it going?"

"It's alright," I said, still trying to catch my breath. "Same ol' crap." I wondered if Javier was playing me—much like Tony had played me in the past.

I must have responded with too much sentiment, because his respond was, "You want to grab a cup of coffee and talk about it?"

"No, I'll be fine. It's nothing." I hardly knew Kenneth, so I certainly wasn't going to confide in him. Besides, I didn't know what was going on yet. "How's everything with you?" I tried to remove myself from the focus of the conversation.

"Lee, my partner, he started his tour duty last week. He's going to be gone for six months."

"That's the life of a Navy wife," I said, half joking.

"You ain't lying."

I gathered my towel and iPod off the treadmill after taking it to a complete stop. "I'll be here around 10:00 a.m. tomorrow if you want to workout. Maybe I'll take you up on that coffee then."

"Sounds good, playa."

"Tomorrow then," I said, and headed to the locker room.

I felt a little guilty. I knew making plans with Kenneth was—in a small part—my way to get back at Javier, and for what? I didn't know. I guess I figured if he could have secrets, then so could I. Kenneth was an attractive brotha, and I had the distinct feeling he felt the same towards me. I was playing with fire.

Once inside my car, I checked my voicemail. I had one new message from Javier. "Hey, Dee, it's me. Don't be upset, but I had to drive to L.A. to check something out. I will explain it all tonight."

I felt a little better hearing from him, but his voice didn't sound very reassuring. Something was wrong. What the hell was going on?

Later, I was going crazy at work thinking about what Javier was doing in L.A. or what had gone wrong. Every time my cellphone rang, I hoped it was him. I tried calling him a couple of times and got no answer. I never met Liz, and already I didn't like her. Did he really expect me to believe that crap about her getting beaten up by her boyfriend?

Ring!

It was Rafael.

"Hello," I answered, dryly.

"What's up?"

"Nothing."

"Devon … you're a horrible liar."

"Why are you so damned perceptive?"

"I'm not," Rafael said. "You just seem to always have drama. If I bait you, it's usually good for a juicy bit of gossip. So … what's wrong?"

"I don't know what's wrong yet, but Liz, Javier's ex-girlfriend, dropped something on him yesterday during a phone call, and he's been acting strange ever since. He says she got beat up by her boyfriend. I think that's bullshit. He skipped work today to go off to L.A., then he simply leaves me a voicemail saying, 'I'll explain it all tonight.'"

"I'm sure you're overreacting."

"Nice try, but I don't think so."

"Yeah, that *does* sound bad," Rafael concluded.

"Do you think he's bi?" I asked.

"How would I know? And even if he is, he's with you. He loves you; everyone can see that."

"I bet he likes those video ho types with the big asses. You know the type, all shakin' their shit in the club, gyrating like some hoochie."

"Is that what he likes?" Rafael asked, in a mocking tone. I was too caught up in my thinking to recognize the sarcasm.

"Yeah, that would be him all the way."

Rafael was now laughing. "Just get the story before you start jumping to conclusions."

I heard Rafael's service radio going off in the background. "Shit! I got to go," he said. "Let me know what happens."

"Bye."

This is the one time I wished I *was* overreacting. Something wasn't quite right, and I could feel it.

I made it a point not to get too involved with anything at work that might keep me late, so I left work in a timely manner. I drove into my parking space at 12:30 a.m. As I pulled in, I saw Javier's car out front, parked on the street. At least he was home. My heart began pounding as I climbed the stairs to the second floor. I was fearful of what he had to tell me.

I envisioned Javier waiting for me with his bags packed, ready to tell me he was leaving me for Liz. At least he would be man enough to tell me in person.

My hand shook as I attempted to insert the key in the lock. Finally, I inserted it and turned the tumbler. When I entered, Javier was on the sofa. He wasn't playing video games or watching television. He just sat there. He was wearing jogging pants and a tank top, so he didn't exactly look as if he was leaving. I scanned the room for a packed suitcase. When I found none, my heart rate slowed only a little.

"What the hell is going on?" I blurted out, slamming the door behind me.

"Why don't you get changed first?"

Now my heart rate was back up. In the past, when Javier had to tell me something that he thought might upset me or start an argument he made sure I was out of my uniform. We had never been physically violent towards one another, but I understood his point—I wouldn't want to say something to him that may piss him off if he was wearing pepper spray, and carrying a baton and a gun. I cooperated and went into the bedroom to change and locked away my gun belt.

A few minutes later, I emerged from the bedroom in only my undershirt and boxers. I sat on the love seat, not sure if I would want to be next to him after hearing what he had to say. I was slightly calmer now. I told myself that we had survived "take your uniform off" discussions before.

Javier moved to the edge of the couch cushion. He rubbed the back of his neck with his right hand. "I fucked up, Dee."

I was beginning to feel nauseated. I knew his next words were going to be: *I slept with Liz. I love her.* I tried to maintain my composure. "What did you do, Javier?"

His eyes welled deep with tears. He slept with someone else, and he had the nerve to cry about it? He wasn't going to get any sympathy from me. "It's her, isn't it? That girl, Liz?"

"It's not what you think." Tears began racing down his cheeks.

"Oh, it's not? I'm thinking you're fucking her. Am I right? Every time you go running to L.A.? You go fuck her?"

"Listen to me. It's not like that!"

I was on the verge of tears, but didn't want to give him the satisfaction. "Then explain it to me."

"Please, Papa, just don't let this come between us." Javier's cheeks were streaming with tears.

"Don't call me that now. You don't have the right to call me that."

"Please, just listen to me," he pleaded.

"What? ..."

"Yes, I slept with her, but not while we were together. You know Liz and I always stayed friends, and she knows about you and me, but when I went to L.A. to make arrangements for the funeral she was there every step of the way. I don't know what I would have done without her. At the time, I didn't know what was going to become of you and me. One night, after the funeral, we were reminiscing about the past ... we had a little alcohol and ... one thing led to another.... You know I don't even normally drink. I don't know what got into me. You and I weren't even talking then, Dee."

"As I recall, you weren't talking to me. I tried

everything in my power, short of coming to L.A., to contact you. Now, I know you were spending time with your girlfriend."

"I did walk in on you and your ex."

I ignored his statement. "Do you love her?"

"No, I love you." As upset with him as I was, I was relieved to hear that.

"Are you bi?"

"No, it was just a one-time thing that shouldn't have happened."

For a brief moment, I felt like maybe everything could be alright. We could get past this, provided he really wasn't bi or in love with her. But then it occurred to me— Javier had slept with her months ago; this didn't even have to come up if he didn't want me to know about it.

I chuckled, mainly out of desperation. "She's pregnant, isn't she?"

"Yes," he admitted, without hesitation. "I swear, Dee, yesterday was the first I heard of it. I hadn't seen her since the funeral. That's why I drove to L.A. I had to see it for myself."

"Why did she wait so long?"

"She said, I was in such bad shape after the funeral, she didn't think it was the right time. She wasn't sure what she was going to do either. And when you and I got back together, she didn't want to complicate things between us. She said, she wasn't going to tell me at first, but she knew that would be wrong."

I didn't believe that for a minute. Liz and I never met. She wasn't trying to spare my feelings. I got up and went towards the bedroom. Javier followed behind me.

"Where you going? Talk to me, Dee!" He grabbed my arm. I pulled away and continued into the bedroom. I grabbed a pair of track pants from the dresser drawer.

"Where are you going?" he repeated.

"I need you to leave me alone right now." My words were terse. Anger and resentment had supplanted any urge I'd had to cry.

I quickly put on the pants and a pair of running shoes, grabbed my wallet and keys, and headed for the door.

"Dee … I'm just as shocked about this as you are." He looked at me, his hazel eyes pleading, a new torrent of tears wetting his cheeks.

I stopped at the door. "For some reason I think you knew she was pregnant. All that talk about getting a bigger place and wanting kids. You had it all figured out."

"That's not true, Dee."

"Yeah, just a coincidence," I said as I walked out the door.

23

I got in my truck and just sat there. I couldn't tell Javier where I was going because I didn't know. I tried to take a minute to process the information I had just received. As much as I hated to admit it at that exact moment, I had never known Javier to lie to me or ever suspected him of it, but I didn't know what to believe now. Was it just a foolish one-night stand? Did I have one of those down low brothas sneaking around fucking women? I was confused.

After a few moments and a few tears, I phoned Rafael.

"Hello," he answered.

"Hey, it's Devon. You home from work yet?"

"Yeah."

"Do you think I could crash on your couch tonight?"

"Yeah, what's wrong?"

"I'll explain when I get there. I'm on my way."

Twenty minutes later I was knocking on Rafael's door. He pulled it open almost instantly.

"Come in," he said. Rafael was still in his uniform pants and an undershirt. He must have barely been home when I called. "What's going on?"

I walked into the living room and planted myself on the couch where he already had laid out a pillow and blanket. "Do you have any vodka?"

"No," Rafael said, still standing in anticipation. "I have soda or juice."

"What kind of homosexual are you anyway? No liquor in the house."

"You can take away my membership card. What happened Devon?"

"Oh, nothing much. My boyfriend is expecting a baby."

Rafael stood there with his mouth open. He plopped down in the cushioned leather chair. "Get out of here."

"Oh, yes. Remember the chick I was telling you about earlier?"

"Yeah, the video ho."

"Javier got her pregnant."

Rafael got up and headed for the kitchen. "I gotta have some alcohol."

Over minibar Jack and Cokes, I explained to Rafael what I knew. A lot was still somewhat unclear to me.

"So, he decided to fuck some girl after his mother's funeral?"

"Must you use the words 'fuck' and 'mothers's funeral' in the same sentence?" I asked.

"Sorry, but technically you just did it too … but I digress. So is he bi?"

I finished off my Jack and Coke longing for another, but he only found two mini Jacks. I was sure he was holding out on me. "He says no."

"So, why did he …" Rafael searched for the right word. "Why did he fornicate with her?"

"Rafael, you can say fuck, just not in the same sentence with 'mother's funeral.'"

"Okay, why did he fuck her then, if he's not bi?"

"Good question. I didn't stay around long enough to find out. As much as I hate the idea of him fucking a female, they do have a history together. I guess he loved her at some point. Maybe that made it easier. He was probably vulnerable also. I bet that bitch took advantage of him."

"So what are you going to do?"

"I don't know."

Rafael perked up in his chair. "Can I ask you something?"

"What?"

"When Javier came over and found you with Tony … were you going to sleep with him?"

"No, Rafael. Why would you think that?"

"Well, you were all about Tony around that time."

I rested my head on the back of the couch staring at the hideous popcorn ceiling. "I don't know what to do."

"You know, I have no business giving relationship advice."

"And yet," I said before focusing back at Rafael.

"I still don't, but do one thing before you make any rash decisions."

"What's that?" I asked.

"Put yourself in his shoes, and I mean from the time he asked you to meet his mom, to finding you with Tony, to her passing, and everything up until now."

"And?"

"And ask yourself: through all that, maybe you didn't make the best decisions, but were you really out to hurt Devon?"

To be so young, Rafael had a mature outlook on the situation. I could see Rafael's point, but I wasn't ready to be that understanding. "I just need some time to think."

"I have another question."

"What?"

"Why in the hell didn't you tell me he was illegal?"

"As usual, Michael can't hold water," I said. "I don't know. It's not something we want everybody to know. We have to be careful."

"Well, I'm not just anybody. I'm your friend. You see how well Michael keeps secrets."

"I know."

"I couldn't imagine dating an illegal. I mean, how does he feel about your job?"

I never really thought about it. Javier just always listened to what I had to say about work, without judgment. "I don't know."

Rafael placed his half-finished drink on a coaster on the table. "Anyway, I'm exhausted. We were busy as hell," Rafael said. "I'm going to turn in."

"Thanks, Rafael," I said staring up again at the ceiling.

"That's what friends are for. Besides, sometimes your life is better than my Telenovas."

"Good night."

Rafael headed off to his bedroom. I was tempted to ransack the kitchen for more alcohol; instead, I unfolded the comforter and laid it out on the couch, turned out the light, and took refuge on the sofa without even undressing. It was a few minutes later when my cellphone rang. I didn't have to look to see who it was. I wasn't ready to talk to him, so I killed the ringer and attempted to sleep. I suspected it was going to be a restless night.

Several times throughout the night I just wanted to go home, but I felt like if I stayed away, I made a point—much like him driving to L.A. on a whim when he was upset. Sometime after 7:00 a.m. I folded the comforter neatly on the sofa and wrote Rafael a thank-you note on his dry-erase board on the fridge. I knew Javier should have already left for work by the time I arrived home.

When I pulled into the parking lot I didn't see his car anywhere on the street. I entered the apartment and found a note on the dinette table.

Dear Dee,

I was worried when you didn't come home last night. I wish I could take this back. The last thing I ever wanted to do was hurt you. It is killing me to think I may have done something to drive us apart. I won't offer excuses. All I can say is that it was a difficult time for me.

Please believe me when I tell you, you are the one I love and no one else. I am not confused about my sexuality. I just did something stupid. During that time, I just felt so alone. I hope you understand. I can't imagine not having you in my life.

Love Javier.

I didn't want to know that feeling either. I folded the

note and placed it in my wallet. I went into the bedroom and began to undress. The faint smell of his cologne still lingered in the air. After I stripped down to nothing, I crawled into bed. It was still slightly warm from his body. I took a deep breath and took it all in. All of him. Within minutes, I was sound asleep.

Every time Javier phoned during my shift, I pretended to be busy and said I would call him later. I was sure he knew I was lying, but I wasn't quite ready to deal with him. I left work late in hopes he would be asleep when I arrived home.

I undressed, showered, entered the dark bedroom, and skillfully crawled into bed. In the darkness, he asked, "So, how long are you going to avoid me?"

I should have known he wasn't asleep. "I don't know."

"Is this going to come between us?"

"I don't want it to, but I have to get used to the fact that you're having a child with someone else. You're bonded with this woman now. She's giving you something I could never give you."

We were lying back-to-back. I felt Javier roll over in my direction. "It's not a competition, but if it were, you give me things she can't. It was your love that pulled me back from that rough spot when my mom passed. Please, don't take that from me. You promised me you wouldn't leave me."

"Javier."

"Yes."

"I don't want to talk anymore right now. Just ... just hold me."

"Okay, Papa."

I slept soundly, but not before crying myself to sleep.

24

I was in the middle of my last set of curls when I saw Kenneth's reflection in the mirror approaching. His lips were moving, but I couldn't hear him since Mary J. Blige blasted through my earphones. He looked upset. I finished up my set, placed the weights on the rack, and paused Mary.

"What's up?" I asked.

"What the hell happened to you yesterday?"

I suddenly remembered that I was supposed to have met Kenneth yesterday to workout. "Oh, shit. I'm sorry man. I completely forgot. I had some stuff going on yesterday."

Kenneth let out a sigh. "No problem, I guess."

"Did you just get here?"

"Yeah. You?"

"I'm about done. Just have to do my cardio."

"What's going on?" he asked. "You kinda look like shit."

"I'm okay."

"Boyfriend problems, huh?"

"Something like that."

"You want to grab some coffee and talk about it?"

What was it with this man's obsession with coffee? I didn't know him well enough to vent, let alone vent about Javier's baby situation. "Thanks for the offer, but I'll be fine."

Kenneth's eyes began to penetrate mine in such a way that I started to grow uncomfortable. I looked away.

"I just hope he appreciates you," he said.

"Maybe it's me that doesn't appreciate him."

"I don't think that's the case. He better handle his business befo somebody snatches you up."

"How's Lee?" I asked. It was my less then subtle way to remind him that he was spoken for.

His gaze was no longer on my eyes. He was looking me up and down in a predatory like fashion. "He's alright; won't be back for six months. A lot can happen in six months."

I was afraid he was going to pounce at any moment, so I said, "I better go do my cardio."

"Call me if you want to talk or something."

"I'll remember that," I said as I walked away.

No sooner did I get in my truck and turn the key in the ignition after leaving the gym that my cellphone chimed.

Mom.

After everything Javier had been through, I told myself to appreciate these phone calls—no matter how annoying.

"Hello, Mother."

"What's this I hear 'bout you living with this Javier fella?"

Now considering my parents hadn't spoken in years, I found it quite amazing that she had acquired that information. "Where did you hear that?"

"Never mind that. Is it true?"

"Yes."

She repeated the question, because I guess she didn't get the answer she was looking for the first time. "You living wit' that boy?"

I was now annoyed. "Yes, mother!"

"Are you two roommates or something more?" she pried, while putting much inflection on the "something more."

"Yes, he's my boyfriend ... partner ... significant other."

"You know how I feel. I think its wrong, and I'm praying for you."

"Yes, you've told me on *many* occasions," I scoffed.

"Why can't you find a nice young lady, settle down, and have some kids?"

"It's not that simple!" My hands started shaking. I maneuvered my truck to the side of the street and found a parking spot. I didn't want to risk an accident by letting my emotions drive.

"Why isn't it?"

"Because I can't!" I shouted. "For the record, marrying and having kids is not the cure all for homosexuality. It's a wonderful start for a broken home though."

"I see. Now this is about me divorcing your father."

"I'm sorry, Mom. I didn't mean to snap, and no, it wasn't an attack on you. I'm tired of this. I thought we had an unspoken agreement. I wouldn't talk about it, and you'd stop condemning me."

I could hear crying through the phone. "It's just that I worry about you. I don't want to see you ... I don't want to see you get sick. I'm a Christian. I worry about my kid's spiritual well being too."

"It's just who I am Mom. I don't believe it's something I'm going pay for in the afterlife. I want to stop letting this be a barrier between us. There's so much you miss out on because we don't talk about what's really going on in my life."

"Like what?"

"Well, like Javier and me. We've been living together for months now. He's means the world to me. Like most couples, we have our ups and downs, but I love him." I shuddered. I went from not discussing my sexuality with my parents to telling my mother I'm in love. I was afraid because I had decided to reveal my relationship to my parents when it is at its most vulnerable. This wasn't exactly how I'd planned it.

"I'm not ready for this," she protested.

"You don't have to be, but get used to it."

"I'm going to hang up now," she said. "Bye, Devon."

"I love you."

She hesitated, before saying, "I love you too."

I sat in my truck at an expired meter. A half an hour went by before I could drive myself home. My head was like a nonstop slide show: images of Javier caring for a newborn child, my mother on bended knee praying for my soul, a horrible weekend with my dad and step-mom, Javier and Liz basking in the happiness of parenthood, and me alone on the sofa. I wished I could hit the stop button.

Oprah was being played on TiVo when Javier arrived

home from work. As much as I now had mixed feelings about him, I couldn't deny him that he looked good. The five o'clock shadow was the same length as the hair on his closely-shaved head. The black slacks and the dark blue polo with the credit union's logo fit him nicely.

He placed his portfolio and the mail on the dinette table. "Hey, Papa."

"Hey," I said.

He walked over and gave me a kiss on the lips before sitting next to me. "How was your day?"

"I sat here all day eating bonbons and watching my stories," I said, spitefully. "How about yours?"

"It was alright," he said while removing his shoes.

"I talked to my mom today."

"Yeah, how did that go?"

All I could do was shake my head. "She heard through the grapevine that I'm living with a certain young man. She suggested I get married and have kids."

"I'm sorry, baby."

"I couldn't bring myself to tell her you're having one."

"It's going to be one of those nights, huh?. What do you want from me, Dee? I'm sorry."

"I want things like they were."

"I fucked up. Things will probably never be like they were, but it doesn't mean it's going to be bad."

Silence.

Oprah was about to announce her next book choice, when Javier had an announcement of his own. "It's a girl," he said softly.

"What?"

"It's going to be a girl, due mid-June. I found out today. I thought it was a good time to tell you since you were already in a shitty mood."

"I'm sorry, Javier. I'm trying. You only dropped this on me two days ago."

"I didn't want to bring this up now, but June is around the corner. I need some answers."

"What do you mean?"

"Well, for instance, I've talked to Liz, and we're talking about joint custody once the baby is older. She will spend part of the time here and—"

"I know what joint custody is."

"My point is that the baby will be a big part of your life as well as mine—since we live together. I need to know if you're on board for all this."

I hadn't put that much thought into it. The baby wasn't born yet and it had already changed our lives. It had gone from an "it" to a "girl." A girl arriving in less than two months. She was taking center stage and I was dropping in standing. I was sure the baby girl was going to be number one in Javier's life.

How much involvement would I have in this child's life? I would have no biological or legal bond with the child. God forbid if Javier and I didn't make it, I would have to deal with losing both him and her. It's not likely I would get visitation rights. Would I want to see the brat anyway? I mean it would probably be her that would drive us apart. Clearly, my feelings were in turmoil.

I said what I thought he wanted to hear: "I'm on board."

Javier just looked at me. "Doesn't sound like you mean it."

"Remember, I didn't ask for this, Javier."

"Neither did I. Shit happens. I always thought that through thick or thin we would be there for each other."

His statement echoed in my head.

25

The following day was Friday, and if I've ever needed a night out, it was then. I arranged to hang out with Michael and Rafael after work. I had just finished showering and was throwing on clothes when Javier came into the bedroom.

"You going out?" he asked.

"Yeah. I'm going to meet Michael and Rafael."

Javier leaned in the doorway of the bedroom. "You want me to come?"

"No, I won't be long," I said, pulling on a T-shirt.

"I kinda thought we would hang out."

"Sorry, you should have said something."

"Yeah, have fun," he said, tersely, as he left the room.

Neither of us said a word as I left the apartment. The truth was, Rafael, Michael, and I were just going to hang out at Rafael's apartment. I don't know why, but I wanted Javier to think I was going out and having a great time. I guess I needed him to think that, since I was a mess on the inside.

Michael answered the door when I arrived at Rafael's.

"Come on in and give mama a hug."

"I need a drink," I said as I walked in.

"Rafael said you were a wreck. You sound pretty normal to me."

"Please tell me he has alcohol now. That minibar crap didn't cut it the last time I was here."

"We did a liquor run."

"Thank you."

I sat on the couch while Michael went into the kitchen to make me a vodka cranberry.

"Hey, you, how's it going?" Rafael asked, coming out of his bedroom.

"I've been better."

"It'll be okay."

"I hope so."

Michael came out of the kitchen with my cocktail and handed it to me.

"Ok, everyone grab your drink," Michael ordered. He

raised his glass and we followed his lead. "The quarterly meeting of the San Diego Chapter of the Charlie's Angels may now begin." And yes, he was referring to the 70's TV show *Charlie's Angels*. We toasted and took our seats. "The first order of business—I motion Sista Rafael be fined for not having alcohol on the premises."

I again raised my glass. "I second that motion."

"Then it's settled. Sista Rafael will buy two rounds of drinks at our next outing,"

"Why, because I'm not a lush like you two?" Rafael quipped.

Michael said, "Hold your tongue, or you could be looking at another fine. Respect your older, wiser sistas."

"I hate you two," Rafael responded.

"Back to business," Michael continued. "What are we going to do with this pitiful one here?" he asked, pointing at me with the drink in his hand.

"I'm fine. Really!"

"Cut the crap. You're the reason we're here and not out somewhere," Rafael interjected.

I placed my drink on a coaster on the coffee table and leaned back into the sofa. "I love that man, but I'm so upset with him now. I've been such a bitch to him the last few days."

"How's that any different than normal?" asked Michael.

"It's okay to be upset. I think you earned that," Rafael chimed in.

"We haven't had sex in a week. We are barely speaking. No, actually, I'm barely speaking. I feel so disconnected from him right now."

"Oh, God. She's starting with the Oprah vocabulary," Michael said. "You're trying to punish him."

"Well, yeah!"

"Honey, you're just punishing yourself in the process."

"Hit me with more of your wisdom, Dali Mama."

Michael took a dramatic sip from his cocktail with his pinky in the air and sat down. "You want him to feel what you're going through, so you treat him like shit. The only problem is, you're too dick whipped."

Rafael laughed. "True."

"I can't believe you, of all people, are laughing," I said, looking at Rafael. "You were so dick whipped you got your wallet stolen and didn't actually get the dick."

"No, she didn't," said Michael. "She went there on you."

"You know that is a sensitive subject, and I would appreciate it if you didn't bring it up again," Rafael said. "Anyway, I'm not the one who used the data base at work to get the address of a wannabe trick," Rafael said.

"You didn't?" I looked at Michael. "Sounds a little

stalkerish."

"I think we're getting off the subject," Michael said.

"Okay. I guess we've all done some crazy things in the name of love," I said.

"I just want to say that I was robbed," Rafael interjected, "I wasn't dick whipped."

"No, you were just too *dick*stracted to know your wallet was gone," Michael said.

We all laughed, and Rafael joined in reluctantly.

Michael started in on me again. "Back to you. I say, make peace with Javier. He made a mistake he is going to have to live with for at least the next eighteen years. You two made it this far; see how it plays out."

"Maybe you're right."

"I'm sure that before you know it, you'll be back to Will and Jada status," Michael joked.

"Will *does* have a child from a previous marriage, and they make it work," Rafael added.

"Not quite sure it's the same thing, but thank you."

Out of nowhere, Michael jumped up from the chair he was sitting in. "We should watch *Waiting to Exhale*."

In unison, Rafael and I shouted, "No!"

According to Michael, *Waiting to Exhale* was a classic. It was his answer to everything. Whenever one of us was having some type of boyfriend problem and we got together for support, we somehow ended up watching the movie. Of course, it was always suggested by Michael. Michael had just about every line memorized. I was even beginning to memorize them myself.

"You know, technically, the movie doesn't apply here. None of us are going through a breakup," I pointed out.

"Close enough," Michael argued. "Besides, if nothing else, you are about to add 'baby momma' to your vocabulary. Something in the movie applies."

"You know, I like how he jumps up like he just suddenly just now thought of this, like it wasn't premeditated," Rafael added. "I mean, you know he brought the movie with him."

"Of course," I said.

"You know what?... Fuck you two bitches," Michael said, half smirking. "If you don't like it ..." He stood as he prepared himself for his Angela Bassett impersonation. "You can get yo shit ... get yo shit, and get out!"

"I also like how he just attempted to throw us out of my apartment," Rafael said, wryly.

Four drinks later, I was barely awake and watching the closing credits to *Waiting to Exhale*. Luckily, Michael must have been tired also because he didn't make us reenact the last scene around the campfire.

I excused myself and went into the bathroom to call Javier. It was almost four in the morning. I dialed his cell and got the voicemail.

"Hey, it's me. I'm over at Rafael's. I'm going to crash here tonight. I had too much to drink.... Hey, I'm sorry about tonight baby. I'll see you in the morning. I love you."

It was a little after 9:00 a.m. when I got home. Javier was sitting at the dinette spooning down a bowl of cereal and looking over some work manuals.

Without looking up from his reading, he said, "How does 'I'll be back shortly' turn into all night?"

"I left you a message," I said. "Didn't you get it?"

"That's not the point. You said you were going to 'be back shortly.'"

"Look, I'm not in the mood for a fight," I said, collapsing onto the sofa.

"I'm not either, but the bitchy attitude is getting a little old."

I laughed out of frustration. "Can you blame me?"

Javier's attention left the manual and cereal bowl. "No, I guess not."

I held out my hand and motioned for Javier to come over and join me. Reluctantly, he came over and took my hand in his. I pulled him into me so that he fell onto my lap.

"I have been a bitch the last few days, but this is a

lot to get used to," I said. "I'm sorry. I'll try and deal." I leaned in and kissed him.

"I miss that," he said.

"Me too."

"Papa?"

"Yes?"

"You got to brush your teeth. I got a buzz from kissing you."

26

By Sunday, things seemed to be getting back to normal. By no means was all forgotten; surely a bouncing baby would soon be here to start wreaking havoc in my life. But for now, we were finding our rhythm again.

A breeze carrying the waft of spring blossoms blew in from the open window above the headboard. We lay intertwined beneath the sheets naked. We skipped our run; we had lovemaking to catch up on.

I gazed into Javier's hazel eyes. "I could do this all day."

"Are we going to get out of bed *sometime* today?" Javier teased.

"I'm living in the 'now.' And *right* now, this is where I want to be."

"Alright, I'll let you have this one lazy day."

"Oh, that's so nice of you to let me have this day," I laughed.

Leave it to a cellphone to interrupt such a blissful moment.

"Is that mine or yours?" I asked.

"Yours, of course."

I grabbed the phone off the nightstand.

"I thought it was going to be a lazy day. Let it ring."

"I just want to see who's calling." I said, glancing at the phone's display. "It's my dad. It won't take more than five minutes."

"Fine. I'm going to the kitchen. You want anything?"

"Some juice," I said, before answering the phone. "Hello." I watched Javier's golden buttocks leave the bedroom.

"Devon, how's it going?" he asked.

"Good, and you?"

"I'm good."

I sat up in bed. I knew the call had to do with his visit since it was coming up in a couple weeks.

"I just wanted to remind you that Priscilla and I will be in Vegas next week, and we will be coming to San Diego the following week."

"Have any idea of where you're going to stay?" I

probed.

"We're going to stay with you at your apartment."

"Oh ... okay." I was shocked.

"That's all I wanted."

"Alright."

"I'll give you a call next week," he said.

"Bye."

I had just ended the call, when Javier entered the bedroom with a glass of orange juice.

I must have looked dumbfounded, because he asked, "What's wrong with you?" as he got back underneath the sheets.

"My dad is going to stay with us."

"What's the big deal?"

I took a sip of the orange juice he handed me and placed it on the night stand. I burrowed myself into Javier's side. "I'm kinda tripping out. I never thought that my dad would be visiting me and my partner. You're going to be the first guy they meet."

"I better be the last too," Javier said while rubbing my head. "I'm guessing they never thought they would be visiting you and your partner either. Just be happy about it. Your dad is trying."

"If nothing else, this ought to be interesting." I said.

I thought about Javier's previous comment. "Hey, so you mean to say if you passed away in some horrific accident—God forbid—you wouldn't want me to find someone new?"

"Hell, no! I'm your one and only. I'll come and haunt you."

"Well, *that's* selfish."

"You better believe it. I can't have you bringing somebody up into our bed while I'm six feet under."

I laughed. "You're crazy."

27

I was beyond nervous, while Javier seemed way too excited to be meeting my dad and stepmom. I knew the thought of meeting my parents validated the importance of our relationship in his eyes. He felt robbed by the fact that I never had the chance to meet his mother.

My dad and stepmom were arriving in a few hours, and I was beginning to imagine everything that could go wrong during my parents' visit: Javier being too affectionate in front of them, my dad having a flashback and throwing me into a bookcase, or the baby drama coming up. I didn't want them to overdose on gay culture either. I had already put away all the *OUT* magazines, my *Latin Men* calendar, and all the gay literature. It bugged Javier that I went through all the trouble, but he was patient with me. I simply told him, "Baby steps ... I'm taking baby steps." I probably should have been ashamed of myself for already walking on egg shells when they hadn't even arrived yet.

I was debating on removing a picture of the two of us from the end table. We were in an embrace on the beach. Javier put his foot down at the mere thought of its removal.

"Dee, they know we're a couple. You putting that picture away is not going to make it any more comfortable for them. Now sit down and relax."

I relented and joined him on the sofa. "You're right. I'm just a little nervous. It's my first partnered visit. I don't want to overwhelm them with our lifestyle."

"Don't say that. I hate dat. This *is* our life. Styles come and go, we are who we are, and that's all," Javier said.

"Ok, don't get all 'gay activist' on me."

"Well, you know how I feel."

"I know ... I know," I said. I feared how he would react by what was going to come out of my mouth next. "Javier, I know I've been crazy about wanting to make a good impression with my family, but I need a favor."

"What, Papa? You want to get single beds while they're here?"

"No ... I think right now we should keep the baby thing between us."

Javier looked confused. "Why?"

"Well, you're meeting my parents for the first time. We've been living together several months now. I don't really want to explain why you're expecting a child. In perspective, it doesn't really look that good."

"Good point. I can live with that for now, but they are going to find out sometime. I mean I made a mistake."

"I know," I agreed. "Just not now. I want them to know you first, before they come up with any judgment on the whole baby thing."

"You got it."

Later that evening, we were in an intense game of John Madden football to pass the time. I was only losing by a mere touchdown in the third quarter. I suggested loser bottoms, but Javier declined. He said, "Your parents are going to show up any minute." *Who was nervous now?*

The house phone rang.

"Pause the game," I said as I got up to answer it.

"Hello," I answered.

"Hey, Devon. We're downstairs."

My stomach dropped like I was on an amusement park ride that tortures your insides. "Okay, I'll be right down."

I slowly placed the phone back on the cradle. "They're here."

"Well, get moving," he said, turning off the game.

"Wait!" I shouted.

"What's the problem?"

"I was losing by my lowest point margin ever, and you didn't save the game."

Javier smirked at me while he continued to put the game system away into the hideaway entertainment center. "Oh, you wanted to finish the game later?" he asked, with mock innocence.

"You didn't like the fact that I was almost winning, did you? You're a poor sport."

"What is 'almost winning'? You weren't winning."

"I wasn't badly losing, and it scared you."

"Whatever."

I kissed him on my way out the door. "We'll continue this discussion later."

"Yeah, maybe you can almost beat me later."

"You're threatened."

I collected myself and went downstairs to greet my dad and stepmom. I could already see them outside the door, under the security light as I approached. Priscilla, my stepmom, was already smiling. My dad stood at her side, expressionless. Both were in their late fifties but could easily pass for being in their mid-forties.

I would be happy to look as good as my dad when I'm his age. I wondered how Javier and I would look in twenty years or so. Who would look younger? Latin genes versus black genes; it would be one hell of a race.

I opened the security door.

John, my dad, was getting more salt than pepper creeping up his sideburns. He had a few stress lines stretched across his forehead. His face was slightly rounder than I had remembered, and I notice the beginnings of a middle-aged gut underneath his Las Vegas T-shirt. Still, his muscular frame could distract someone from his minor signs of aging.

Priscilla had no visible gray in her black shoulder-length hair. I wondered if she had dyed it. She appeared shapely in fitted workout pants and an identical Las Vegas T-shirt. She had a shape most women would be happy with but insisted she was a bit overweight. Her fair skin was splashed with a few freckles on her cheeks.

"What's going on?" John said. He gave me one of those half-handshake, half-hug greetings.

"Nothing much, Dad," I replied. "Hey, Priscilla." I received a regular hug from her.

"Hey, Devon! It's so good to see you," she beamed. "I see you lost a few pounds."

"You know how we Californians like to stay in shape," I said. "Well, where are your bags?"

"They're in the car," John replied.

"I'll let you boys get that. I have to use the bathroom," Priscilla said as she started walking into the courtyard.

"What's your apartment number?"

"Sixteen. On the second floor," I said, a little reluctantly. I felt I should be there when she met Javier. "You want me to take you up?"

"I'll be fine. You go ahead."

I followed my dad toward the street. "How was the drive?" I sounded like him with the trivial conversation.

"It wasn't bad. Should have been here sooner, but Priscilla had to stop at every outlet store between here and Vegas."

I envisioned Javier and me on a road trip. It would probably be Javier who would want to stop at every point of interest and me who would want to stick to a timetable and get there. He would cuss me out in Spanish when I would say, "I'm not stopping." Of course, by then, I would be fluent in Spanish, know what he is saying, and curse right back at him—in Spanish. He would make it a point to drive us home, just so he could stop at every place that I wouldn't.

I love him.

We hadn't gone anywhere other than L.A. since we met. That mainly had to do with his illegal status. With all the talk of immigration reform in the upcoming election, I prayed that Javier's status would change, that he would be officially forgiven and pronounced legal. Of course, that would be contingent upon the government coming up with a sensible plan for identifying, screening, and legalizing the millions of illegals here, as opposed to sending everyone back (as if deporting them would even be possible or in the best interest of the economy). Javier forced me to watch *A Day Without a Mexican* on one of our DVD nights, and it really did make me wonder what would happen if the entire illegal population suddenly vanished. So many organizations and companies would be scrambling for low-wage, part-time, and graveyard-shift help, as well as those willing to carry out backbreaking physical labor in construction and landscaping. That's not to mention the void that would be left from a cultural experience so many of us have become dependent on.

"We're right here," John said, breaking me from my thoughts.

We were in front of a newer model Ford Explorer. "You rented an SUV, huh?"

He hit the keyless entry and opened the back hatch. "No, Priscilla rented the SUV. I don't know why she didn't get something more practical. A mid-sized sedan would have been fine."

That was my dad, always trying to save a penny. We each grabbed a suitcase and headed up the apartment stairs. I hoped Javier was doing alright alone with my stepmom. Upon second thought, I knew he was alright—he could be quite charming. As we got closer to the door, I could hear Javier and Priscilla laughing. When we entered, both were standing in the kitchen, Priscilla holding a glass of water.

"What's so funny?" I asked, passing through the doorway.

They both replied, "Nothing."

Javier walked up to my father with a welcoming smile. "Hello, Mr. Wallace. I'm Javier." He shook my father's hand then reached for the suitcase. "Here, let me that that."

"Nice to meet you, Javier. Call me John."

"Can I get you anything? Something to drink?" Javier asked.

"No, I'll just have some of Priscilla's water."

"You better get your own," Priscilla protested.

"I guess I'll have some of my own water," John said.

Javier took the suitcase I was carrying as well. "I'll put these in the bedroom. Well don't just stand there, get your dad some water," he grinned.

Javier and I figured they would be more comfortable in our room, so we were going to sleep in the guestroom on the futon.

I had just handed my dad his glass of water, when Javier reemerged from the bedroom.

"Well, have a seat, take a load off," I suggested. We all shuffled into the living-room. Javier and I sat on the sofa while John and Pricilla occupied the loveseat. I'm not sure if I did it intentionally, but there was plenty of space between Javier and me on the sofa.

"How was the drive?" asked Javier.

"I love road trips," Priscilla said. "But somebody gets cranky after a while."

"So, you guys hungry?" I asked.

I noticed dad was staring at the photo of Javier and me on the end table that I had wanted to remove only hours ago. I couldn't gauge his thoughts over the photo, but I was sure he was thrown by it. "Yeah, I'm starving," he said, finally removing his gaze from the photo.

"Do you like Mexican food?" Javier inquired.

Priscilla said, "Does *Baja Fresh* count?"

Javier laughed. "It's a start. There's a restaurant, not far from here, called *Ortega's.* Devon and I go sometimes. He loves it. They prepare authentic Mexican cuisine from recipes created by the Ortega family of Puerto Nuevo, Mexico. The recipes date back to the 1950's when Puerto Nuevo started booming as a fishing town.

Javier only called me "Devon" when he was upset. Usually it was "Dee" or "Papa." Now, he was the one putting on a show. Yes, I liked Ortega's and yes, we had gone a few times, but when did he become such an historian on the restaurant?

Ortega's was also in Hillcrest, the gay mecca. I wasn't

sure I was ready to take my parents there.

"Or we could go to *Chili's*. It's fairly close too," I interjected.

"*Chili's*? They can go to *Chili's* anywhere. Let them try something new. Something they may not get back home," Javier suggested. "That is, if it's alright with you," Javier said, looking towards John and Pricilla.

"You all decide; I need to wash up," John said. "Where's the bathroom?"

"Well, that *Ortega's* sounds fine with me," Priscilla concluded. "I'm down for something new."

"*Ortega's,* then," Javier said.

John and Priscilla went into the bedroom to freshen up. I joined Javier back in the kitchen where he was putting their glasses in the dishwasher.

In a mocking tone, I said, "Let's go to *Ortega's*."

"What's wrong with *Ortega's*? You love that place."

"It's in Hillcrest."

Javier closed the door to the dishwasher. "So?"

I took a seat at the dinette. "I don't want to take them to Hillcrest!"

Javier sat across from me and took my hand. "We've talked about this already. You can't continue to shelter them. If they didn't think they could handle it, they wouldn't be here."

"I hope you're right."

28

We all piled into the Ford Explorer and made our way to *Ortega's*. My stomach began to feel like it was on that amusement park ride again. It was a Friday night, so I knew the kids would be out in full force. Luckily, we made it to the restaurant without passing any gay parades on the way.

Ortega's had been a cozy little restaurant up until its recent expansion into the empty lot next door. The new and improved *Ortega's* boasted an upstairs dining area, a larger full-service bar, and a crackling fireplace. The restaurant was finished with a contemporary décor that included splashes of Mexican accents here and there. The restaurant bordered on casual and classy.

Like most nights, *Ortega's* was busy. Dad and Priscilla

were seated in the waiting area, while Javier and I stood. We were told it would be a thirty-minute wait for a table.

Everyone in the waiting area couldn't help but notice the two attractive men that strolled in the door. Both were runway-model height with the clothes to match. One had dark hair; the other was blonde. They both appeared to have spent incredible amounts of time at the gym. They easily could be fitness models for Men's Health magazine. You didn't need gaydar to know they were a couple, especially since they walked in holding hands.

I looked on, along with everyone in the waiting area, as the dark-haired one exchanged words with the hostess. The blonde seemed annoyed that they would have to wait for a table. My eyes shifted back and forth between their exchange and my dad. The couple must have decided not to wait; they turned and walked out, still hand in hand. To my surprise, not a grimace from dad or Priscilla.

Soon, we were seated by a table near the patio, so we could look out onto the street. We were looking over our menus when a tall, lanky blonde guy approached. He was wearing the restaurant's uniform: black slacks, an apron, and a teal polo.

"Good evening. I'm Mark, and I'll be your server," he stated.

My gaze bolted to Pricilla—*please, don't say it!*

"Hi, Mark. I'm Priscilla, and this is John, Javier, and Devon. We'll be your customers."

She said it. It was sort of a ritual with her.

"Well, good to meet you all," Mark said. "Can I start you off with some drinks?"

We all looked at Priscilla.

"Such gentlemen they are, Mark. I'll have a glass of your house wine. White, please."

"Get me a Bud Light," John said.

"Me too." I really wanted a pomegranate martini, but I was worried the glass it would be served in wasn't butch enough.

Javier looked bewildered. "You're getting a beer?"

"I drink beer … occasionally."

"I'll just have water," Javier said.

"Great. I'll get those drinks for you," Mark said, before dashing off to another table.

"So, what's good here?" John inquired.

"Why are you asking them?" Priscilla asked. "The waiter was just here."

"Well, they eat here all the time, so I'm asking them."

Javier smiled at their banter. "Actually my favorite is the Kobe Beef Bistek."

Priscilla noted Javier's choice. "That does sound

good."

"Devon likes the Chicken Mole Enchiladas. Every restaurant we go to, he finds a favorite and sticks with it."

"I do, huh? Well, I know what I'm having then."

Dad closed his menu. "So what do you do for a living, Javier?"

"I work for Southern California Credit Union. I'm in their management training program."

"How do you like it?" Dad continued.

"It's alright for now, but someday I think I want to own my own business."

I was caught by surprise by his answer. "Since when? And what type of business?" I asked.

"I've just been tossing the idea around," Javier said. He diverted his attention back to John. "I used to manage a bar when I was back in college. I liked the people and the atmosphere. It was a lot less stress. I would love to go into business for myself."

I was a little bothered that Javier had never shared that with me, but this wasn't the time to bring it up.

Priscilla smiled. "Bars and restaurants are so hard to get off the ground."

"It's like I tell Devon: put your twenty years or so in with the Federal government, then go do what you want to do," John said.

I sighed noticeable. "Don't you think someone should have some job satisfaction? I mean, I sit most of the day wasting away in a Jeep."

"Yeah, but they pay you good."

"I guess that's what's most important," I said. I began searching the restaurant for Mark in serious need of that beer … but longing for a pomegranate martini.

Underneath the table, Javier took his hand and placed it on my knee. Any stress I was feeling dissipated.

After Mark returned with our beverages, we ordered. Javier and I both went with our usual. Priscilla ordered the Mixed Green Salad with Mahi Mahi, and John chose the lobster.

Over salad, Priscilla asked, "How did you two meet?"

It wasn't a question I would have expected from my stepmom; nonetheless, Javier and I both grinned at the memory of our chance meeting.

Javier began to tell the story, while my dad focused his attention out the window. It was a story I loved telling, but to hear it told in front of my father, who I knew didn't care to hear it, tied my stomach in knots.

"It's a park not far from here that we both run in. One day, I was doing my run and I see Dee in front of me, so I started pacing myself after him. We're running along for a while, then all of sudden he just takes off."

Smiling, I said, "I didn't know him. I was trying to lose him. I thought he was following me."

"But I kept up," Javier added.

"Excuse me. I have to use the bathroom," John said, abruptly … before leaving the table.

"Don't pay him no mind," Priscilla said.

"Yeah," I said, sadly.

The rest of dinner, we kept the conversation light in order to appease John. We danced around topics of the weather, sports, and current events.

29

I was already lying down, when Javier entered the guestroom. He took off his sweatpants and climbed onto the futon.

"I like your folks," he announced.

I put down the magazine I was reading. "Just remember there is still one more to meet, not to mention the siblings."

Sentiment washed over his face. "I miss her."

I kissed Javier on his forehead. "I know, baby." I pulled him close.

"You know a little sex right now would make me feel a whole lot better."

I playfully pushed him away. "You're such a freak. My dad and stepmom are in the next room, and you want to have sex. That's just gross," I said. "Anyway, the condoms are ... Oh, shit!"

"What?"

"The lube and condoms are in the nightstand in our room," I gasped.

"So? I'm sure they would be happy to know we use them."

"Yeah, but also in that drawer are handcuffs, porn, and a host of other things I don't care to mention."

Javier laughed. "Let me get this straight. You de-gay the entire apartment, but you forgot to take your bag of tricks out of the bedroom you put your parents in?"

"Well, I forgot," I said. "You think they will look?"

"Hell yeah! They are going to find out their baby is a freak."

"Thanks. You're a big help."

"There's nothing you can do about it now, unless you want to go in and grab all your toys."

"Oh, so they're *my* toys now. I use them all by myself."

"Well, it takes a lot of creativity to keep a freak like you happy."

I could only grin. "Shut up, Javier."

"Dee," Javier said, suddenly, with some urgency in his voice.

"Yeah?"

"What do you think if one day we go get tested? A complete checkup and be done with the condoms."

"What?"

"We're a monogamous couple. I trust you; you trust me. Why not?"

I had heard of couples doing that, but I'd never given it much thought. I mean, giving up condoms is the ultimate act of trust. "I don't know Javier; I would have to think about that."

Javier rolled his eyes. "That's always your answer. You say that—that you'll have to think about something—and hope that whatever it is will go away. At least have the balls to say no."

"That's not fair, Javier. This is big."

"And that's why we would take the necessary precautions. We get tested now and again in six months."

I played devil's advocate. "Ok, suppose someone has an indiscretion."

"Well, that shouldn't happen … but if it does, that person should be smart enough to at least do it safely."

"How about we continue this conversation after my parents are gone?"

I couldn't believe he was talking to me about condom use. He was the one having a baby out of wedlock, but now he wanted to take our relationship to a whole new level by not using condoms.

Javier rolled over and pulled the sheets up to his neck. "As usual, you have to have your way."

I rolled over and turned off the lamp. There were no "good nights" or "I love yous."

It was 6:39 a.m. when I felt Javier nudging me. He was standing over the futon fully dressed.

Groggy, I said, "What's going on?"

"I have to go to L.A."

"What?! You have to go now? Is this about last night?"

"No, it's not about last night. It's Liz. She's in labor."

"Labor? She's not due for another month."

"I know, but I'm kind of worried."

"You have to go now?" I protested. "My parents are here. Don't leave me alone with them."

"She's going into labor, Dee. I have to go."

"What am I supposed to tell my parents?"

"I'm sure you'll figure it out."

"Fine. Go," I said, not at all happy about it.

Before Javier walked out the door, he said, "Dee, don't be upset with me. You understand why I'm going, right?"

"I understand. It doesn't mean I have to like it."

"I love you," he said.

"I love you too."

His "I love you" felt flat to me. He was preoccupied. It may have been more convincing if he had remembered to kiss me goodbye.

The aroma of bacon and eggs lured me out of bed some time after 8:00 a.m. I had been lying awake there since Javier left—unable to fall back asleep. I wondered how this baby would affect us if it was a special-needs baby. With premature births, any number of things could go wrong. *What have I signed on for?*

I got up and put on the sweatpants Javier had worn the previous night. I found my stepmother in the kitchen preparing breakfast.

"Good morning," I said, taking a seat at the dinette and yawning.

Priscilla was stirring a pan of scrambled eggs. "Good morning," she beamed cheerfully.

A pile of cooked bacon sat on a plate near the stove. "We have bacon?" I grew up on bacon, but now made it a point to cut back on pork and red meat.

"No, I went to the store and picked up a few things this morning. Don't worry; I cooked some of your turkey sausage too."

"Thanks."

"Why don't you call in Javier and your dad for breakfast?"

"Yeah ... Javier had to drive to L.A. this morning for

some family business."

"Oh…. He's a very nice young man," Priscilla said, while buttering a stack of toast. "He's obviously crazy about you—and cute."

"I know. I care about him too," I said, choosing my words wisely.

"Please—you two are in love."

I laughed. "I guess you can say that."

Priscilla turned the burner off under the eggs and placed them on a cool burner. She brought a glass of orange juice over to me at the table and sat down. "I came into your life when you were around ten years old, and I love you like my own, Devon. Maybe because we're not exactly blood, I don't have any expectations. People seem to have certain expectations from their own kids. They plan out their kids' lives before they even know what it is their children want. No expectations here," she assured. "Your dad is different. He wanted different things for you. But believe me when I tell you, he *is* trying. He's making an effort, Devon. He loves you."

"He has a funny way of showing it."

Priscilla stood and went back to minding the food on the stove. "Can I offer you a piece of advice that my mom gave me when I married your dad?"

I was puzzled. I wondered how advice given to her when she remarried related to me. "What's that?"

"I guess with it being my second marriage, she felt I needed to hear this. I think she believed I gave up on my first marriage too soon…. Anyway, she told me, 'if the joy out weighs the pain, then hold on to him.' They are going to make mistakes, and there are going to be hurdles. That's to be expected. Relationships aren't all candy and flowers—Lord knows."

I wasn't sure if our walls were thinner than I perceived or if she sensed something was going on between Javier and me. Maybe it was simply a piece of advice for someone starting out in a new relationship. I just listened, then said, "I'll remember that."

After a trip to the zoo and dinner at *The Hard Rock Café* in San Diego's Gaslamp District, we arrived back home late in the evening. Javier's car was parked on the street. I didn't expect to see him back so soon. I assumed he would be staying in L.A. overnight.

I found him lying on the futon in the guestroom. I lay next to him.

I could already tell he was sulking, but about what, I didn't know. "Hey," I asked, "how did it go?"

"She was having Braxton Hicks contractions."

"What's that?" I asked.

"False labor. They basically sent her home."

"That's good; at least nothing's wrong. Right?"

"Yep."

"Then, why do you sound so down?"

Javier rolled onto his side. "First I was scared something was wrong, and then I was relieved. I know its weird … but now I'm a little disappointed. I thought I was going to be a dad today."

"Well, don't rush it. The longer she stays in, the healthier she'll be."

"There's something else."

"What?"

"Liz wants to meet you … I thought maybe we could drive up next Sunday for the day."

"Why does she want to meet me?"

"Well, the baby will be spending some time here eventually. She just wants to meet you."

"No, she wants to check me out," I protested. "She wants to give a seal of approval before letting the baby come visit in the future."

"Maybe so, but I don't think it's too much to ask. She's a concerned soon-to-be mother"

"Well, I don't know … I may be working."

"You're off next Sunday. Your schedule is posted on the fridge."

"Okay, I'm not sure I'm ready to meet her."

"Why?"

I wanted to shout at him, but I didn't. Instead, I spoke quietly, an underpinning of frustration in my voice. "Because she used to be your girlfriend, you fucked her, and now she's pregnant with my boyfriend's baby. Sorry; I'm not at all ready to meet her."

"Yeah, and I've been paying for it every since."

I stood up. "Stop playing the victim," I whispered. "Not only did you get your rocks off, but you're having a baby. You can deny it if you want, but I know it pleases you to no end to be having a baby. You just said so a minute ago."

I hoped our argument didn't escape the guestroom.

"Fuck you," Javier said.

I left the room and sat on the sofa fuming. I switched on the television and began to channel surf. Twenty minutes must have passed before Priscilla came out of the bedroom.

"Don't mind me. I'm just going to grab a glass of water, then we're headed off to bed. We want to get an early start." She walked past me to the kitchen.

I continued my assault on the television remote, pressing buttons mindlessly.

Returning from the kitchen, she asked, "Is everything okay?"

"It's fine."

She simply said, "It will all work out" before heading

back into the bedroom.

I was embarrassed that tension between Javier and me was so obvious to her. We couldn't even portray a happily married couple for a single weekend.

After an hour of watching nothing in particular, it was 10:06 p.m. I started for the guestroom but stopped before reaching the door. I could see no light escaping from underneath the door and figured Javier was already asleep. Not ready to face him, and needing a break from the family, I grabbed my keys and secretly left the apartment.

From my truck, I dialed the number I stored in my phone weeks ago, but had no intention of using. I guess I was lying to myself. Thirty minutes later I found myself on Kenneth's couch.

30

The plan was to just blow off some steam, but for every Corona I had, the more I opened up. By number three he knew *almost* everything about Javier and me—I wasn't buzzed enough to divulge Javier's illegal status.

"That's some deep shit," Kenneth said, sitting a cushion-length away from me.

"Who *you* tellin'?"

"I mean, I don't know what I would do if I found out Lee was doing bitches, not to mention if he got some bitch pregnant."

"When is Lee due back, anyway?"

"Four fuckin' months."

Feeling bolder, I said, "Can I ask you something?"

"Go for it bro."

I took a sip from Corona number four. "Do you and Lee mess around?"

Kenneth laughed. "Of course we do, he's my boyfriend."

"Very funny. You know what I mean."

Kenneth started to look as if I had asked him the bonus question from Jeopardy. Damn, he looked good. I was sure he wore the tank top especially for me. I wanted to feel those biceps around me and his solid body against mine. I felt guilty and hoped it was the alcohol lusting after him and not me.

"We mess around, but it wasn't always like dat. Our first year together, we fucked like rabbits befo he had tour duty. I love him, but months at a time without seeing each other—dat shit ain't workin.' I know a lot of couples are into that open relationship bullshit for the fun of it, but it's something we do only when he's out to sea. The military don't give a shit about you having a wife, not to mention a fucking boyfriend…. So, three months into his tour, we both were going crazy. We couldn't even have phone sex with him being on a ship and shit. So we came up with this arrangement. We figured it was either this or break up."

"What was the arrangement?"

"We can have sex with other people, but never the same person twice. Always wrap yo` shit. Neva fall in love. And when we're together, the shit stops."

I took another swig from my bottle. "How does that work for the two of you?"

"The shit works when you follow the rules."

I belted out a drunken laugh. "I hear another story coming on. What happened?"

"Damn yer full of questions," Kenneth noted. He continued, "Well, I met this brotha I started seeing regularly. He knew the deal. I'm always up front. He tells me he's falling in love and shit and wants me to leave Lee."

"What did you do?"

"I start thinking maybe the dude is right. I mean, he has a regular nine-to-five; I won't have to deal with dis military bullshit, so I'm giving it some thought…. Now this is over a period of two months, and I talk to Lee once a week, and we send e-mails everyday…. Well, I guess I'm acting different over the phone and through emails because the next time I talk to Lee, he says 'pick me up from the airport.' Lee dropped over two g's on a ticket to come see me from Japan. When I see him at the airport, I knew that's where my heart was. I cut it off wit ol' boy and never broke the rules again. Just six more years of this military crap, and he's out…. Damn you got me talkin' like a bitch and shit. I was hoping to get my dick wet."

Up until the last remark, I was thinking I'd had

Kenneth all wrong. Sure his relationship wasn't conventional, but they were making it work; and who was I to judge? They were faced with unusual circumstances and they adapted.

Kenneth started to stare me down like I was prey again. "So, tell me something," he said.

"What?"

"Why are you here?"

"I don't know," I said.

"Did you come here to fuck or talk?" he asked, rather bluntly.

"I don't know. I mean I thought about it."

"I think yer pissed at yo boy, so you thought you'd come over here and get back at him."

"Maybe," I said.

Before I knew what was happening, Kenneth began stroking himself through his shorts. "It's right here if you want it."

A strange desire overwhelmed me. I felt a mixture of lust, shame, and excitement stir in me all at once as I watched him stroke himself. It wasn't as if I wasn't familiar with my old friend, lust. It just seemed that Javier was always around when he came to visit lately.

Luckily, shame won out. "I better go," I said, quickly jumping to my feet. I placed the unfinished Corona on the coffee table and started for the door.

Kenneth also got up. "You know you want it!"

I reached for the door knob. Before I could turn it Kenneth forcefully pinned me against the wall. I could feel his breath on the back of my neck and his erection on my ass even through his clothing. The strange feeling in my gut was growing.

"So what's it going to be? Are you going to get even, or go home and play nice?"

"I ... I'm leaving." *What was I doing here?!*

"I knew you would be a cocktease," he said, before backing off me.

I fumbled with the knob and deadbolt, and raced out the door.

I crept into the apartment sometime after midnight. All was quiet. I went straight for the bathroom and ran the shower. I removed my clothes and stepped into the tub. The water was hotter than I normally cared for, but I didn't bother adjusting the temperature. Steam started to fill the bathroom within minutes. The water stung my skin, but I didn't care. I could only think about what I nearly went through with Kenneth. I almost betrayed Javier's trust simply out of spite, and that's the worst type of betrayal.

In that shower, I did something I hadn't done in quite some time. I prayed. The events in my life seemed be out of my control and I needed help. I could no longer handle it on my own. I prayed Javier and I could make our relationship work in spite of what is thrown at us. I prayed for his safe passage to and from L.A. considering he may be taking these trips more frequently with a baby on the way. I prayed that my parents would no longer condemn me. Finally, I prayed for forgiveness.

My skin throbbed as I toweled dry. I gargled away the taste of Corona and lime, gathered my things, and slipped into the guestroom.

"Where the hell you been?" Javier asked as I climbed onto the futon.

I laid my head on his chest. "It's not important."

Javier wrapped his arms around me. "You're such a fucking pain in the ass."

"I know. I'm sorry."

31

Sunday morning, after breakfast, I was helping my dad load the suitcases into the Ford Explorer. He placed the last suitcase in the cargo area and closed the hatch. I started back towards the building.

"Wait a sec, Devon," he said. "I want to talk to you about something."

My father never struck me as a communicator, and he was also predictable, so I braced myself for the "I disapprove of your lifestyle" conversation. I was determined to hold my ground. I wasn't the young boy he was nearly ready to pummel years ago.

"What's up?"

"You know you were always the independent one out of all the kids. After leaving home … all these years …

not once have you called asking for money, or any kind of help for that matter. I wish your siblings took after you in that respect. I can't pretend like I understand your lifestyle or accept it. But one thing I can say is, you're doing all right for yourself, and that's all I can ask for. You're a different person than the one that left Chicago.... You're a man ... I'm proud of you."

I was speechless as I tried my best to hold back tears. I was both ecstatic and ashamed. I was ecstatic that after all these years, my dad was making an effort. I was ashamed that I still sought his approval, and approval wasn't being offered. I was settling for tolerance, but I guess that was progress. "I ... thanks dad."

For the first time in my adult life, my father gave me a real hug.

"Javier ... he seems nice too."

"Yeah, he is."

He placed his hand on my shoulder while we walked back to the apartment. "I'd better get Priscilla. She likes that Javier a little too much," he joked.

"Yeah, I think they really hit it off."

Javier and I stood on the curve as they pulled away.

"Your stepmom invited us out to Vegas the next time they're there."

I laughed. "Oh, really?"

"Yep."

"I wonder how *that* would work."

"What do you mean?" Javier asked.

"The sleeping arrangements. At their place, they would probably have us in separate bedrooms."

"Naw, I think they would be cool with it."

"You're probably right," I concluded. "Javier …"

As the Explorer turned the corner and drove out of sight, Javier turned to me. "Yeah, Papa?"

"Thank you."

"For what?"

"For making me be real with them."

Javier took my hand. "It was all your doing. I just highly suggested."

"More like kicked and screamed."

"Well, sometimes you need a little direction," Javier chuckled. "But I know something you can do to show a little gratitude."

"Let me guess.… Does that involve sex?"

"Yeah. It's been a long weekend."

"Well, not before we play John Madden football."

32

It was a drive I had made only a couple of times with Javier. It was a drive he would do on a moment's notice to visit his sister or to get away when I pissed him off. The drive from San Diego to Los Angeles was just under three hours—two hours if you sped and there was no traffic. With every mile, I grew irritated and nervous. I didn't know if it was because I was going to meet Liz or because we were approaching the San Clemente, California checkpoint. If caught, Javier stood to be deported, and I would be probably looking at possible jail time and loss of a job since I lived with him and had full knowledge of his illegal status.

We approached a highway sign much like those reserved for Amber Alerts. It flashed Be Prepared to Stop for Inspection.

"Shit!" I shouted.

"What's wrong?" Javier asked.

"The checkpoint is open." The previous times I had gone to L.A. with Javier, we were lucky enough not to have to stop at the checkpoint due to it being closed.

"Well, don't go getting all nervous. That will get us sent to secondary inspection."

"I don't know about this, Javier."

"Dee, these are your people—relax," he soothed. "Let me do the talking. It's not the first time I've driven through the checkpoint while it was open. And if worse come to worse, we're just friends and you know nothing about me being illegal."

I couldn't relax. For the first time, Javier's problem was taunting me. It was waiting for the right time to rear its ugly head. It waited until we were going to visit Liz to remind me that Javier is illegal. It wanted to see if I could take the pressure. I asked myself, "Did I really think this through?" I loved him, but I had a lot to lose.

A half mile from the checkpoint, my stomach was tied in knots. His problem threw another taunt my way. It was a road sign I'd seen many times over, but didn't pay much attention to anymore. It seemed to scream "Caution!" at me. That may be because that is what the sign actually said: Caution. It featured a Mexican family—father, mother, and child—in black silhouette. The sign is nearly obsolete now, but in the nineties the signs were necessary to warn motorists to be aware of illegals—or pedestrians, if you will—who might cross the highway at any moment. Many lost their lives, and more often than not, they were running from the Border Patrol.

I looked at Javier while he drove us closer to our fate. *Is he worth all this?* I hated myself for even asking the question, but his illegal status was no longer buried in our hall closet. His problem was now cruising north, up the I-5 freeway ... mocking me.

We eventually came to a stop in a line of cars while two agents on either side of the vehicles inspected the motorists and their vehicles. Most cars were merely waved through. Others were stopped while an agent standing on the driver's side engaged motorists in conversation. The agent on the passenger side was a backup. Maybe they would switch places when one got tired of questioning motorists and needed a break.

Just ahead of us, the agent had been speaking with someone in a Toyota Prius for at least a minute. We were next in line. I didn't realize my leg was shaking noticeably, when Javier told me to stop it. The AC blasting didn't prevent beads of sweat from forming on my forehead.

Javier turned to me. "Dee, you know why I think my

mother took me being gay so well?" he asked.

I wondered what his question had anything to do with us approaching the agent at the checkpoint. I complied anyway. "No, why?"

"She always knew. She had time to deal with it."

"How do you know that?"

"Because when I was eight years old I begged her to let me join Maria's Girl Scout troop. She said no, but who do you think sold all of Maria's cookies?"

Suddenly, a vision of young Javier in a Girl Scout uniform going door to door selling cookies entered my head. A loud, uncontrollable, boisterous, laugh passed my lips. Javier joined in.

The agent pointed and directed the Prius to secondary inspection. We slowly pulled forward. The two of us were still laughing when he asked us to state our citizenship. We barely got out the words U.S. citizen between laughter. The agent shook his head, sighed, and sent us on our way.

Finally, after regaining my composure I said, "You made that up, didn't you?"

"I'll never tell."

Once in L.A., we exited the 101 freeway.

"We'll be there in a few minutes," Javier informed me.

It seemed like it would be a memorable occasion.

In a few moments, I was going to meet Javier's baby's momma.

A sign told me that we were in Silver Lake, a neighborhood of Los Angeles. Javier was soon making his way down Sunset Boulevard. After several blocks, he turned right on some residential street I didn't catch the name of.

Javier studied the street for parking. He pointed to a dingy fourplex built between two Craftsman-style homes and said, "That's her place." We found a spot a couple of blocks away.

Before getting out of the car, Javier said, "Please be nice, Dee."

"Got it. Be nice to Javier's baby's momma."

Javier shook his head. "How long you been waiting to work that into the conversation?"

"Since we left. I'm sorry. I'll be good."

"Thank you."

We walked the two blocks and up the walkway of Liz's building. Javier hit a few buttons on the call box. It wasn't long before we heard Liz's voice answer from the box.

"Yes?" she said.

At least she sounded sweet as pie.

"It's Javier."

"I'll be right there."

Liz was apparently on the first floor because she emerged in a matter of seconds and opened the security door. I've seen a couple of pictures of her before, but I have to admit she was even prettier in person. Maybe pregnancy gave her that glow everyone spoke of. Liz was a little on the short side and obviously pregnant. She looked like a petite woman with a basketball under her blouse. Her face wasn't round and her ankles looked normal. Liz was fair skinned, almost white, with short cropped hair. She looked cute in her black Capri pants and white maternity blouse.

She smiled. "Hi! Come on in."

She hugged Javier and offered me her hand. "You must be Devon. I'm Elizabeth."

"Nice to meet you," I said.

"You cut your hair," Javier noted.

"I'm trying to make things as easy as I can in the next couple months. I figured this is low maintenance…. Come on in." she motioned us to follow her through the small foyer.

Liz's apartment was to the right. She led us into the living room. Stacks of baby gifts occupied one corner. There were pampers, a crib, bottles, a playpen, a car seat, and some gifts that were still wrapped.

"Sorry about all the stuff. The shower was yesterday," she explained. "Excuse me while I check on the food. She waddled into the kitchen.

Javier went over to look at all the gifts. I never heard Javier mention anything about a baby shower. Yes, it's usually a women's affair, but I was surprised that Javier didn't try to come up and help in some form. Although … I was glad he didn't.

"There's a lot of stuff here. You shouldn't need much of anything," Javier said, projecting his voice to reach Liz in the kitchen.

"Yes it is," Liz replied. "Your sister was such a big help yesterday too. She should be here any minute."

"I think she was a little surprised by the whole baby thing," Javier commented.

"You can say that again," I mumbled.

Liz reappeared in the doorway of the kitchen. "Where are my manners? Can I get you all anything to drink?"

"I'm fine thank you," I declined.

"Nothing for me," Javier said.

"Well then, excuse me and lunch should be ready shortly," Liz said, before returning to the kitchen.

As we waited, Javier became preoccupied with all the baby products. I just sat there feeling uncomfortable. He managed to pull himself away when he heard the clamor of pots and pans.

"You alright?" he shouted. "You sure you don't need some help in there?"

"I'm fine."

"I think I'm going to go help her," Javier informed me. "You alright?"

Putting on my best happy face, I gleamed, "I'm good."

Javier smiled. "Okay."

After Javier left the room, I looked over the magazines on the coffee table. There was *Parenting, Women's Fitness,* and *Time.* At least she was well-read. I was reaching for the *Time* magazine when the call box buzzed.

"That should be Maria," I heard Liz say. "Would you let her in?" she asked Javier

Javier entered from the kitchen and made his way to the call box by the door.

"Who is it?" Javier blurted into the call box.

"Open the door, faggot," Maria shouted through the speaker.

Javier hit the button to temporarily disengage the security door and opened the door to the apartment just as Maria reached it.

Maria was about six feet tall in her four inch heels. Her dark jeans hugged her hips like bodypaint. She adjusted the spaghetti strap to her cream-colored halter-top as she slid the large black designer purse off her shoulder. She took off her Prada sunglasses and ran her fingers through her straight, long, black hair. The few times I'd seen Maria she always looked as if she was a rich bitch right off of Rodeo Drive. She struck me as the type that dressed up just to go to the corner store for a gallon of milk. She was high maintenance.

"Tell me you didn't dress like that for the shower yesterday," Javier complained. "You look like a hooker."

Maria and Javier always went for each other like hungry pit bulls. It was a little unnerving when I witnessed them together for the first time. For them, it was all love. I got over it quickly when Maria started taking aim at me. It actually made me feel like part of the family.

"Shut up!" Maria shot back at him.

They hugged, probably longer than one would expect after hearing such an exchange. It was a hug that said *we're still suffering from the same pain: the loss of a loved one.*

"Enough. You smell like a li'l bitch in all that cologne," Maria said, breaking their embrace. I knew it was all talk since she was the one who bought the fragrance, Issey Miyake, for Javier. "Where's my Devon?"

"Hey, Maria…." I blushed, walking towards her.

"Give me some love." Maria greeted me with a hug. "Now handsome … when you gonna ditch my loser-ass brother and get with all of this?" she asked, as she spun around. She was the perfect ice breaker for this luncheon.

"It's tempting," I said.

"I know, right," she squealed in her best chola accent.

"She looks like Slutty Barbie," Javier chimed in.

Maria turned in his direction. "Don't hate. Appreciate."

"Whatever," Javier scoffed. "I'll be in the kitchen."

"Hi, Maria," Liz shouted from the other room.

"Hey, Liz."

"Lunch will be served shortly," Liz reminded.

"Well you girls handle your business in there." Maria teased.

"Shut up, Maria!" Javier shouted from the confines of the kitchen.

I laughed. Maria had a way of getting under Javier's skin that even I hadn't mastered yet.

"Come over here and talk to me," Maria coaxed, ushering me over to the couch.

"How you doing?" Maria asked with concern.

"I'm good."

Maria whispered, "No, Papa. I mean … how you doing … with all this?" She waved her hands looking for the right words. "This baby stuff."

"I don't know. I guess I'm holding up. One minute I think I'm fine with it, and the next …"

"Let me guess. Ya'll fighting."

"Exactly," I agreed.

"I don't know what he was thinking, but one thing I do know is he loves his Devon."

I smiled. "Really?"

"You two punks better work it out."

"I was so nervous about coming here."

"Who wouldn't be?" Maria added, "I have known Liz as long as Javier has known her. She was never one of my favorite people. When they were dating she had my brother all wrapped, but I guess the bitch is going to be family now."

Javier entered with a stack of plates and silverware. "You think you two can stop gossiping long enough to set the table?"

Maria groaned, "I am not the help; besides, I did enough yesterday."

"I'll do it, Javier," I volunteered.

"Thanks, Dee," Javier said as he deposited the plates on the dining room table and escaped back into the kitchen.

Maria followed me over to the table to continue our discussion. We began to distribute the plates and silverware.

"Devon, can I give you some advice?" Maria asked, again dropping her voice to a whisper.

"What's that?"

Franco Ford

"Keep an eye on her."

That piece of advice didn't quiet my nerves; it actually made me that more on edge. Maria wasn't particularly fond of Liz, and she had known Liz for quite some time. For me to come to that same conclusion after just meeting Liz carried no weight. I was biased. But Marie's sentiments gave me concern.

"Let me ask you something," I said, taking a chance.

"What?"

"Do you think Javier got ... taken advantage of?"

"I don't know, Devon, but it has crossed my mind."

No sooner had Maria and I finished setting the table Javier and Liz began bringing out the food. Lunch consisted of baked chicken, roasted red potatoes, steamed vegetables, and dinner rolls. We seated ourselves at the sizable round table with Javier in between Liz and me.

"I know this is not the chicken from yesterday...." Maria protested.

"Yes, it's leftovers," Liz acknowledged.

"Can you believe this bullshit? Inviting me over for leftovers," Maria mumbled.

"Maria!" Javier shouted.

"Shut up Javier! The girl knows I'm just messing with her."

We passed around the serving platters of food, helping ourselves. When everyone had their desired share, Liz asked, "Would someone like to say grace?"

We all looked at each other. It wasn't that Javier and I never said grace when we sat down for dinner, but I think everyone was taken by surprise. It seemed, at least to me, that she was trying too hard.

Silence.

"Fine, I'll do it." Liz bowed her head, and we all followed her lead. "Oh, heavenly Father, thank you for the food we are about to receive, and may it nourish our bodies. Thank you for this time with friends, new and old. Amen."

Everyone repeated, "Amen."

Maria went for the bottle on the table and gawked at the label. "Please tell me you have something harder than sparkling cider."

Liz sounded agitated when she said, "I told you yesterday, Maria, I don't have any alcohol."

"I know, but I figured you would have gone out and got some since yesterday for me."

"You might want to start keeping a sixpack in the fridge," Javier suggested. "Watching her go through withdrawal gets ugly."

"That all you got Javier?" Maria asked. "You gettin' rusty down there in San Diego? You're not a challenge anymore."

"I'm just biding my time. I'm going to hit you when

you least expect it."

"That's enough, you guys," Liz interjected. "Please, not today."

"Honey, this is the family you married ... I mean 'got knocked up into,'" Maria said.

I nearly choked trying not to laugh.

Liz was determined to get lunch back on track. "So, I hear you're a Border Patrol Agent."

I quickly chewed and swallowed. Up until then, I was simply eating and enjoying Maria and Javier taking swings at each other. "Yes, I am."

"How do you like it?" Liz pressed.

"It pays the bills."

"So ... you carry a gun?"

"Yes, I do."

Liz continued. "Do you keep the gun in the house?"

"Yeah, I do."

I could see Liz was beginning to play the part of concerned mother already. "Hmmm ... that could be a problem with a baby visiting," she said. "Don't you think, Javier?"

Before Javier could respond, I said, "I don't leave guns lying around the house." Javier added, "Dee is good about keeping it locked up too."

Maria downed some of her disappointing cider. "If this child is growing up in L.A., the sooner she learns to shoot the better."

Javier and Maria exchanged high fives. Everyone except Liz laughed.

"It's a concern Liz, but that's down the road," Javier assured her.

Javier was going out of his way to make things comfortable for Liz, and that was beginning to annoy me.

Liz dropped her fork and placed both hands on her belly. "She's kicking Javier.... Feel here." Liz held out a hand to guide Javier's hand to where she felt the kicking.

The sight of watching Javier place his hand on her stomach turned mine.

"I feel it," he beamed.

"She just kicks like crazy sometimes," Liz gloated.

After the kicking extravaganza, Javier and Liz resumed eating.

After a moment, Liz asked me, "How is your lunch?"

"Good," I expressed, rather dryly.

"Good job, Liz," Javier complimented, raising his glass of cider to toast the occasion.

"It's alright," Maria said, reviving her chola accent.

I was working on a heaping mouthful of potatoes when Liz asked, "So tell me Devon, do you like kids?"

I was beginning to think she was purposely waiting

until my mouth was full to engage me in conversation. I chewed franticly before saying, "Yes. Yes, I like kids."

"You plan on having any of your own?"

I considered that to be a rather shady question, so I admit I lost control and hit back. "I hadn't planned on it just yet, but if I do, you can be sure they will be just that— *planned*."

Everyone was silent. Okay … maybe it was a bit much, but she started it.

Javier attempted to move us past the awkwardness. "The potatoes are really good."

"Thank you, Javier."

"So anyway, girl, when is your last day at work?" Maria asked.

"I think in a couple weeks, and then I'm done."

"What is it you do?" I asked.

"I work in Human Resources at Cedars-Sinai."

I pretended to be interested. "Sounds challenging," I said.

"You wouldn't believe the amount of sexual harassment cases we are receiving lately. One doctor in particular is in some pretty hot water. He deserves it though."

We all listened while Liz went on and on about the wonderful world of human resources. Between the endless adventure of human resources and questions for me it was the longest lunch I had ever attended. It felt more like an interview.

Lunch was finally nearing an end. Javier and Liz cleared the plates. I wondered what kind of signal I could give Javier to let him know I was ready to leave if I didn't get him alone.

"We have cheesecake," Liz said, coming out of the kitchen.

Damn it. Dessert.

We resumed our previous spots at the table. At least this time, I was picking at cheesecake and not yesterday's chicken.

"So, can you believe it?" Liz asked. "In less than a month we will have a baby girl,"

"No, I can't," Javier said. He looked to me for a reaction; I didn't provide him with one.

"When's the due date?" I asked Liz.

Liz fumbled with her fork, nearly dropping it. "Late June."

I wondered if anyone else found it strange that she didn't recite the exact due date. "That's a Cancer, right?"

"I really don't know," she said.

I wanted to probe deeper. "When is your birthday?"

"It's April 4th."

"Ah … an Aries. And what year?"

Liz apparently didn't like my line of questioning. She rolled her eyes and barked, "1982."

"What's with all the interest with birthdays?" Javier asked me.

Now it may have appeared I was suddenly trying to be Liz's BFF—Best Friend Forever—but there was a reason to my friendliness and sudden interest in the zodiac.

"Oh, I have a friend at work that's into astrology and does charts and stuff."

"I never heard you talk about astrology before," Javier snickered.

"That's because it's a *new* interest for me."

"Well, I'm dying to know what my chart would say," Liz added.

"You all need a life," Maria said, licking cheesecake off her fork.

Liz looked at me. "You don't like cheesecake?"

I looked at Javier "Yes, but my stomach is a little upset."

"I'm glad you enjoyed lunch, but maybe you shouldn't have eaten so much," Liz said.

"I'll have to remember that."

Somehow, I made it through dessert.

A while later, Maria and I were talking in the living room. Javier had insisted on helping Liz with the dishes. I wanted to tell him she's pregnant, not helpless. He wasn't that helpful at home.

After several minutes, Javier and Liz reappeared from

the kitchen.

"We better head back to San Diego," Javier said. "We both work tomorrow."

"So soon?" Liz protested.

"Yeah, Dee is not feeling so well either."

"Sorry, you're not feeling well," Liz said, with a sad face, as if she was talking to a kindergartner.

"It must have been something I ate," I said as I stood up.

Maria said, "I told you not to serve us leftovers."

"There was nothing wrong with that chicken, Maria."

Maria turned to Liz. "All I know is if my stomach becomes upset, I'm coming back here and sharing the wealth, if you know what I mean.... Now walk me out, faggots."

Javier grumbled. "I guess we're walking her out."

"Thanks for everything yesterday," Liz said to Maria.

Javier and Maria exchanged hugs with Liz. Liz turned to me. "Well give me a hug, silly."

Reluctantly, I did. It felt forced and mechanical on both our parts.

We said our goodbyes to Liz and walked Maria to her car.

"It was good seeing you, homos," Maria said, extending her arms and hugging us both at the same time.

"Love you," Javier whispered into her ear. Maria whispered the same.

After Maria was in her car, we started down the street towards Javier's car.

"So?" he said.

"So … what?"

"What did you think of her?"

"I thought the point of coming down was to find out what she thought of me."

Javier sighed. "Don't be like that."

"Does it really matter what I think?"

"Yes."

"I don't think you can handle it."

"Try me," Javier said, hitting the keyless entry remote.

We both got into the car.

"Ok. You asked for it. I don't like her. I think she's kind of sneaky too. I think quite possibly she stills love you."

Javier started the car and pulled away from the curve. "Get out of here."

"You saw how she acted towards me."

"You're just trippin.'"

"Every chance she got, she tried to belittle me. You asked. That's my opinion."

"I don't know what you're talking about."

I rolled my eyes. "You didn't notice?"

"No."

"Then ask your sister."

"I think you're overreacting."

"What do you really know about her, Javier? Sure you dated in high school, but what has she been up to lately? Do you know her dating history or anything?"

Once on Sunset Boulevard, Javier was driving well over the speed limit. "I see where this is headed," he said.

"I'm sorry. I just think these are things you should ask yourself. And slow the hell down. You don't need to get pulled over."

"You know what I think? I think you're jealous."

"Whatever," I said. "Let's just drop it."

"Let's"

Every conversation, for that matter, was dropped the entire drive back. We didn't say much of anything to each other the rest of the day.

33

The following day at work, I drove out to my assigned area. I was a little anxious. What I was about to do wasn't so much illegal as it was pushing the boundaries of my authority. Normally, it could be done over the service radio, but I didn't want an audience. I used my cell phone to dial the direct line to dispatch.

A female voice answered, "CBP dispatch, San Diego sector. How can I help you?"

With as little as a name and a birthdate, Liz's criminal history was a phone call away. As much as I disliked her, I didn't think she was a felon. My inquiry would probably turn up nothing, but it was worth a try. I was desperate.

"Yes, this is Yankee 586. Can you run a criminal records check by name and date of birth, please?"

"Sure. Proceed with your information."

I got Liz's full name from the magazine subscriptions on her coffee table. "The name is Elizabeth Montez."

"The birthdate?" the dispatcher asked.

"It's April 4, 1982."

"Stand by while I run it."

"Thank you."

A minute went by before she returned to the line. "Okay, the individual is not in our immigration system." I didn't expect her to be since she is a United States citizen. "She's pretty clean except for an arrest a few months back—destruction of private property."

"The dispo?" I asked. Dispo, or disposition, is the result of the arrest, whether it was time served or a slap on the wrist.

"She was arrested, but it appears the charges were dropped."

"Thank you. Can I get a hard copy of that in my station mailbox please?"

"Will do. Anything else?"

"That's it, thanks."

The hard copy, the criminal history on paper, would give me a little more information, but probably not much more. I would pick it up on my way into the station at the end of my shift.

As I figured, Javier was sound asleep when I arrived

home. I figured he would be, since I wasn't one of his favorite people after the drive in from L.A. the day before. I pulled Liz's criminal history check from my breast pocket and sat at the dinette table before bothering to remove my boots. As I suspected, it wasn't much. There was an arrest number with the L.A.P.D., but something told me to dig deeper. I had another idea, but it would have to wait until morning. It involved calling for a favor from an angel.

On the way to the gym the following morning, I called for that favor.

"Hey, Bitch," Michael answered.

Bypassing small talk, I said, "I need a big favor."

"Let's hear it."

"Remember that guy you were doing on the L.A.P.D.?"

"I spent some quality time with a gentlemen caller, if that's what you mean."

As I recalled, one weekend before Javier and I started dating, Michael, Rafael, and I went to L.A. to hit the clubs. Michael met Lyle, a police officer for the L.A.P.D., at *The Abbey*. They were inseparable all night. On occasions, Michael would go up to L.A. to see him, and Lyle would sometimes come down to San Diego. That all ended when Lyle introduced Michael to his whips-and-chains fetish. Michael was down for a little experimenting, but things got out of hand when Michael found himself chained and tortured for two and a half hours because he couldn't remember the "safe" word. He soon ended it with Lyle. It was a scene Michael couldn't get into. Michael said, "I can't even look at my own handcuffs the same."

"I need some info on an arrest. No hard copies, just the info would be good enough."

This was a lot to ask of someone, so I figured it raised my chances if I didn't ask for any paperwork. In instances like these, you didn't want to leave a paper trail when doing such a favor.

"No. *Hell*, no. I just got the feeling back in my nipples."

I pleaded, "It's important. I wouldn't have asked otherwise."

"What's this all about anyway?"

"I did some research and found out that Liz was arrested a few months back for destruction of private property. I just want to follow up on it."

"Sounds like a scorned girlfriend."

"Exactly what I was thinking."

"You've piqued my curiosity," Michael said. "Give me the arrest number and I'll see what I can do. You will owe me big."

I gave Michael the number.

"Give me a few days,"

"Okay," I said. "Thanks."

"Later."

I was doing crunches in the aerobics room when Kenneth entered. I feared I would run into him sooner or later, but I wasn't changing gyms just to avoid him. I continued with my crunches as he approached.

Kenneth kneeled beside me. "I was hoping to run into you."

I removed my head phones and pressed on with my crunches. "Oh, why is that?"

"I wanted to apologize."

I stopped and was now lying on my back. "What?"

"I wanted to apologize," Kenneth repeated. "That day you came by my place, you had me going down memory lane. I got kind of angry and frustrated. With Lee gone, it gets hard sometimes … but then you come over … and I'm thinking, this fool don't know how easy he got it. I was like, at least ya man is home. I guess I was trying to punk you out for coming to me and not working things out wit' ya boy."

I sat up. "Maybe I deserved it. I probably shouldn't have been there anyway."

"No, I was wrong." Kenneth said raising a fist.

I gave him a fist bump. "Thanks."

"So, how are you and yo … maybe I should stop referring to him as yo boy."

I laughed. "Javier. His name is Javier, and we're good."

"Is he good to you?"

I reflected for a moment. "Yeah, he is."

"Then that's all that matters," Kenneth said. "Well, I'm going to let you finish your crunches. I'm sure Javier would appreciate that."

"Take it easy, Kenneth."

34

I was watching television, expecting Javier in from work any minute, when my cellphone rang. It was Michael.

"Hello," I answered.

"Do I have an earful for you!"

My pulse quickened, figuring this concerned the information on Liz that I asked Michael to look into. I muted the television.

"What's up?"

"Oh, you owe me. You know how much ass-kissing I had to do for this information?"

"Alright, I owe you big. What you got?"

Michael implemented a dramatic pause. "… Well … it turns out 'girlfriend' was arrested for taking a bat to this doctor's Mercedes."

"Really?"

"Oh, it gets better. Apparently, this doctor works at the same hospital she's employed at. One day, girlfriend follows him and his family to a restaurant, and when they go inside, she goes all Barry Bonds on his beautiful piece of German engineering."

"Damn." I moved to the edge of the sofa.

"At the arrest, some witnesses say she was going on about how he was a dog and a liar as she vandalizes the doctor's car. She herself told the arresting officer that Dr. Townsend, the man she was seeing, completely cut her off when she told him she was pregnant."

"Oh, shit!" I nearly choked. I rose from the couch and began to pace. "You think he's the father?"

"I was wondering that myself. That's where it's unclear. I mean, more than likely yes … but there's the possibility that she simply told him she was pregnant by someone else and he dumped her."

"Yeah," I agreed and settled back on the couch in defeat. "Wait a minute."

"What?"

I dashed to the bedroom and pulled the record checks out of a dresser drawer where I'd hid them. I skimmed through the paperwork. "The arrest was in September, and Javier's mom passed away during the first week in

October."

"Before Javier's and Liz's infamous one night stand," Michael concluded.

"Exactly!" I said. I couldn't help but think this theory only rang true if Javier and Liz only had the one time together as Javier said.

"One last thing," Michael said.

I couldn't imagine what else he had to tell me. I wasn't sure I could handle any more. "Go ahead."

"I have the name and work number for the good doctor."

"One sec." The search for a pen led me back into the kitchen where I took down the number for Dr. Alex Townsend.

"Thanks, Michael. I appreciate this."

"My pleasure. It was fun. I felt like a real angel hunting down leads. That feeling will probably pass when I'm chained to a bed next weekend."

I laughed. "It was for a good cause though. This needed to come out."

"How you going to break it to him?" Michael asked.

"I'm not sure, just yet." I heard Javier fumbling with his keys at the door. "Hey, I got to go. He's coming in."

"Let me know how this soap opera ends."

"Okay," I agreed. I quickly closed my phone and

stuffed the record checks in my pocket.

Javier mumbled, "Hey," as he entered.

I went up to him and wrapped my arms around him. I felt weighed down from what I learned and I could only imagine what it would do to him. How would I tell him? Would he be mad because I checked Liz out? Now wasn't the time. I needed to think first.

"What the hell is your problem?" Javier asked.

We had been bickering since Sunday, so he was probably surprised by my gesture.

"Nothing, I'm just happy to see you."

Javier smiled and gave me a peck on the lips. "You're up to something."

I kissed him back. "No, I'm not."

Javier loosened his tie. "I know what this is about."

"What?"

"You want to get laid."

I grinned uncontrollably. "That's not true, but it does sound like a good idea."

Javier did his Austin Powers imitation. "You horny baby?"

"Yeah, baby," I laughed.

Javier's lips greeted mine again. Clothes hit the floor as we slowly made our way to the bedroom.

An hour later we were sprawled across the bed.

"What's for dinner?" Javier inquired.

"Now, did you smell anything cooking when you got home?"

"You had all day to cook."

I chuckled. "Well, I had to spend half the day in the gym to look good for you."

"That I *do* appreciate," Javier said as he rolled over and began stroking my back.

"Besides, when was the last time I came in from work and found a hot meal?"

"You get off too late," he said.

"Lame excuse. Go order some takeout."

"I love your crazy ass."

Will he still love me when he finds out what I have learned?

"You better go order some takeout." I said.

Javier began to get up. "Don't get mad but I promised Liz I would drive up Sunday and help put together the nursery."

At that point I guess I no longer felt Liz was a threat, but Javier had horrible timing. Why couldn't he have brought that up later? Why now, after we just made love?

"Okay."

"You fine with that?"

"Yes," I said.

"Now, I *know* something is going on."

"Nothing is up. Now go order us some food. I worked up an appetite."

I watched as his naked body left the room. Javier always strutted around naked after sex. I guessed it's the little things you start to love about someone.

35

The next morning, I was seated at the dinette table in my robe with a mug of green tea, my cell phone, and the police report. I took a sip of the tea before I dialed the number.

A young woman answered, "Dr. Townsend's office. How may I help you?"

Not expecting Dr. Townsend to be available, I asked for him. "He's seeing patients at the moment. Can I take a message?"

"Yes, can you please have him call Agent Wallace?" I left my number. It was a little risky throwing around titles since I wasn't working in the scope of the law, but I figured it might get me a quicker response than if I was simply "Mr. Wallace."

"I will give him the message."

"Thank you."

A few hours later, I was dressing for work when Dr. Townsend returned my call.

"Hello."

"This is Dr. Townsend," he said. "Who are you?"

"Yes, Dr. Townsend," I said. I sat on the bed not entirely sure what line of questioning I was going to implement. I was just hoping he would cooperate. "I'm Agent Wallace. This is a bit awkward, but I was hoping I could ask you a couple of questions concerning Elizabeth Montez."

There was a brief silence. "Maybe you should contact my lawyer."

"You don't understand. See—"

Dr. Townsend cut me off. "What more does she want from me? She won't be happy until she destroys me. She accepted the terms of the agreement. That should be the end of it."

I was confused. "What agreement?"

"The child support agreement. I'll pay for the little bastard, but I want nothing to do with it. I already have a family."

"So, you are the father?" I asked. I stood anticipating his answer.

"Wait a minute. Who are you?"

"I was trying to explain to you sir, an associate has had ... a run-in with Ms. Montez. Ms. Montez has led my associate to believe he is the father of her baby."

Dr. Townsend began laughing. "That greedy bitch. The terms of the agreement only apply if the bastard's mine. We're definitely getting a DNA test."

"Thank you, sir. I think I've heard enough."

Before I could hang up, Dr. Townsend continued, "She came on to me you know. She was supposed to be on the pill. We're fucking for a few months, then boom! ... She's pregnant. On top of that, she files sexual harassment charges against me. I give her one thing though—she's a nice piece of ass."

"Thank you, doctor!"

Angrily, Dr. Townsend said, "Make that bitch pay for what she's doing."

"Bye, Doctor Townsend." I quickly hung up.

Dr. Townsend provided far more information than I had expected. It appeared that Liz forced a nice child support settlement from the good doctor. I believed that Dr. Townsend was telling the truth when he said, "she came on to me." Liz was ruthless.

36

It was Sunday. Javier was supposed to help Liz with the nursery. He shuffled around the bedroom getting dressed and preparing to go to L.A. I remained in bed pretending to sleep. I hadn't taken any action yet concerning Liz.

When Javier was done dressing, he kissed me on the cheek and was gone. After several minutes, and when I was sure he was on the road, I got out of bed. I freshened up and sat down for another cup of green tea. I reached for my cell phone, this time armed with a different number. This one was taken from Javier's cell phone.

The night before, I decided I wasn't going to be the one to tell Javier what I had learned. Liz was.

Liz answered on the second ring. "Hello."

In my best perky morning voice, I said, "Hello, Liz,

this is Devon."

"Javier isn't here yet," she said sharply.

"I know. He's on his way.... I'm going to cut to the chase. I know what you're doing."

I could hear Liz clear her throat over the line. Silence. "…Excuse me?"

"I know about Dr. Townsend. I know the baby isn't Javier's, and don't waste my time trying to deny it."

Once again, silence. "… How did you find out?" she said flatly.

"That's not important. Javier is on his way. When he gets there you're going to tell him everything," I instructed.

Liz began to sob. I wondered if she could cry on command. Over the phone she didn't have to produce real tears.

"I bet you think I'm a horrible person," she started.

I didn't respond.

"It started off fun, you know? I didn't have any intention on falling in love with him.... He told me he was going to leave her. I figured a baby would be the incentive he needed. When I got pregnant … he cut me off completely. He said I set him up. I only contacted a lawyer after he started treating me like shit."

"And you decided to drag Javier into your drama."

"The week of his mother's funeral, he was so

vulnerable. I had just found out I was pregnant, and Alex wasn't taking my calls…. I didn't plan it … it just happened. I always cared for Javier … even after he came out to me. I guess wanting men I can't have has always been my problem." Liz's voice quavered with tears.

"And you were just going to let him believe the baby was his," I asked.

Liz tried to explain, her words punctuated by sobs. "I know Javier … always wanted kids, and I … I needed a father for my baby…." I guess I did sort of hope … that … he would want a family too."

"You should consider getting some help."

"What I need is a father for my baby! Both Javier and I grew up without one, and … it's no treat." Her voice now sounded nearly desperate.

The thoughtfulness of wanting a positive father figure for her baby was extraordinary, but her methods were demented.

"So, were you going to milk Javier for child support also?" I asked.

"It wasn't about the money with Javier. We haven't even discussed child support."

"I expect Javier to know all of this today. And we never had this conversation."

Liz sniffled then sighed. "You're just having the time of your life putting me in my place, aren't you?"

I didn't respond.

"Your precious Javier will know the truth."

With that said, I ended the call.

I figured Javier didn't have to know my part in this. I didn't feel right being the one to deliver the blow. I also thought that it allowed Liz to possibly save face if it appeared she came clean on her own accord. The important part was that he would know the truth. It wasn't my goal to destroy Liz; besides, she clearly needed professional help. I just prayed the baby wouldn't suffer for her mother and father's ignorance, let alone their irresponsible indulgence.

It was getting late in the evening, and I hadn't heard from Javier. I was dying to know what transpired, but I knew he would call when he was ready. I was more concerned with how he was doing, and how he took the news. I just hoped she wasn't cold enough to spring it on him after he spent all day working on the nursery.

I was in bed trying to watch the news, but it just didn't hold my attention. I turned the television off when I heard Javier enter the apartment. He came into the bedroom and stood at the foot of the bed. He looked tired and stressed, almost like the night I saw him after he returned from his mother's funeral in L.A. I wanted to scoop him up into my arms, but I held my position considering I wasn't supposed to know anything.

"Why didn't you just tell me?" he asked.

"Damn it! She told you?"

"About the baby? Yes. But I didn't need her to tell me that you had something to do with her telling me the truth," he said.

I was afraid he would misinterpret my motivation. "I just thought you should know the truth," I explained.

Javier started to pace at the foot of the bed. "Can you believe that at first I was upset with you?" he admitted. "I thought, 'why couldn't he just let me have this?' After I calmed down, I realized that was stupid. I spent the last few years of my life trying not to live a lie, and this wasn't just about me. This involved me, you ... a baby. I guess it was better to know now than to have her throw it in my face after a disagreement sometime down the road."

Javier managed to stop pacing. He sat on the edge of the bed and turned to face me.

"How're you doing with all this?" I asked.

"I never in my life wanted to hit a woman so bad," he confessed.

"I think the feeling will eventually pass."

"I hope so. I think I spent most of the day calming Maria down. She was convinced she could 'whoop her ass,' as she put it, without harming the baby. She promised she would only deliver blows to the face."

"I'm sorry Javier."

Javier crawled the length of the bed to me and rested his head in my lap. "What would I do without you?"

I wiped away the tears rolling down his cheek. "I ask myself the same question everyday."

37

A few weeks had passed since the baby fiasco. Things had gotten better. It seemed that Javier and I were getting used to having drama over our heads. We did agree that we wanted to start a family sometime in the future.

A month earlier, we both got HIV and STD tested and received clean bills of health. We've talked about going au naturel, but I decided against it, even after we're tested again. That didn't sit well with Javier, but he perked up when I told him it would be up for discussion again after we're married.

Javier had started working on a business plan to start a nonprofit organization—a halfway house for runaway gay teens. After things cooled down with Liz, and against my wishes, Javier did eventually contact her to see how she and the baby was doing. I guess if he could forgive her, I could do the same.

It turned out that Dr. Townsend had visited Lena, his and Liz's daughter, once a DNA test proved he was the father. It was too soon to tell if he would be a permanent fixture in the baby's life.

To my surprise, my mom announced that she was planning to visit Javier and me. I was sure part of the motivation for the visit had to do with Dad's and Pricilla's visit—she wasn't going to be out done. I was a little worried. Javier said it would be fine—he's usually right about these things.

Rafael started spending time with a Navy guy. This one really *is* in the Navy, and Rafael met him at a coffee shop. Guess who hardly has time for *me* now.

To the delight of both Rafael and me, Michael had finally quit smoking. To our disappointment, Michael took an assignment on the northern border. He said he was due for a change and vow's he'll be back.

I too was due for a change. I didn't feel I was growing on the border careerwise. I was still employed by the Border Patrol, but I had sent my resume around to some other federal agencies. I was hoping to land a position with Customs and Border Protection as a Criminal Investigator (C.I.). C.I.s investigate, arrest, and deport aggravated felons who has committed serious crimes and are in the United States illegally. I will be interviewing for the position in a couple weeks.

We were all doing well. Things couldn't get any better … could they?

38

I heard Javier shuffling about in the kitchen. He had taken the day off.

I was just drifting back to sleep, when he entered with a tray. On it was a rose in a small vase, a glass of orange juice, and a plate of scrambled eggs, turkey sausage, and whole wheat toast.

I sat up against the head board. "Breakfast in bed?" I yawned. "What did I do to deserve this?"

Javier laughed as he brought the tray over to me and placed it on my lap. "You have no idea, do you?"

I shook my head. "What?"

"It's our anniversary ... one year.... You made such a big deal about having an anniversary date, and now you don't remember."

"Well, I didn't know we were going to actually celebrate it."

Javier stood over me. "I took the day off, and you don't even remember."

I looked down at my food. "Can I have some jelly please?"

Javier started for the door. "Are you kidding me?"

"Javier!" I shouted. "I'm just messin' with you. I *know* it's our anniversary. Happy anniversary! Come back and give me a kiss."

Javier pouted in the doorway. "No, you have morning breath."

"On the cheek?" I pleaded.

"Fine."

Javier walked over and planted a kiss on my cheek.

I reached into the nightstand on my side of the bed and pulled out a small black box. Javier's eyes grew big at the sight of it.

"What is it?" he asked as I handed him the box.

"Open it and find out."

He did. Inside the box was a platinum band.

"Try it on," I said.

Javier slowly slipped the band onto his ring finger.

"It fits perfectly, Papa."

I held up my hand since he had failed to notice my own matching band. I had slipped it on after he had gotten up to prepare breakfast.

Immediately, at the sight of it, a tear crept down his cheek. "Oh my God," he exclaimed, "you have the same ring!"

"Yep."

Javier grinned. "What if someone at work asks you about it?"

"I guess they'll get an earful," I said. I took his hand. "I wish I could marry you and make you legal."

"You worry about that a lot, huh, Papa?"

"I guess I do."

"Wait a sec." Javier went over to his dresser drawer and pulled out an envelope, and walked it over to me. "I guess it's kind of my present to you." He held the envelope out to me.

Javier sat on the edge of the bed next to me. I instantly recognized the seal from the Immigration and Naturalization Service as I unfolded the letter.

Before I could read one word, Javier blurted out, "I got a visa number."

Incredulous, I asked, "How?"

"When Maria turned twenty-one, she petitioned for my mom and me. It finally came through. I mean, I'm still not a citizen, but it's the first step ... and now you don't have to worry about me getting arrested."

I placed the tray of food aside so that I could hug

him. "Come here, baby. I'm so happy for you."

"You don't have to worry anymore."

"I guess we just might be getting married on that beach in Hawaii after all."

"Looks that way," Javier said, lying in my arms. "Dee."

"Yeah?"

"You didn't have anything to do with me getting my visa so soon? I mean, I was told it could take up to ten years."

Javier looked up. I just smiled. "Of course not. Some things are even out of *my* control."

"Why don't I believe you?"

"Don't question it. It's a blessing."

"You're a blessing," he said. "Happy anniversary."

"Happy anniversary, Javier."